Vampire God:

The New Evolution

Iran Reynolds

ISBN: 979-8-89212-862-9

Dedication

I dedicate this book to my late mother. She was my strength in all the bad times throughout my life. My mother was bold, brave, independent, sassy, and opinionated; she always stood beside me no matter how difficult the times were. She made those dark and lonely nights brighter, and she inspired my imagination and my creativity. Thank you for being the best mother you could be in my life. I love you.

Acknowledgment

Thanks to everyone on the Delta writing team who helped me so much with editing, designing the best-looking book cover I have ever imagined, and creating a website to communicate with my readers. My project managers, Casper Smith and Alan Hill, for keeping me on schedule and providing honest feedback.

Contents

About the Author

Iran Reynolds has been writing thrilling short stories since his childhood. With every story, he set out to explore his imagination, bringing intriguing characters and world to life. Letting his creativity take control, he built new gripping storylines, intertwining fantasy with emotional depth.

Married with two kids, he is an entrepreneur and an extreme gamer. With every new idea, he imagines being in a new world full of possibilities.

Preface

I've always been curious about the celestials and vampires growing up, and I combined the two curiosities into one imaginative piece. In this celestial realm, where stars burn like forgotten promises, a cosmic drama unfolds. Lucifer's ethereal brother, once bathed in the heavenly glow, succumbs to treachery from his brother and transforms into a creation of the night—a vampire born of celestial dissent. Follow the descent of an angel turned vampire and the ascent of a fallen brother seeking redemption. As you embark on this journey, witness the celestial sibling rivalry that transcends the boundaries between heaven and the underworld, where the heavens themselves bear witness to a struggle that echoes through eternity—a tale of celestial blood ties stained by the shadows of destiny.

Chapter 1
The Resurrection

"Stay put, brother," a command announced from the west.

Zephyr spun around. He was ever compliant with his brother's orders. This instance was for the sake of being called upon. Whatever it took, this one stood its ground.

And there, he placed his eyes upon the other one of his kind; the Star that mornings celebrated, his luminance unmatched. Each step put forward omitted brilliance of some sort. Who could question? After all, it was Lucifer Morningstar himself.

The angel's radiating being reached out to Zephyr, who was, in no manner, lesser. He was replicated evenly so. Both were built sturdy yet so fragile. Silken feathers so gentle, and yet when they glided, they could tremble mountains.

The two lacked any contrast. Neither found in their mien nor their egos.

"Brother," Lucifer uttered in a low, deep voice, still commanding Zephyr to stay.

"You have lost any more right to name me so," Zephyr roared indignantly.

The waters in heaven quavered to his fury.

"Yes," Lucifer responded in a softer manner. "Yes, that is the truth."

He looked toward the grounds in frustration. And suddenly, all his expressions shifted. They now suggested otherwise. Was it a fulfilled smile amidst this chaotic quarrel with the only other one of his kind?

Zephyr was baffled at this audacious angel. His confusion grew as Lucifer now laughed maniacally.

"You are not my brother." Lucifer spewed his words of spite. "You are an imbecile, created merely as a loathsome being."

Zephyr's protest was just as passionate, "I was created by The Most High!"

"YOU ARE A DISGRACE TO THE MOST HIGH," Lucifer's raging proclamation broke out.

"I am an Archangel. This is who I am," Zephyr spoke in a low, calm tone. He did not budge from his position, standing as still as ice in the deepest frozen seas. "I am far from being a disgrace. It is you who enrages me, infuriates me, and challenges me each day to fight my vicious urges." He maintained his tone, "Perhaps it is you, brother. Perhaps you are the disgrace."

"Such insolence," Lucifer's squinting eyes would have been burnt to a crisp if they could be. "All the angels who have ever paraded the skies, all the men who have ever walked the earth, and all the demons that creep in the dungeons know that I indeed am the Archangel of the highest most decree." He continued, "I congratulate your audacious impudence."

Lucifer's gaze grew harsher as he paused, letting his words steep in the purity of his emotions. "But know this; there will be consequences."

"Highest?" Zephyr chuckled. "Merely my equal," he said, grunting past the end of his sentence.

"YOU FOOLISH CREATURE," he screamed with all the intensity he possessed in his angelic lungs. "I CURSE YOU," he declared as he began to chant spells under his breath. "You shall crawl and creep on among mortals for the rest of the times to come. To us heavenly bodies, you shall be a futile being. But for mortals, oh for mortals, YOU SHALL BE A MONSTER."

Lucifer's hostility did not end there, "They shall despise you, be fearful of you, and shun you." He paused before continuing, "JUST AS I SHUN YOU OUT OF HEAVEN."

Zephyr did not utter a single word. Standing there in disbelief, all that his heart could imagine were the times of joy that the brothers had together. But now, hearing what he had just heard, his eyes were agape. He had known that there was friction between the two, but he had never fathomed that Lucifer would declare such words. That Lucifer, his fellow archangel, could... curse him.

One might have comprehended how Lucifer's malice for Zephyr had been relieved. However, the ethereal creature spoke again. In all his glory, he continued to state the conditions, proclaiming his brother's fate. "You will be a creature of the night." His eyes were as cold as the frigid gales of winter. "You shall know no light until all the days to live have been lived by all the mortals."

***

drip

One after another, the droplets plunged to the ground from the stalactite as if their misery had been put to rest.

The cave was large, with plenty of hiding spaces tucked into its crevasses. Cain sat hunched over in one of them. His head was crammed between his legs, and he trembled in oscillation to every splash of the droplet. His mind flashed memories of what had just happened.

Blood. Splattered, splashed, and smeared. It was the blood of Cain's brother and, in a way, his own. He strengthened his clench around his legs as his stomach turned. *But what was this?* His tight fists had, instead, wrung the blood out of his clothes. *Was his brother's blood on him?*

"I did not want to do it. I did not. How?" Cain shrieked as loud as his lungs allowed him to. The shame of what he had just done took over the entirety of his soul. He felt as if his heart was being clutched from the inside and then slowly squashed. "I love you, Abel. Come back, please."

Frantically, he managed to get on his knees and began praying. "Most High, please. Please reverse this. This could not have happened."

His eyes were closed with full force. With all that was left in him, he prayed to the Most High to undo what had just happened. Embracing himself in panic, he kept uttering words of regret, then of shame, and then surprisingly, of denial. "I did not do it, My Most High. I don't know who did. Someone killed my brother." There was no end to his lunacy.

And while he was hysterically mumbling, a clear and firm voice commanded, "Rise."

"The Most High?" Cain responded, with his eyes still closed.

"No, stand and see for yourself."

Cain did not stand, but he did open his eyes gradually. His first sight was the ground. And the horrid instance of what he witnessed next made him fall back on himself.

A rugged cloak. And through it peeped out a pair of feet. However, one could not discern it to be humane. The skin was reddened and peeling, and it smelled burnt. Long rotten nails almost fell off of the cuticles of the decayed limb.

Cain forced his eyes shut as he fell back. He grew fearful of what the fore could possibly be like.

"Open your eyes, Cain," the voice commanded once more.

He was afraid of the coming grotesque reality. However, if it were a monster, he did not want to be consumed by it.

"Open," the voice now said more affirmatively.

Cain finally opened his eyes.

***

Zephyr's spirit was cast onto the earth. He had been shunned out of the heavens. And to his surprise, he was not a spirit anymore. He noticed himself covered in flesh. A peculiar feeling of being weighed down took all over him. He felt the physical sensation of mass on his body.

His bare body lay under the shade of an overarching rock. The coarse, grained texture of the ground covered with hefty rocks instinctually stimulated him to move. Making sense of his surroundings, he grabbed a rock in his reach and pulled his mass toward it. Inch by inch, he was exposed to the sun.

"Aaargh," he screeched as he felt a sharp burning sensation piercing through the skin on his hand.

And then, the very sensation began to make its way through his entire body, from his arms to his chest, and from there, up toward his head and down toward his toes.

Now turned to man, he lay there continually experiencing shrewd aches deep in his bones, all the way from the surface of his skin. He quivered, squealed, and gnawed progressively as his skin began to redden. It burned so strong that one could see smoke rising.

Hours passed, and the former archangel was left to suffer in the sun. But finally, the massive burning star set in the west, and Zephyr's agony began to dim.

Exhausted, he panted hectically as he crawled toward the river. Struggling to reach just the edge, he dunked his head in the water as soon as he could. He drank the water, looking to quench his thirst. But as soon as he was done drinking, he felt the thirst once more.

So once again, he began to drink. However, each instance of drinking water resulted in only a drier throat. He howled some more before managing to stand on his two feet. He moved gradually with heavy steps.

Hours spent walking landed him in a cozy cove. He sat in a corner, weeping, grieving his misery. "I shall have my vengeance, Lucifer," he screeched.

And then suddenly, he heard some clamor.

He hid in one of the crevasses immediately to notice the cause. Two men made their way into the cave. One was carrying the other. The man being carried had a huge cut on his shoulder and was uncontrollably bleeding out of it.

Placing the bleeding man on the ground in the cove, he began to clean the blood off of his friend with a soft white linen cloth.

Zephyr's observation of it was keen. However, compassion was not the reason for it.

The real reason why Zephyr was so pulled by the situation was his newly developed olfactory senses. He smelled blood. And it made him salivate. Without thinking twice, he moved toward them.

The two men saw a figure appearing from within the cove, and what they witnessed left them in utter fright. They immediately feared the burnt beast that emerged before them. As their first instinct dictated, they tried to make a move but failed to do so as their bodies had endured the shock enough to freeze.

Zephyr came closer to the man, sniffing the blood from right where his nose almost touched the man's blood-soaked skin. And before his nose could meet the skin, his tongue did. One strong lick was enough for him to realize that his quench was not for water.

***

"Who-who are you?" Cain managed to utter.

"Rise," the voice commanded again in a low, grainy, but sturdy tone.

Life left Cain's body with every passing moment. He gasped for air through the sobbing. The atrocious creature in front of him convinced him that he may perhaps have even been dead.

"Are you the Angel of Death? Did the Most High end my misery of life?" he asked the cloaked monster.

"Your life mustn't be miserable," the voice responded. "Your life mustn't be worthless any further, for I am here."

"Please, who are you? And what do you want of me?" Cain dared to ask again.

"Behold! You stand in the presence of the King of Darkness. I am Zephyr, a vampire and the first of my kind."

Cain's baffled eyes spilled tears some more. His heart nearly burst out of his chest.

"Cain," Zephyr uttered gently.

"How do you know my name?"

Zephyr's malformed hands reached the hood of his cloak. His nails were piercingly sharp, and the burnt cuticles were merely seen to exist. He placed them on his forehead where a hairline would be and gradually pushed it back. Cain's angst boiled as he was aware that whatever he would witness now could shiver him to the spine.

Zephyr halted midway. The air was soaked with the fright of the man before him, and for now, this was not his aim. Hence, only revealing his wrinkled mouth, he began to speak.

"I know that you are the son of Adam, Cain," he said. "And I know the misery that engulfs you now."

Cain's frozen body and frenzied mind could not yet comprehend what he had heard.

"Abel is dead. And you did it," Zephyr stated. "And I am able to fathom how a common mortal would presume you to be at fault. But imagine me to be your friend. For I do not believe so."

Cain hesitantly asked, "What-what does this mean?"

"I have been eyeing you and your brother. I see that your anger overwhelms you and the hatred you have for your brother caused you to kill him."

Cain glared at his lips while Zephyr attempted to comfort and, yet, convince him.

"You, too, were tricked and shamed by the deities above, for I am just like you," Zephyr said.

"My Lord, what happened to you?" Cain finally spoke, with real words in a voice that was familiar to him. Even if Zephyr had not convinced him yet, Cain established that he knew he was not to be harmed... yet.

Zephyr's restrained lips glided onto his cheeks ever so slightly as he formed a smile. He could see his mission clearly from here on.

"I was cursed by Lucifer and frowned upon by God," Zephyr revealed.

Cain rose and yet stood at a distance from the unearthly creature. "What do you want of me, My Lord?"

"I want to make you better."

"How so?"

Zephyr took a step forward toward Cain. His arm reached out while he spoke, "I will give you a gift of immortality. You shall not die the humane death. And the world shall see you for the ages that are to come until the end of time."

Perplexed, Cain asked, "How does this aid me, or even make me better?"

"You might see this as a burden, but to die for your sins is an easy pass to the afterlife."

Cain was stunned yet intrigued. He could have probed further, but the surrealness of the scenario sealed his lips. So he let Zephyr speak uninterrupted.

"I can also feel the presence of the angel who placed me here, for he has fallen as well. Let me tell you, he also had a role to play in placing you where you are now."

"How is that possible, my Lord?"

"When you see your birth givers again, ask them about Satan, the Serpent."

Cain had a grasp of the Serpent's work. His eyes almost bawled out when he realized how Satan had tricked both his parents and him. He reached such misery due to Lucifer's schemes.

Zephyr noticed Cain afloat and lost in his thoughts and reasoning. And before Cain could utter another word, he took the chance to propose an offer, "Will you accept my gift of immortality? Envision how together we can seek vengeance on the Fallen Angel. The one who caused our damnation."

Fallen Angel, Cain contemplated. *How can this be? Is the renowned Satan that caused doom to my family... an Angel?*

***

Zephyr's newly discovered thirst for blood had no quenching to meet. But the fear of persecution remained. He had to survive and yet meet the needs of his newly given body.

He lived near the cave where he had found the two men. And whenever men visited, he would hunt them down. It was a smaller one, and there was space for no more than one person. He hid there, slept there, and brought in whatever was left of the hunted men.

Eight days had passed ever since he fell from the celestial skies. The new vessel was still alien to him. The skin was like that of mortals but paler. And with each day, it lost its color more so. This is when he would want to feed again. It was as if his own body was incapable of producing new blood, and he would need a man's blood to keep his vessel alive. However, then there was the verity of him being immortal in this abominable world.

Zephyr's new being was complex. He would often sit down and fantasize about his celestial vessel; what regal elegance; the one that knew no hunger or thirst, sturdy and yet fragile—radiating the light of life. And then he would look at what he had become, a creature of dungeons, a being outlandish to light. He was merely captivated in ever-rotting flesh.

Although with the great absence of ease, Zephyr began to embrace what was now his. In the next few months, as his body turned paler, so he could better fit in the shadows, he also grew sharper teeth. Canines that could rip bone when pierced through the flesh. His eyes adjusted to the darkness that was almost metaphorical now to his existence in hiding.

Even with the ever-rotting flesh and a vessel that tied his being down, his powers were limitless. He possessed the ability to move mountains, read minds, persuade through words, and emit unearthly charisma.

"You shall suffer, Lucifer Morningstar," he uttered under his breath. Then a stream of rage shot through his spine, and he was immediately on his knees.

"YOU SHALL SUFFER TOO, MORNINGSTAR. OF THAT MUCH, I AM CERTAIN," he screamed at the top of his lungs.

***

Zephyr's time as a heavenly body had just come to an end. And Lucifer's boasted chest could not grow any larger now. The appreciation of his own powers filled his being with an electric-like flow of *amour propre*.

Morningstar had imagined himself as the most high being among all angels. But now, it seemed as if he had transcended from that very level.

An angel appeared right when Lucifer was buried in his vain thoughts.

"The Most High calls onto you," the angel spoke.

"Ah! Finally, a being worthy of addressing," responded Lucifer. "Inform Him that when I am finished with my business for today, I will pay him a visit," he uttered as he proudly turned his back on the angel.

The angel was baffled. How could another angel, although of a higher rank, reject the Creator's summoning?

"Are you certain?" The bewildered angel confirmed.

"Yes, yes, I am certain, you halfwit," Morningstar spewed fury at the poor being. "I am done appearing to each of His commands as a dunce. You all may perhaps admire to adhere to them, but I, I am in every way superior. This foolishness does not suit me."

The angel's disbelief in Lucifer's disgrace to the Most High caused him to freeze. He only stood there to hear, dreading the consequences of this.

"I am the Star of the Morning, the highest being and equal to the Most High," he claimed. "You shall see my reign to now prosper until the ends of time."

This... was it. As the next moment appeared in the celestial time, the presence of Lucifer Morningstar had been banished from the Heavens. Covered in dirt, he lay on a shore.

He could not open his eyes in the piercing rays of the sun, but when he finally did, he looked around. He could not help but notice that this was Earth, where he had been thrown to.

Lucifer's eyes shot blood as he screamed in disbelief. He touched his body, which immediately felt alien. His celestial feathers snipped.

"YOU DID THIS TO ME BECAUSE YOU KNEW THAT I COULD BE BETTER THAN YOU," he shouted at the skies. "Now you shall see my wrath and what damnation I bring upon to your Creation."

Morningstar's vanity was his downfall.

***

"Yes... yes, Lord Zephyr, I will accept your gift," Cain's trembling voice declared.

Zephyr's burnt lips emerged, smiling out of the hood. And then, gradually, he lifted it. He revealed himself to Cain. A horrid array of emotions bulked up in Cain's heart.

He was intimidated, and the overwhelming emotions were so profuse that he had gooseflesh all over. However, yet, for some reason, he remained staggeringly inspired.

Cain was inspired by Zephyr's pain, not just physical or emotional. It was the kind of pain that cannot be put into a single word. The kind of pain that empties your soul. Something so inordinate happens to your entire being that it fills you up with torment. All the torture and affliction rise to the brims of your cups, and then the cups run over. Then, one by one, the cups begin to empty. They are drained of all the contents in them. What remains then is only void.

This is the very feeling that Zephyr, too, empathized with when he saw Cain's pain.

Cain rose and stood before Zephyr. There was no fear lingering in his heart anymore. It transformed from conformation to the respect that Zephyr's persona commanded.

"What command do you have for me, My Lord?" Cain urged.

"I want to build an army with you."

"An army?"

"Certainly. More earthlings must adhere to my cause. They must understand the ways of Zephyr. I want my kind, this new kind, to dwell." Zephyr was indefinitely unshaken of his cause, but he was reluctant to reveal it yet.

Cain understood the need to not immediately probe the King of Darkness. He did not have the slightest notion of what it could be, but his newfound master's word was to be his command. He discerned how adamant Zephyr was for his cause, so he decided to remain patient and trustful.

"I must live for all eternity and will create a flock of followers to your cause," Cain claimed. "Thank you for this gift. I shall live up to what's needed of it."

Zephyr forwarded his arm toward Cain. He kept it on his shoulder and lightly caressed it. "Be not afraid, for you are my Prince now. I shall treat you as my right hand for all the ages to come."

"I-I am forever grateful, My Lord," Cain began to bend to kneel in front of his new Lord.

However, Zephyr stopped him right there. "You are not to bow to me. But bring the people that shall."

Cain nodded in affirmation. He had not seen such a lord before.

The mere importance of being blessed by someone in order to join their cause brings a sense of purposefulness. This is the very purpose that humans sometimes strive to achieve. Cain's murdering of his brother placed him in a vulnerable void where this purposefulness or any sense of direction was emptied. He became the wet clay that could be formed into anything by the one handling it. When a person feels everything at once and then nothing at all, he is destined to feel something again. And before a man can feel again, there appears a thin line of immense vulnerability. This is the exact moment of a man's true weakness. This is where all his defenses recess into nothing. If you want to truly control someone, this is the very moment to approach them and sway them.

Zephyr kept his eyes on Adam and Eve's children. He knew that someday catastrophic chaos would birth from Lucifer's doing. So, he kept a watch. He saw the family closely, and he studied their mannerisms. He took notice of their individual traits and predicted their tendencies. He kept such close monitoring that one could not truly be sure if he may or may not have directed an act or two toward his purpose. This angel had been cast out of the heavens, but in no way did he settle into the mediocrity of the earthlings. His cognizance remained vastly superior.

Zephyr moved even closer to the man. He was intimately positioned next to Cain. His arms began to circle Cain's torso, and in a moment, he embraced him. Cain felt the warmth that emerged from this grotesque creature of the night. He had never imagined such horror to be so comfortably radiant.

Zephyr brushed his fingers against Cain's back and gradually embedded his mouth in Cain's neck. Before his lips could touch the man's skin, he took a good sniff. He could smell fresh, strong, and warm blood beating against the walls of the vessels. Zephyr could even hear them. Then his tongue slid out of his mouth and lightly glided over Cain's neck, wetting the skin. Once it was ready and warm, his sharp canines emerged out of his jaws, and he pierced them through Cain's skin right where the most blood was running through the widest arteries.

Once the fluid lost its direction and began to spill, it was now time for Zephyr to devour it. He circled his lips around and suckled on to the blood that spilled out of the pierced skin. Soon, he let go of the stronghold of his teeth, still maintaining his mouth above the two punctures in the skin. When the neck was relieved of his canines, blood gushed out through the two holes that it had created. So, he suckled onto them some more, satisfying his appetite for tonight.

He had now drained all of Cain's body of the red fluid. So he stepped back, watching the lifeless corpse fall to the ground. Cain's earthly body lay pale, emptied of all its blood and human essence.

Zephyr then uttered a spell under his breath, whispering the words of rebirth. And Cain's finger began to tremble. Slowly, his entire body endured an electric-like flow of energy. A single shiver ran through his body, and he was awake. His eyes were immediately wide open. He managed to stand his ground as soon as he could. And with every passing second, he transformed into a godlike creature of the night, like Zephyr himself.

His skin was paler than snow, all his hair shed, and one could see his branched vessels lifelessly peeking through his skin. His gaze was bloodied; his eyeballs turned into a crimson red color, yet vibrant as ever. It seemed as if all the blood in his body had now been stored in his eyes. All else was gray. This was the first vampire created by Zephyr and certainly was not to be the last.

This was when Zephyr uncloaked himself, revealing his true self to the reborn man as a vampire. His eyes were the same shade of deathly crimson.

Zephyr looked up in the sky and saw that the light was fading away. It was time for him to make a move; the full moon was full, and the night was as clear as his seraphic vision.

"I must take leave now," Zephyr said.

Cain could not yet speak. His body was still transcending into a more ethereal being. So Zephyr only planted a brief kiss on Cain's forehead and moved out of the cave.

However, he had uttered a few words of insight before he left.

"Be wary of your brother's children. They have found out what you had done to their father," he said. "This world shall not be pleasant to you anymore."

Even if Cain could not speak yet, his intense sense of hearing had already developed.

Chapter 2
The Royal Twins

Although the King of Darkness had been robbed of many things, his keen understanding of power did not fail him. As a celestial being constantly dodging Morningstar's shadow, Zephyr had learned how to climb the ranks without ruffling too many feathers. Or perhaps, one should say, he knew exactly which feathers to ruffle.

He had been cast down to earth, stripped of his powers, and turned into a beast. But that did not stop him. If Lucifer wished to see him like this, Zephyr would take his punishment and wage war against the arrogant angel. Zephyr's plan formed before him slowly as he turned possibilities over in his head.

He had found Cain in a lonely cave, cowering under his power. As the vampire continued his solitary stroll toward the nearest settlement, he saw flashbacks of Adam's son turning into a superior, immortal being. There was no ethereal celestial glow as Cain's irises turned crimson, but Zephyr knew that his first vampire would not disappoint him. Cain's power was unmatched, and the desperation in which he had consented to follow him would only ensure his loyalty to his newfound god.

Naturally, the next step was to find a man of influence and start at the top. If Zephyr turned someone at the top of the hierarchy, there would not be many people who would present any opposition. Weaker humans were always first to give in, but Zephyr needed followers that would become warriors and fighters. When Lucifer would look down upon him next, he would find that Zephyr was not alone and that his kind had grown much more than the archangel could ever imagine.

The King of Darkness decided that he would track down a royal bloodline. After all, who better to turn into immortal beasts than those already born for greatness? Zephyr solidified his plan as he set foot on the outskirts of a small town. The place held no identifiable marker, but the scattered houses upon the rolling hills could only mean a greater settlement ahead.

As night fell and the moon reached its highest, Zephyr noticed how every home lay dark and silent, where townsfolk slept, unaware that a monster walked amongst them, passing through their slowly thinning streets as the town opened up before him.

As the small buildings began to gradually grow in number, Zephyr found what he was looking for: it was a small tavern where candles still glimmered inside, the heavy door blocked the clamor of drunkards and fistfights, but a small plume of smoke from the chimney told Zephyr that the night was young, and people plenty.

He halted before the entrance to the pub, wondering why a crippling sense of hesitation suddenly overtook him. The vampire urged himself to reach for the door, but his hands failed him. Zephyr grunted in frustration.

Suddenly the door flung open, revealing a big, burly gentleman with a heavy beard. The heavyset man eyed the cloaked vampire and shrugged.

"What're you waitin' fer? Come on in," he said.

It was as if the utterance of those nonchalant words freed Zephyr of some unknown bind. The vampire's brow furrowed as he followed the man into the pub, eyeing the patrons inside it. It was fairly quiet. Only the din of casual conversation continued as he made his way to the bar. Zephyr seated himself on a rickety wooden stool and sighed.

Silence had prevailed as all eyes turned to look at the cloaked figure. Zephyr was a giant by human standards. At 7 feet tall, the vampire turned heads left and right, and as the cloak fluttered to reveal his slim form, people felt inclined to stare.

"Whiskey," Zephyr grunted, letting the deep gravel of his voice shun the glares that focused on him still.

The barkeep made an affirmative noise in response, and with the clinking of the glass on the table, the conversation seemed to resume. The burly man that had greeted him sat beside him, "You're new."

Zephyr turned his head to fix the man with a serious look. He waited for him to go on.

"Man like you is hard to miss. If you were from 'round here, we'd've known ya." He went on, "What do you want from us?"

"Why do you think I want something more than a drink?"

"The look of ya." The man shrugged. "Yer eyes are hungry."

Zephyr blinked as if to draw the man's attention to his own crimson eyes. "I need a name."

The man swallowed thickly, "Who-"

The vampire nodded at the barkeep, who placed his drink before him. "Your king, where is he?"

"Pardon?"

"I'm looking for your king." Zephyr kept his tone level and emotionless as he lifted the glass to his lips.

The burly man shook his head as if he was snapping out of a reverie, "We're not far from the palace, but we're far enough for his majesty to ignore us. If you keep headin' north for another day, you'll see how the trees grow fewer, and the houses start lookin' better. You'll end up reaching a small bridge that helps you cross a ravine."

The man looked up at Zephyr to see if he was following and then quickly looked away. "There's a stone wall with a massive gate. It's hard to miss. King's castle is dead in the center of town. The rest of the place is beautiful, well kept. Not like this town here."

Zephyr nodded. "His name?"

"Edward Moon the Third," he snorted. "Stupid name for a careless king. He's got more money and power than is good for him."

The man eyed Zephyr once more, taking in the cloak, pausing at where it fell open slightly to see if there were any weapons concealed at his waist. "His wealth makes him blind," he paused. "Easy to kill."

***

Zephyr had gotten enough information from the man at the bar to know where he was headed. The townsfolk were bitter, giving up their king's weaknesses with ease. The castle would be easy enough to approach. Once he was inside the four walls of the city, the smaller enclosure would be easier to surpass. It was a summer night, which favored the vampire. The longer the moon shone down on his dark path, the sooner his teeth would find the throat of a king.

The whiskey had burned his throat but in a good way. It was warm and almost fiery in taste, but it reminded him that his thirst was not for ale or water. Zephyr had wanted blood then. He wanted to feel the skin break beneath his fangs so blood could pour forth and flood his mouth. He wanted to devour a living being and rob it of its life, but none in the tavern had seemed worth the hassle.

Zephyr would be patient, he had his sights set on a worthy target, and until then, perhaps a small animal would suffice.

After what had felt like hours, the castle rose before him. The moon seemed to make its windows glitter as it bathed the building in the moonlight. The vampire neared it and admired how the small metropolis seemed to grow in its might the closer he got to it. Zephyr found himself on the bridge before the city gates. The dark metal gates were massive, guarding the city against monsters like him.

The King of Darkness approached the gates slowly. Though his demeanor gave nothing away, the vampire found himself recalling how the tavern had seemed to repel him until he had been invited inside. Would this city do the same?

Two soldiers stood on either side of the gates, leaning against the stone wall, close to dozing off. Upon the approaching footsteps, one straightened up quickly and gripped his spear tightly, muttering something to his partner to rouse him from his sleep.

Zephyr neared them and stopped only when a foot of distance remained between them. The guards' eyes traveled up his form, taking in the height and menacing might of a dark stranger.

"Let me into this town. I pose no threat," Zephyr began.

The more awake of the two spoke up quickly, "Sir, we cannot let you in. The town gates are to remain sealed until sunrise. You may demand entrance then."

Zephyr took one step forward, fighting off a smile as the guards froze in place, "I will do no such thing. Let me in now, lest you wish trouble and suffering finds its way to you soon."

"We're going to have to ask you to leave, sir," the one on the left spoke.

"If you do not comply, we will have to use force," the other joined in. As he finished his sentence, the two guards tightened their spears and pointed them toward him.

Zephyr finally let himself smile. He blinked slowly, steadying the trembling hands of the young footmen. They had never seen the face of battle, nor had they ever used the weapons gripped unsurely in their hands.

"Nervous?" The vampire teased. He enjoyed how the guard on the right shifted his foot ever so slightly in the hope that he would be able to attack him.

Zephyr eyed the gate wearily, and his smile widened when he noticed that the metal entrance was open ever so slightly. Good. He could move quickly now. The guard on the left seemed to notice the shift in Zephyr's demeanor and stepped back just as he lunged at his companion. Zephyr placed his hand on the back of his neck and sunk his nails into the flesh. Before the boy could scream, the vampire snapped his wrist and grinned at the resounding crack of the snap of his neck. Before the second guard could react, Zephyr struck the boy across the face, sending him reeling back. The guard's back slammed against the stone wall, and he slumped down slowly.

The vampire plunged his hand downwards, letting his talon-like nails dig into the flesh, and yanked out his heart. He tilted his head slowly, pondering over whether or not to sink his teeth into the organ.

No matter. Zephyr kicked the metal gate and watched it swing open. The King would make for a hearty meal.

By the time the moon had begun its journey downwards, Zephyr had found his way to the heart of the town, where Castle Moon had stood proudly. Its gates opened in ignorant welcome, and its walls were easy to scale up because of the stones that jutted out from the tower. Perhaps the king had thought it beautiful, but to the King of Darkness, beauty lay in the ease with which he would take over the throne and drain an arrogant king of his power.

The Vampire's days on earth had taught him that sunlight was not kind to him, but shadows were gentler. If he had a hearty drink of blood in a day, it would even bring some color to his cheeks. He could survive daylight if he had new blood pumping through his veins. But he had timed his attack well. The King would be dead before dawn if all went according to plan.

The stairwell he had landed in was pleasantly dark. The vampire straightened up, enjoying how the darkness concealed him. He waited for a moment, taking in the noise around him. His senses were sharp, and he could hear voices from a floor below and above. Zephyr closed his eyes, focusing on the booming laughter that emanated from the floor above him. The vampire went out on a limb and decided to chase the laughter.

Despite being cursed with a form that was an insult to his celestial beauty, one thing Zephyr appreciated was the speed this new form had. His vessel was swift and lithe, allowing him to do his business as a vampire with far more ease than a human vessel would. On days where he fed well, he would even go as far as to say he looked charming.

The vampire darted from column to column, crossing the vast corridor with relative ease. The gilded wooden doors lay open before him, allowing him a glimpse into the tiled throne room. The cream tiles glistened as they reflected the light from the candle chandeliers that dotted the enormous room. A red carpet led to the throne that sat upon a regal platform elevated at the room's northern end.

King Edward Moon sat upon his throne in white. The deep maroon of his cloak contrasted the starkness of his shirt. Two children stood on either side of him, holding golden staffs in their left hands. They framed the king elegantly. Zephyr studied them from the shadows, noticing how both the girl and the boy had eyes identical to the king's. The cut of their jaws was similar, too, leading the vampire to conclude that the children were Edward's offspring.

Zephyr had been moving swiftly along the wall, letting the low-hanging tapestries hide him from the bored eyes of the children as they listened to Edward drone about his greatness. He was mere paces from the king when the arrogant lord said something fascinating.

"The only reason I insist upon such rigorous training for the both of you is that your mother was raised by the most cunning minds this world has to offer. You have her brains; your tutors seem bent on teaching you strategy at only twelve summers old." Zephyr peeked behind the final tapestry and watched as Edward sighed, "Then there's the matter of the Castle's Mystic. He seems to prophesize greatness for you both."

Zephyr inched his way to the back of the platform. He was now cloaked in the looming shadow of the throne itself.

Edward laughed, "Then again, that fool says I'll die young."

The vampire stepped into the light, wrapping one hand around the King's neck as he gasped. Zephyr's reflexes were quick. Edward had just opened his mouth to let out a blood-curdling scream when the vampire tilted the king's head back, leaning over him from the left side to bare his fangs over the exposed neck.

Zephyr could hear the beating of blood beneath the blue vein that teased him. It seemed to stand out against the pale flesh. Zephyr sank his fangs into the flesh and drank. He felt the blood sprout forth like a fountain, and he relished the sweetness of it. It filled his mouth and began to drip down his chin as he swallowed hungrily.

The children backed away from the dark figure as Zephyr drained their father of his life. Edward's eyes had rolled back, and his mouth hung slack as Zephyr licked at the blood, feeling it flood his mouth again and again as he drank like an animal.

Outside, the moon seemed to change color. Its white sheen had shifted tones to something darker. At first, it was a cream-colored orb in the night sky, but as it grew darker, it seemed almost red. Villagers awoke from their slumber to witness the moon shift colors. It turned red as if to announce the realigning of earth's fate.

A steady murmur turned into scared shouts of "Blood Moon!" as the night lost all its luster.

As the townsfolk chanted at a moon that no longer looked like what it once was, the throne room in Castle Moon lay eerily silent. Zephyr had drained the King of his blood, and Edward lay slumped and pale on his mighty throne. As the vampire pulled away, his crimson eyes glowed with indulgence. He straightened up, feeling stronger and invincible. Zephyr's eyes met the curious and mildly horrified eyes of the children that had stood beside Edward moments ago.

They had backed away from the platform and now stood a few feet away from the scene of the crime. The boy clutched his sister's arm tightly, and both of them pulled their eyes away from their father and to the vampire who stood before them in all his might. Zephyr studied the girl, letting a smirk cross his lips as he took in the curious awe in her eyes. The boy's eyes darted between Edward's corpse and Zephyr as if silently asking if the children were to follow the same fate their father had.

The vampire was not hungry, and the king's last words sparked some interest in him as well. The sight of the curious twins set in motion a plan that he had not fully considered until that very moment. Power children from a royal lineage would serve as excellent specimens of Vampiric might. Zephyr mused over turning the children and being a father to them as they took over the kingdom.

They were young, and their minds would easily mold into the vision that dominated the vampire's mind. Having children of his own to raise would be an interesting task.

Zephyr held out his hands in a friendly gesture, letting his gravelly voice sink into the hearts of the twins.

"Children," he began softly. "I am your father now."

The girl tilted her head skeptically.

"I have drained your father, and his blood runs through me now. It fills my body and pumps through this vessel as we speak. Accept me as your father now, for I will never leave you."

The twins exchanged a look and shakily got down on their knees. They knelt before Zephyr, postures uncertain but not daring to defy him on account of how the stranger before them had just drained their father. As they bowed their heads in fearful reverence, the heavy oak doors on the other end of the room opened, and a small child entered the room. He ran up to the twins, ignorant of the dead king on the throne and the vampire that stood in front of him.

"Who is this?" Zephyr inquired.

"Our younger brother," the boy responded. "His name is Sebastian."

"He's eight," the sister cut in, as if stating the child's age would ensure that the monster before them wouldn't hurt their brother.

Zephyr took a few steps toward the children. The vampire bowed slightly and inhaled deeply, his nose picked up three different scents, and he could easily determine which was the fresh blood of a child. If he had turned the smaller boy at this age, he wouldn't survive it. If his royal lineage granted him any leeway, the child would remain eight summers old forever and essentially useless.

The vampire hummed, dismissing the boy as he turned away. Perhaps the youngest would grow up to be the next King of Castle Moon; maybe then he would be of some use. Zephyr's heightened hearing caught the elder brother whispering to the younger one to scurry off to his room.

The obedient little runt did as instructed, not daring to look back at the scene he had just witnessed.

"I understand you're scared. I know you do not trust me." Zephr crouched before the children, bringing himself closer to them in height so they would not be craning their necks at a dark, cloaked figure.

The vampire pulled his hood back, letting it fall about his shoulders. He had just fed moments before, which brought life back to his face. Zephyr's features looked less severe, and his crimson eyes shone with power. He looked healthier now, and the children did not cringe at the sight of him.

"You're confused," he continued. "But what I did was necessary to bring you closer to your fate... as prophesied.

You must be no more than fourteen, fifteen summers old. But what I am about to grant you will give you power beyond your wildest imagination. You will change, but not so drastically. You might grow a bit despite my turning you, but that is because of the age of transition you're already in."

"Turn us into what?" The girl spoke up. Her eyes were sharp and inquisitive, and they did not turn away from his heady, crimson gaze.

"Children of the night," Zephyr announced. "Children of greatness."

"What would that entail?" she persisted.

"Give me your wrist," the vampire snapped, suddenly tired of this pointless line of questioning. He would show them what he meant. "Both of you."

The girl held up her wrist first. It trembled with fear, but she looked at him bravely. Zephyr smiled softly, "Trust me, child."

With that, Zephyr lifted the nimble wrist to his lips, eyes closing as he felt the pulse in her wrist as loudly as a drumbeat. The vampire inhaled, composing himself as the fresh blood called out to him. His pupils dilated as he bared his teeth ever so slightly, letting the fangs slip down from beneath his lips.

The girl gasped as they pierced her skin. She closed her eyes as the fangs sunk deeper, spilling blood on either side of her wrist as Zephyr refused to drink more than what was needed to turn the child. Her eyes were scrunched shut when the vampire pulled away, licking over the wound gently to watch as it healed soon after, blood congealing so no more would be lost. She fell backward, pale and helpless, as she was drained within an inch of her life.

Her brother cried out, lunging at Zephyr, "WHAT HAVE YOU DONE?"

The vampire held out a hand, grabbing the boy by the throat, "Patience, child."

Zephyr turned his attention back to the fallen girl and whispered a spell. The words of rebirth seemed to fall upon the girl's form gently. Her body began to tremble as the spell breathed new life into her. Her eyes flew open, dark and crimson. She began to sit up, her body twitching as if it was alive with something entirely otherworldly. As she stood, Zephyr was fascinated by how she seemed taller now. Her form was the same as before, but she was deathly pale now. She met Zephyr's gaze with a smile that seemed to thank him for what he'd done. Suddenly, the girl beamed, baring her newfound fangs in appreciation.

They both turned to look at the boy whose throat was still in the vampire's grasp. Zephyr grabbed the boy's wrist instead and held it to his lips. As he started to struggle, the boy's sister spoke up. "Trust him, Eugene. He's going to make you all better now."

At his sister's words, the boy fell limp, watching his sister warily, who sounded much more calmer after the vampire had drained her of blood.

Zephyr lifted his wrist to his lips once more and bared his fangs, sinking them into the soft flesh. His teeth found the blood instinctively, sinking in where the skin was thinnest and where the blood beat against it restlessly. Zephyr drank, conscious of his previous attempt on the girl. She still maintained her human form but appeared stronger and paler. Perhaps all he had to do was drink almost enough to kill so that the bodies had no choice but to cling to the spell of rebirth.

The boy whimpered as he grew weaker, and the blood left him. Zephyr pulled away in time, watching the boy fall back onto the floor. The King of Darkness whispered the spell once more, conscious of how the girl watched him aptly.

An eager student, the vampire mused as the spell finished. The boy's body twitched as he lay unconscious on the floor. His body jolted as the spell took effect, and his vampiric powers became active. The boy opened his eyes, staring at the ceiling as his irises turned crimson. He blinked slowly before sitting up shakily. He looked to Zephyr and then to his sister, his eyes questioning.

"Your survival," Zephyr said as he rose, wiping his mouth with the sleeve of his cloak, "is testament to your strength. You are worthy of the powers given to you, amongst which is immortality. You are stronger and faster, and your senses have improved far beyond human capacities. You are of a more superior race, Children of the night."

The children shared a look of apprehension, but the smiles on their faces were grateful. It was clear they appreciated the gift Zephyr had bestowed upon them.

"As Children of the night – and as first of your kind, I will name you once more. You are to forget the titles you once knew yourselves as. Your new names will demand respect, and they will be reflective of your power," Zephyr put his hand on the boy's shoulder, "my son, Zedkiel."

The boy moved his lips as if he was practicing the name on his tongue. The vampire put his hand on the girl's shoulder next, "And my daughter, Ariel."

The twins looked at Zephyr with reverence, their crimson eyes aglow with promise.

"You will find that you do not need to sleep as much anymore. Your immortality gives you that luxury. But like children who have just been turned, you may need to rest tonight. Tomorrow, I will teach you how to feed, and then, we shall begin your training."

"What are we training for?" Zedkiel asked.

"As children of the night, you will train to strengthen your abilities, and then you will use your powers to build an army. There will be strength in our numbers, and we shall use that to face our enemy."

"And who might that be?" Ariel inquired.

"The first glimmer of the morning, the brightest spark in the universe. Lucifer Morningstar. God's favorite."

***

Zephyr spent his night watching over his children. As he lurked in the shadows, the twins spoke to each other in whispers. They were awed by their renewed strength. The twins felt more lithe and graceful.

"He killed Edward," Ariel mused. "But he has given us greatness in its stead. He promises to be our father too. He's training us as his children."

The brother listened to his twin intently, but he still seemed timid and confused. "And what about Sebastian?"

Ariel shook her head, "Sebastian is too weak. He is a child, and he could not handle the transformation we took on. We only have each other now, Zedkiel." She smiled softly at her brother and held out her hand for him to take. Zedkiel took it and squeezed it gently, grateful for the comfort she offered.

Zephyr could tell their bond had been strong before, but sharing the transformation had brought them closer. As silence prevailed, the King of Darkness witnessed as a conversation transpired between them through their gazes alone. Their bond would make them inseparable and, in turn, stronger.

When the sun rose the next day, Zephyr was there to shield them from its rays. Heavy curtains fell upon every window, shielding them from the sun's unkind light. As they sat together in the throne room that morning, he addressed his children candidly.

"How do you feel?" he inquired, watching the twins closely.

"Hungry," Zedkiel spoke up, "and thirsty."

"And water does not quench it." Ariel nodded, exchanging a glance with her brother. "But we still feel stronger than before."

"Good," Zephyr hummed, "What you thirst for is blood, and I will not have you hunt small prey to quench your thirst. My children deserve a hearty feast for their first meal."

The twins smiled, excited at the prospect of a meal that would quench their thirst.

"There is a festival taking place in your town today, and when the sun dips below the horizon, we shall visit." Zephyr paced the hall languidly. "I want you both dressed in your finest clothes. You will visit as prince and princess of the kingdom and let the townspeople adore you."

"But, Father," Zedkeil began, "where will you be?"

"Always near, my son." He smiled softly. "Look to the shadows, and you shall find me."

"And what shall we do about Edward Moon?" Ariel looked to the throne where the drained body still lay, slumped over and bloodless. It was still early morning, and the castle staff was asleep.

"We will hide his body for now. When we return, you must pack to leave the castle. We will train elsewhere. We will raise the alarm for Edward's demise before we leave, and a regent will raise your younger brother."

"You seem to have it all sorted out, Father," Zedkiel's smirk had a hint of menace in it.

"What sort of father doesn't have all the answers?" Zephyr smiled back. "Now, I suggest you prepare for your first public appearance as children of the night. A feast awaits at the end of it."

Zephyr felt a strange sense of pride tugging at him when the twins emerged from their room. They were both dressed elegantly. Ariel wore a deep emerald floor-length dress over which she had draped a regal, black velvet robe. Zedkiel wore a cream-colored silk shirt and a navy blue blazer over dark trousers. The twins looked like royalty, and their features made them look more mature now, with their eyes crimson and expressions seemingly composed. Zephyr admired his children, smiling at them slightly.

"Ready for the festival, children?" The King of Darkness pushed open the wide oak doors, letting the twins through. As he followed after them, Ariel turned to look at him inquisitively.

"What's our course of action, then?" she asked.

Zephyr hummed as if he was musing over the night's plan: "Enjoy the festival," he shrugged. "Bask in the glory of your royalty and let the villagers fawn over you as their prince and princess."

"Surely, that's not all, Father?" Zedkiel inquired.

The vampire smiled, "I know your hunger plagues you now, and you have spent most of the day trying to quench it with whatever came your way. But once you're in the festival, all will become clear." Zephyr was eager to see what would happen to the twins when they were suddenly surrounded by so many humans so soon after being turned. "As I said, enjoy the festival, and then you may retreat to the tent they leave reserved for loyalty. I will always be close by."

As the twins followed the lights and enthusiasm of the festival, Zephyr retreated to the shadows, eagerly watching his children. The moment the duo noticed their father had left, Zedkiel held out his hand to his sister. Ariel took it and passed him a smile.

"It feels different, doesn't it?" Ariel asked.

"I feel stronger. I feel better even," Zedkiel responded. "And I don't even miss Father– "

"You mean Edward." His sister corrected him, squeezing his hand when he nodded quickly. "This will be good for us, Zed. I trust Father. And you know of the prophecies too."

"I hadn't realized this greatness the mystics spoke of would have such a violent beginning."

When his sister didn't respond to him, Zedkiel shot her a sideways glance. He found her grimacing. "Are you alright?"

Ariel shook her head, squeezing her eyes shut. "They're so loud," she winced. "The festival is so far away, but I can hear everything already."

"Do you think these could be our powers?" Zedkiel cast a gaze around, looking for Zephyr.

"They must be," Ariel gritted her teeth. "Can't you hear it too?"

Zedkiel made an affirmative sound, setting his sights on the entrance to the festival before them. The light seemed brighter, and his hunger was rearing its head again. Zedkiel focused on the streamers and the candles that dotted every stall. He tried to enjoy the colors of the banners and all the people milling about, yet he found it hard to breathe.

"Zed–" Ariel trailed off, her eyes glassy as her vision became blurry. She felt weak, and suddenly, it felt as if her nostrils were on fire. They were aflame with so many different scents, so many human scents, it was dizzying.

"Why can I tell what a five-month-old child smells like?" Zedkiel scrunched his nose. "And how can I tell it apart from a grown man or a prepubescent girl?"

Ariel whipped her head around, "You can sense it too?"

"It's like I can feel their hearts beating as we pass by them," Zedkiel muttered, lowering his voice as they entered the path that led through the maze of food stalls and trinkets. "I'm having trouble breathing."

Ariel closed the gap between her and her twin, letting him lean back on her ever so slightly. "I'm here, Zed." She took a deep breath. "I feel it too. It's too much. Their scents, their hearts, I can hear everything."

Zedkiel tried to take a deep breath but froze when it hitched. Ariel rubbed his back, waiting for him to exhale. As she did so, she felt a pair of eyes on her. She turned her head and met the gaze of an older man at a soup stall.

"Y-Your Highness?"

Ariel shot the man a thin-lipped smile. She was more focused on ensuring that her brother didn't pass out from sensory overload. Several other heads turned in their direction at the older man's words, and a hush fell amongst the crowd. The twins could feel several pairs of eyes zeroing in on them, gazes widening in surprise. After all, it was not often that royalty blessed such a humble festival with their presence. They were not known to mingle with the townsfolk, let alone on occasions such as this. Edward Moon was known to make an appearance now and then, but he had kept his children sheltered and protected.

"My word," a lady breathed out in surprise, "look how the twins have grown!"

At her exclamation, another voice joined in, "Oh, she has her mother's face."

"Welcome, Your Majesties." One vendor bowed awkwardly, his hat falling off as he did so. The twins tried their best to offer polite smiles, but it had become harder and harder to focus on decorum with the heartbeats of several human beings assaulting their ears.

"Ariel," Zedkiel whispered weakly. He had closed his eyes briefly, swallowing the lump in his throat as sweat beaded his forehead. He felt feverish, and he was shaking from the loss of control he felt. Surrounded by so many people, the boy was uncertain about what his body needed at that point in time. And yet, he found himself fighting off an almost carnal urge to rip into the flesh of the first person that stood in his path. He wasn't certain if he wanted to devour the person before him or slaughter them.

The thought of blood had him swallowing hard once more. Flashes of visuals of blood made his mouth dry. Zedkiel struggled with the realization that he felt a desire for blood. He craved it, the warmth of the coppery fluid to fill his mouth and wet his throat.

Panicked, he glanced at Ariel. She met his gaze as she licked her lips, her brows furrowed in confusion and yearning that matched his. She smiled sheepishly at her brother.

Zedkiel gasped at the sharp fangs that protruded from her lips.

At her brother's alarm, Ariel was hit by a realization. The twins were no longer like the people before them. They were more than human, and they were far superior. Their needs no longer matched those of common folk. If her brother was feeling any of the things she was, there was a high possibility of him lashing out at the next person that stepped closer to him. She had to do some damage control before things fell out of hand.

Ariel spotted a teenage girl pushing her way through the crowd to get a glimpse at the prince. She had long auburn hair that fell to her waist even when it was braided. Her green eyes sparkled with excitement as she broke through the crowd, easily capturing her brother's attention.

Ariel looked around for Zephyr, hopeful that their father would emerge from the shadows and usher them to safety, but he was nowhere to be found.

Her ear twitched at the sound of the girl talking to her brother. Ariel whipped around. Her jaw clenched as a strange, envious fire sparked within her.

"Is there someplace quiet we can go?" Ariel inquired out loud. "Our father mentioned a royal tent. My brother feels a bit feverish, and we would like to rest for a moment before we join our people again."

At her words, Zedkiel snapped to attention as well. "Yes, it would be rude of us to leave when we have just arrived. We wish to stay among our people, but a place to rest would be wonderful."

"Oh, of course, Your Highness," the auburn-haired girl piped up. "The royal tent is just this way. Allow me to guide you."

Ariel gritted her teeth when Zedkiel assented, following her as the townsfolk cleared a path for them. She was starting to feel tired all of a sudden, a full day of unsatiated hunger had been draining enough, but all these townfolk and their scents had left her with a headache.

Father, where are you? Ariel thought blearily.

***

The King of Darkness had watched his children from the shadows. He admired how they relied on one another as their heightened senses assaulted them. They braved the brunt of it with ease, only needing to slow down or gather themselves a couple of times before the crowd noticed them. But Zephyr could tell their hunger was affecting them greatly. He smiled at how Zedkiel looked at the villagers, his crimson eyes ravenous as he subconsciously licked his lips.

His smile broke into a grin when Ariel had passed her brother a sheepish grin. Her smile revealed her brand new fangs, sharp and eager to sink into flesh. Of course, the girl was not certain if it was blood she craved. The sweat beading on her skin indicated that she was fighting her urges, but Zephyr knew the children were ready to feed.

When a younger girl led the twins away, Zephyr knew it would be time to let the children feast for the first time. As Zephyr darted through the shadows, a larger tent caught his attention. Villagers had gathered outside the tent and were peeking inside. A signboard outside stated the name of the act. In large gilded letters upon dark wood were the words: 'The Mysterious Animal.'

Zephyr poked his head inside, curious. Inside, he spotted a large cage within which a large black cat circled its bounds. The animal was large with yellow eyes that glimmered as it took in the bystanders that studied it in awe. It was clear that the animal was from the cat family, but its sleek body and shimmering fur made it look both ethereal and strangely sinister.

A man that looked to be the animal's tamer released a fox in front of the cage. The cage was locked, and the mysterious animal had no way to come out to grab the fox that had been set in front of it as a prize.

The animal stared at the fox for a moment, and everything stilled as the animal inside the cage turned into a blur. There was a clang, followed by a squeal. When the cat stilled again, the fox was nowhere to be seen. Zephyr narrowed his eyes and spotted the blood spattered outside the cage. He followed the minute trail into the cage and met the animal's gaze as it coughed up what looked like the fox's skull.

***

When Zephyr entered the royal tent, the twins lay upon a settee, clearly exhausted. Ariel shot up at the sight of him.

"Where were you?" she questioned.

"I was here all along, Ariel," Zephyr answered simply.

"Why didn't you come to help us when people surrounded us? Couldn't you see we were unwell?" Zedkiel sat up, rubbing his eyes as he whined.

"I cannot hold your hand through every trial. I needed you two to experience the hunger, the craving, on your own for the first time. I needed you to question what it was you felt and what you think you needed at that moment."

"What did we need?" Ariel snapped, clearly enraged.

Zephyr smiled. Clearly, the hunger was making the children wilder.

"Where is the girl that led you here, Zedkiel?"

The prince blushed. "She left the tent to bring us water."

"Excellent." Zephyr crossed his hands behind his back. "When she comes back, you will feed on her."

Ariel's jaw dropped. "Excuse me?"

Zephyr laughed. "You're not turning her." He patted Ariel's head, annoying her further. "You're draining her of her blood. You're drinking her."

Zedkiel swallowed hard. He took a shaky breath. "Blood."

"Yes, I'll teach you how," Zephyr answered patiently.

"You're telling us we've been hungry for blood all this time?"

The vampire nodded. "It'll make sense after your first blood. The first drink is always the finest."

When the girl entered the tent again, Zephyr stood in the shadows, watching as the twins tried to pin down their first prey. Ariel pretended to be indifferent to how Zedkiel grabbed the girl's hand when she turned around to leave after bringing the water.

"Stay," Zedkiel whispered, "what's your name?"

The girl glanced sideways at Ariel before blushing. "Anna."

Zedkiel rose from the settee, taking a step closer to the girl, her hand still in his.

"Anna," he smiled, trying out her name.

The girl's breathing hitched as her flush deepened. Zedkiel took his other hand and tucked a stray lock of hair behind her ear. Anna didn't notice when Ariel walked up behind the two, close enough to grab her waist.

Zephyr had told them what to do, and he watched critically as Zedkiel brought his face closer to the girl. His hand was already at her neck.

"May I?" Zedkiel whispered. Ariel made a face behind Anna's back, and Zedkiel smiled at his sister over her shoulder.

Anna nodded, unsure.

At her approval, Ariel brought a hand and covered Anna's mouth, catching her off guard as Zedkiel tilted her neck back. Ariel bared her teeth, her fangs extending over the girl's carotid artery. She glanced up at Zedkiel as she did so, the point of her fangs just above the flesh.

Zephyr nodded as Zedkiel swallowed thickly.

Anna struggled against the twins' grip when Ariel's teeth sank into the flesh. Ariel moaned as her teeth sank in, the blood gushed out, and the girl quickly sealed her mouth over the puncture, drinking hungrily.

Zedkiel's breathing grew heavy. "Ariel," he demanded.

Ariel pulled away to take a breath, blood spilling over Anna's neck and down Ariel's chin. She nodded downwards, motioning for her brother to do what she just did.

Zedkiel bent down, placing his mouth over the wound. As he began to drink, his eyes fluttered closed, and a small grunt left his lips as he drank his fill, the girl shriveling in his arms. When he finally pulled away from the drained girl, he met Ariel's gaze.

Their crimson eyes glittered as they met, both a reflection of each other as blood dripped from the edge of their lips, their fangs tainted with their first blood. They turned to look at Zephyr, who had just emerged from the shadows.

"Call in the next villager," Zephyr smiled.

***

It was well past midnight when the twins emerged from the tent. Zephyr had decided the best way to leave the festival would be to set a small fire in their stead, letting it grow and wreak havoc. By the time villagers would get it under control, the bodies outside the royal tent would be charred beyond recognition. He hadn't anticipated his children to be quite so famished, but they had drank a quarter of the town clean. As they left the festival and headed toward the castle, the siblings shot each other sheepish glances as if they were embarrassed by what had transpired between them.

"Did you have any idea...?" Zedkiel trailed off.

"I hadn't known this is what it would turn into, Zed," Ariel confessed, her voice low. "But it was...."

"Amazing." Zedkiel nodded as he exhaled.

"I didn't realize I could feel so—"

"Powerful?"

"Complete," Ariel finished.

He offered her his hand, which she took gratefully. She lifted her brother's hand to her lips, kissing it briefly.

Zedkiel stiffened as he felt Zephyr's presence behind them.

"You did well tonight, children." The first vampire did nothing to hide the pride in his voice. "You've set foot into your new life. You've learned how to feed. We're setting foot into the next stage of your training."

"We're leaving the castle?" Ariel asked.

Zephyr nodded, "You need to train somewhere away from home. Where people do not know you, and where your past cannot haunt you."

The twins nodded in understanding.

"You cannot carry the name of Moon any further," Zephyr added. "You are now part of the first vampires. We are the first and original three, and you shall help me raise an army in our name. Our kind must expand, but we must do this carefully. Our growth must be slow but insidious."

"So, what name shall we raise this army under?" Zedkiel asked.

The vampire looked at the twins, recalling their first prey. The Mysterious Animal flashed before Zephyr's eyes as he did so, and Zephyr felt like something had clicked into place. The vampire realized he had found the name that would be the sole identifier of the generations of vampires that would follow. It would be telling of their royal blood until the end of time. The mysterious animal had torn apart the fox mercilessly, and his spirit would live in the royal vampire bloodline. They would tear apart Lucifer and his army in the same way when the day arrived.

"Eleazar," Zephyr answered. "Ariel and Zedkiel Eleazar."

The name meant 'God Helped', and it would infuriate Morningstar to no end when he would find them one day.

After the first feast, the walk back to the castle was quiet. Zephyr had watched how the twins leaned on each other, looking to one another for support. A single look would leave Zedkiel at ease, and a nudge from the brother would result in a shift in Ariel's demeanor.

It was good, the vampire decided. They were the first vampires that mankind would know. And they would need a strong bond to last millennia. They were children now, but life would be unkind and unwelcoming to them over the years. It would do them good to have someone to trust.

The flames of the festival had turned into dark smoke as the villagers scrambled to save what was theirs. When the smoke would clear the next day, bodies would be counted, and the king would be dead. The twins would be gone, and the villagers would assume they were amongst those that perished in the fire. Zephyr hadn't anticipated how wonderfully things would fall into place, but he appreciated it nonetheless. The castle gates lay open in wait for them, and the children rushed in.

"You must be prepared to bid this life farewell, my children," Zephyr's voice echoed through the corridors.

"Take what you need and all you hold dear, but know that you are no longer the kin of Edward Moon."

"Of course, Father." Zedkiel agreed. He stood in the center of the throne room, eyeing where some blood had spilled over. The stain was dark and dry now, but Zedkiel pushed aside the feeling that rose within him. He could not miss a father who was not his. He was Zedkiel now, a superior vampire.

"Everything alright, my son?"

Zedkiel forced himself to look away from the scene of the crime. "Yes, Father. I was just about to get my things."

"Hurry, Zedkiel. Check on your sister too." The vampire called out. "We must leave before the sun is up."

The boy rushed off, his face set with determination. He was a different man now. He could not hold on to the life he had before.

Zedkiel went straight to his room, eyeing the belongings that decorated every shelf and surface. He pulled out a trunk from under his bed and threw it open. Every item he picked up felt meaningless and meaningful at the same time. But they were all tethers, Zedkiel realized. He could not afford to be tied down when his new life promised him greatness. The boy ended up leaving most of his belongings behind. Other than the necessities, Zedkiel left his room with only a notebook under his arm and his mother's ring strung about his neck.

He stopped outside Ariel's room. She was closing up the trunk when Zedkiel knocked.

"Ariel?"

His sister smiled at him warmly. "Come, help me close this."

"What did you pack?" he asked as Ariel pushed down on the top of the trunk while he closed one of the clasps.

"Some clothes, rouge–a few of mother's things. My blade as well," Ariel patted at the ornate dagger strapped to her side. "Nothing serious."

Zedkiel nodded, helping her close the final clasps.

"Nothing seems to matter quite as much anymore, does it, brother?" Ariel asked. She had dropped her voice to a whisper. Zedkiel picked up the note of confusion in his sister's voice. They had felt numb since they had been turned, and although Ariel maintained her vigor and quick wit and Zedkiel was cautious and quiet as ever, there was a sense of apathy that dominated everything else.

"All I can think about is my next blood," Zedkiel confessed. "And all I can care about is you."

Ariel's eyes snapped up to meet Zedkiel's. The twins gazed at each other silently for what felt like hours. The girl saw in her brother's eyes that he was telling the truth. And he spoke for both of them. They felt like a reflection of each other.

The sound of a door opening shook the two out of their trance. Zephyr stood in the doorway.

"Ready?"

***

Zephyr had coerced three horses out of the stable by the time the children were ready. The vampire had attached a cart to the back of his horse's reins for the twins' belongings. He had also packed some food, uncertain about what a young vampire would require. He had felt himself at a loss when he stood in the castle pantry, an empty basket in his hand. Lucifer cast him down in this form, but what of the two who had been turned into this? What would they need? And how would they carry on?

Zephyr fought off the uncertainty and doubt, shaking his head with the understanding that they would all learn with time. He had to train and polish their skills first. When the children followed him out of the castle, he made sure to avoid the throne room. The twins had been packing when Zephyr had dragged Edward's body back to the throne room. The staff would discover him in the morning.

They set off quietly, their horses' hoofs clacking against the stone pathway that led beyond Castle Moon. The twins were silent, stealing glances at one another for comfort. Their hearts did not sink as they left the city that they had known to be their home all their lives. Instead, the two felt unsettled by how little this shift mattered to them.

"It doesn't feel human," Zedkiel muttered, not realizing that he spoke out loud.

Zephyr smiled. "What doesn't?"

Ariel thought about how she could steer the conversation away from Zed.

"Let Zedkiel answer, Ariel. You can't always answer for him." The vampire paused. "I do not want you to fear me. I need you to trust me. The same way you trusted me when I taught you how to feed."

Ariel opened her mouth to say something, but her brother raised his hand to silence her.

"I suppose we're still getting used to the fact that we're vampires now, Father. That's all there is to it. We hadn't known the prophecies spoke of a change so great. The shift is sudden, and at times I feel I need time to absorb what is going on. It feels like I'm drowning," Zedkiel confessed. He stared at the back of Zephyr's head, waiting for a reaction.

They journeyed onwards into the forest.

After a while, the vampire spoke, "It's natural to wonder why you don't want the things you once did. Why aren't you reacting as a human being would? Why didn't the sight of several dead bodies disturb you when you were the one that drained them, right?" Zephyr turned his head slightly to let the twins know he was speaking directly to them. "It is simply because you are no longer human. The terms no longer apply to you."

A few more moments passed before Zephyr spoke again. "Bring your horses up to the front. I would like to see you as we travel."

The children obeyed, eying the distance between them in the form of the first vampire.

"You might not believe this, but I was an ethereal being once. I was an archangel, mighty. I had seen God himself, and I had spent time with his children, with his most favored creations." Zephyr took a deep breath. "I was cursed by God's favorite child, Lucifer Morningstar. He was the cherub that cast me to this flesh. He dreamed of being God's equal and could not stand anyone who was ambitious or well-liked."

Zephyr glanced at Ariel with a sad smile. "I had wings once, silken and elegant. They spanned wide enough to cover you both under their shadow and still have room." He shook his head. "He cast me down to curse me as a monster and strip me of all my blessings. But here, I wish to be more than just a monster to mankind. I want you two to see that.

We are vampires, but that does not make us any less than humans. If anything, we are now far superior."

Zedkiel's brow furrowed as he tried to understand his father. Zephyr, like him, had gone through a sudden and cruel shift.

"After I train you, I want you to help our number grow. Choose your family wisely. The people you turn will become your kin, and no one shall have to suffer the curse of loneliness that he cast upon me. We shall have an army big enough to stand up to Morningstar."

***

The first three vampires journeyed in silence. They would take shelter just past dawn and only emerge after dusk. As the scenery changed, the twins wondered how far they would go. Zephyr taught them how to drain small prey during a journey where humans were tougher to come by. Of course, a hare or small deer wouldn't have the same effect as a human being, but it would still suffice. Ariel had scrunched her nose up the first time Zephyr had held up a small rat up to her.

"No," she shook her head, "I refuse to drain a rat."

Zephyr shrugged and held it up to Zedkiel instead.

The brother took it gingerly from Zephyr's hands and drained the small creature.

"That's absolutely disgusting, Zed."

Zephyr motioned the kids to follow him through the foliage. "We'll see how you fare when the hunger kicks in, Ariel."

It felt like days before their small caravan finally came to a stop. The last leg of the journey had been rocky, with most of the greenery falling away and being replaced by a desert, except for the idle cactus and small tree scattered in the distance.

"Where are we?" Zedkiel finally inquired. The horses had started moving down a slope and into what looked like a cavernous canyon. Night had fallen, and the rocks began to rise on either side of them as they climbed down into the valley. The desert looked icy blue in the moonlight, with only dark silhouettes giving the place any detail.

"The Grand Canyon," Zephyr announced. He stretched his arms on either side of him. "This canyon of caverns and dust will look fiery in the daylight, and this will be your training ground for the years to follow. Humans do not frequent this path often, but you will still be able to learn how to hunt, turn, and fight others."

Ariel and Zedkiel climbed off their horses, turning in a slow circle as they took in their surroundings.

"Our home is now a desert?" Ariel asked.

"Far removed from Castle Moon, I am aware." Zephyr walked toward a dark silhouette in the mountain wall. "Follow me."

The twins followed Zephyr into the darkness as he entered the cave. The siblings were surprised to realize they could see perfectly in the dark. As Zephyr continued forward, the cave opened up into a wider space. The cave walls rose on either side of the opening, with a small opening at the top that was reminiscent of a skylight.

The space was wide enough to house all their belongings, and it felt as if Zephyr had scouted the area before. The opening was cordoned off into sections, and it looked surprisingly comfortable.

"I will not bind you to this place, do not worry." Zephyr placed his hand on Zedkiel's shoulder. "But think of this as a safe space. This is home for now, and this is where you will train. It would be best if you learned to practice patience. This immortality can turn into a curse if you aren't careful."

Zephyr faced Ariel. "All you two have is each other. Rely on that. I will teach you how to fight but learn to fight well. Hold no punches back. You need to be trained enough to take on any enemy that crosses your path. This matter can take years, my children, centuries even."

"Are we only to train until we are needed?" Ariel pouted.

"No," Zephyr laughed. "You are to train until you are ready."

"And when will that be?" the girl argued back.

"When you can match me in battle."

The twins hadn't known what to expect when Zephyr initially started training them. Their uncertainty gave the vampire room to mold them into the mighty vampires they were destined to be. Day in and day out, Zephyr would start their day with training in hand-to-hand combat within the cave. It was not until the duo was completely exhausted that he would take a break, calmly strolling away from the panting children, not breaking a sweat himself.

After hand-to-hand combat, he would teach them how to wield their weapons. First came swords, followed by daggers and small blades. The day would end with target practice at dusk when the sun's rays were no longer scorching. Zephyr would give them moving targets as well as stationary ones, teaching them how to master every weapon one by one. They were immortal, so it was up to them to learn how to fight with whatever weapon mankind developed. They could not afford to be overpowered or have the luxury of ignorance any longer. They had to be aware, on their feet, and perpetually prepared to master every tool the inferior race developed.

Ariel had taken to the smaller blades quicker than her brother, but Zedkiel seemed to wield broadswords with unearthly grace. The twins struggled initially, overwhelmed by everything the first vampire put upon them. Still, Zephyr watched with pride as they picked themselves up repeatedly, their eyes narrowing at how he dodged every hit they sent his way.

When Zedkiel fought Zephyr in close combat, the vampire encouraged the younger man to bring his dagger to the fight. After all, there was no wound a fresh drink of blood would not heal. Ariel watched from the sidelines, studying the fight instead of simply watching. She nodded subtly, noting how Zephyr tended to dart to the right when Zedkiel approached from the front. The girl watched for patterns, her gaze rapt as the fight went from a tussle to a graceful battle that was no less than a dance.

Ariel was always the second to follow in battle. At times, she used to wonder if fighting him in second place would give her an advantage. Perhaps her brother would weaken her father, leaving her to outsmart him with the patterns she noted from the first battle. But one smile from her father would tell her that she knew nothing, and the way the vampire fought his son would greatly differ from how he fought his daughter.

The twins would sleep after dawn, the exhaustion of the fights knocking out the young immortals. By noon, they would wake up again and start their lessons within the cave. The fighting and lessons would move out after the sun would set. They would hunt for prey after moonrise. Occasionally, there would be the lonely, unsuspecting traveler that would be their victim. Still, Zephyr taught the twins to use their speed and agility to capture smaller animals on most days.

The King of Darkness witnessed the twins' appetites grow, and his eyes shone with pride when they learned to fight each other uninhibited. They were vampires, children of the night, and their strength was matched only against each other. A hearty feast would heal their wounds, and so they fought dirty and they fought smart.

The vampire had not realized how easily he had fallen into a routine with his children. When the days turned into months and years, he did not know. But he knew that Ariel preferred the blood of deer to the occasional hare. He also knew that Zedkiel wasn't quick at close combat, but his strength in sword fighting had almost bested him in the first year. Above all, he knew the twins were closer than most siblings tended to be, that something transpired in their silent looks to one another that he could not read into.

But what did it matter? They were no longer who they had been when they were born into royalty. When it came to companionship, one required a partner that understood their life experiences, and the twins had only each other. As far as Zephyr was concerned, their closeness did not bother him.

***

"Argh!" Ariel yelled in frustration, whipping her head back to get her dark hair out of the way. "Stay still."

Zephyr laughed, swiftly blocking a blow from Zedkiel as Ariel struggled to get up. It was their fifteenth year of training, and he had taken to fighting the two at once now.

Zedkiel was a silent fighter, while Ariel relied on her words, attempting to enrage her opponent to the point where the enemy would lower his guard to respond to her snark.

"Slow," Zephyr teased, swinging his leg forward, not waiting to see if it connected with Zedkiel's side. He knew it would.

"Arrogant," he commented, bringing his hand up to block Ariel's blow. She did not notice when her father had launched a counter-attack, but suddenly the ground was gone from beneath her feet.

Zephyr spun around, ducking out of the way in time. When his punch did not connect, Zedkiel was thrown off balance, running past his target and stumbling as he did so. "And unsure."

Zedkiel stood beside his sister, who gazed up at their father from the floor of the desert.

"You have learned well over these past few years. But you need to stop overthinking every fight you have with me." He dusted his clothes off as he spoke, fixing the cuffs of his jet-black shirt. "Fight, and let every battle teach you something new. If you come into the rink thinking you can defeat me, you will fail every time."

"So, we go into the battle already accepting our defeat?" Ariel asked. She wiped away the blood that had started oozing from a cut on her cheek. Absently, she held her hand up to her lips. "We'd never win, then."

"No," Zephyr shook his head. "When you're fighting me, look forward to the lesson, not the victory. Who knows, maybe someday, your knowledge might surprise you."

"Father," Zedkiel panted. "At times, I feel you enjoy never letting us win."

"Let?" the vampire's tone lost all its humor. "I will never let my children win, Zedkiel. You will earn every victory. Be it against a human that knows his way around a blade or me. You can never match my power, and you will always be slower, less capable than me. I am the first of our kind, and every vampire will follow will only be a reflection of the power I wield."

"Yes, Father," his voice grew small. "And no reflection can compare to the real image."

"I am the master of the undead, King of Darkness—you are merely the prince."

Silence descended upon them. The canyon grew quiet in the first vampire's respect as the trio was left alone with their thoughts.

"For now," Ariel began, "it's just the three of us against the rest of mankind, Father."

"You are indeed the most powerful of us all. But when do we become more than just us three? How will we have children of our own?" Zedkiel looked down at his sister.

"Let us create more vampires, Father. Let us outnumber men and rule a kingdom of darkness that is ours alone," Ariel continued. Her eyes glimmered in the dark.

Zephyr studied the twins' expressions in silence before turning around and gesturing at them to follow him. As they walked back home, the vampire let the twins turn their thoughts over in their heads for a while before he finally spoke.

"Children, pay heed to what I'm about to tell you both," he took a deep breath. "If you ever happen to fall for a human being, you find yourself incapable of holding yourself back. Remember that if you wish to change them, there will always be the possibility of their becoming formidable opponents. You will fall for a human, but once they have been turned, they might not be the human you found yourself in love with."

"Their power might corrupt them and turn them against us," Ariel mused quietly, her voice barely a whisper as the words sank in.

"You do not want to create more than two vampires in your lifetimes. If there are only two, it will be easier to keep an eye on them. You must train those you turn in the same way I train you. Do not be hasty about who you choose to turn; because if you make an enemy of the vampire you create, and they kill you, they will become more powerful."

They had reached their cave by then. Zephyr proceeded to head inside. He placed their equipment and weapons by the entrance, knowing the twins would get to work immediately and begin putting everything in its place.

"Pass this on to your children, and we shall have order within the Vampire Order. We can't afford to have opposing armies within the House of Eleazar when the time to fight Lucifer is nigh."

Ariel was laying out the daggers on the giant stone slab that served as their weapons table. "Vampire Order? Isn't it just the three of us?"

The King of Darkness smiled fondly at his daughter. "At this point in time, yes. But the time is not far when you and your brother will be out making armies of your own, in our name. I have been thinking about the future of our Order, and the Grand Order will consist of four regions."

Zedkiel glanced up from the sword he had been turning in his hand, wide-eyed at his father's plans for him and his sister.

"I will be the Lord of the Regions, and the four would be the Northern, Southern, Eastern, and Western Regions. Each region shall rule over one thousand factions, and each faction will consist of ten quadrants."

Ariel had been doing the math on her fingers. "Meaning each quadrant will carry a thousand vampires."

Zedkiel looked at his father. "But if we are permitted to turn only two vampires, this will take eons."

"Patience, my son," Zephyr smiled. "I am training you both to the best of my capacity, but every vampire will not spend decades under your care. You will have to be smart about the systems you implement, the training, and the rites of passage you will set for each of your regions. You will have to learn to trust vampires who are not your own but are an extension of you, regardless."

Zephyr joined the twins at the weapons table. He picked up a rag and began polishing his favorite blade. "Zedkiel, I will place you in charge of the Northern Region. You shall be its guardian and protector. If any threat befalls it, you are to fight back and vanquish it. Ariel, the South is yours, and your responsibilities are the same."

The siblings' eyes met, wide and afraid.

"You're separating us?" Zedkiel panicked.

"Not yet, my son," he shook his head, smiling.

"And the East and West?" Ariel inquired.

"Those will fall under my domain until I find a successor."

***

The twins sat on their beds with their legs crossed. The King of Darkness had laid out his plan for them moments ago, and they pondered over the weight of the eternity that lay before them. They felt like children sometimes, unaware of how quickly time passed. All Ariel could think of were the years that stretched out before them.

Zephyr tried to sympathize with his children, "I understand it seems daunting. Time stretches out before you, and your immortality feels like a curse. But are you aware of how long you have been training with me?"

"I know it's been a few years."

"It's been fifteen years, Ariel." The vampire studied their expressions. "We have spent every day of the last fifteen years together in this canyon. We have journeyed to small towns for prey and trade, and we have fought off caravans of thieves. I have trained the finest warriors this earth has had to offer."

Zedkiel spoke up, "I hadn't realized it had been so long, Father."

"It felt like nothing."

"Another fifteen years shall pass like this, and it will all feel like a flicker," he explained. "I hope you understand why I'm laying this all out for you like this."

Ariel narrowed her eyes. "Why?"

"I believe it's time you two left this nest. It is time for you to venture out on your own. You must now flourish on your own, explore your powers and abilities, and pursue what the fates offer."

"Just us?"

"You must be independent of the covenant. When you leave this canyon, you will be truly tested for the first time because you won't have my shadow to retreat to for help. You will learn what you are capable of and what your restraints are. I will leave this land and head toward the regions that still require a successor. And in the meantime, I will also explore other lands to find a permanent home for us."

"You're leaving?" Zedkiel asked, his voice wavering.

The gravity of the situation seemed to hit the children just then.

"Father, you can't leave us," Ariel pleaded. "Was it not you who said we were not yet strong enough, that we had much to learn?"

Zephyr's voice was soft. "And you must do that on your own for now. I am not leaving forever, Ariel."

"Don't leave us, Father. Please." Zedkiel's eyes were glimmering in the light that reflected off the cave walls.

Zephyr rose, walking toward his children. The King of Darkness placed his hand on Zedkiel's head. "You'll be fine, Zed. You'll do well. I believe in you."

He looked at Ariel, who looked both distraught and angry.

"And you too, my daughter."

Ariel shook her head, petulant.

"When I return, there will be a massive army at our feet. They will be waiting for the next and final order to attack. The army I will amass will help me exact my revenge on the Cherub that cursed us with this immortal life." The heat in Zephyr's eyes was evident. "Morningstar's light will die the night we fight, and he shall never rise again. He damned us, but we turned his curse into our strength. He wanted humanity to fear us, but I will make sure humanity turns for us."

The King of Darkness nodded at his children, his final words a promise he had every intention to keep. He would see to the end of Lucifer's reign.

"Father," Ariel began, rising from the bed. She clutched his arm desperately.

"You'll do well, Ariel. There's no doubt about it."

"Don't say that like it's a farewell."

Zephyr smiled sadly at his children, his heart cinching at the sight of the twins in pain. He had grown attached to the duo, and the thought of leaving them upset him. A part of the vampire was surprised. He hadn't expected to feel so deeply for the twins, and yet here he stood, a lump in his throat as he lifted his hand, raising two fingers to whisper the spell that would cloak him.

Zedkiel's eyes widened as he saw his father's lips move silently in the spell. Smoke began to rise on either side of the King of Darkness as he faded before them. The fog surrounded Zephyr, cloaking him. Ariel dove forward, trying to grab Zephyr, but Zedkiel held her back.

"No!" she cried.

When the fog dissipated, the King of Darkness had disappeared.

Ariel's lips quivered as she stared at the spot where Zephyr had stood moments ago. Zedkiel stood still, the unlikely pillar of strength that his sister held on to as a sob escaped her lips.

He embraced her then, pulling her close as he wiped away Ariel's tears. The girl looked up at her brother, the fear in his eyes reflecting her own. Zephyr had been a presence they had grown accustomed to. There was an affection for the King of Darkness in their hearts that they could never explain.

He had been in the shadows while they fed, protecting them as they had their fill. And his guiding hand had steadied their shaky grips upon their weapons. Zephyr had a subtle sense of humor that the duo had grown to enjoy, and he had always allowed the twins to do what they wanted. Never batting an eye at their closeness.

They had never been alone before. Ariel desperately gripped her brother's shirt, her tight grip communicating how powerless she felt. There was a deep feeling of loss that shook them to their core. Ariel felt untethered and unhinged.

"We don't need to leave right now, Ariel. We don't have to head our separate ways just yet," he soothed, placing his hand over hers.

She nodded. "Not yet."

Chapter 3
The Start of the Southern Region

Left to forge their own path, Ariel and Zedkiel wandered the earth aimlessly. Although both understood why the King of Darkness ushered them on a journey where they had to continue on their own, the underlying feeling of abandonment was inescapable. The only solace they found was within each other. However, apart from this small comfort, the world felt like it was positioned against them.

Neither sibling felt a sense of purpose in their existence, apart from the one their father had assigned. But in trying to fulfill it, perhaps it was he they sought all along. The warmth and acceptance they felt in the presence of Zephyr were unparalleled. Nothing could fill that void.

The best they could manage was to emulate the sense of belonging that they gave one another. And unbeknownst to them, that was where their true strength lay. In their darkest of days, their combined will and power made them rise above. No foe, man or beast, could hinder their being.

However, at the end of the day, reality washed over them like a heavy torrent of rain; they would remain strangers in this world. They knew not of any others of their kind. They could only soothe each other for the pangs of deep-rooted pain they felt. And when they couldn't, they merely trudged along, hoping to be reunited with their father one day and become a family once again.

What they did not realize was just how close their father had been all along. In training them, Zephyr had imprinted much of himself in them, even in their most primal of actions. Every time either of them swung a blade or hunted for food, they felt his essence and the memory that came with it.

Besides this, they had learned how to channel energy from one of the many Moon Banks their father had left them. Any time they felt their life force depleted, they would bathe in its essence to regain themselves. And when this did not prove to satiate them, they hunted and fed off humans, just as they had been taught.

Of course, they were hesitant at first, unsure of what consequences they could face. But with time and each successful attempt, it became second nature to them. The two had learned to be quite deft at the task. Ariel would lead the charge by either acting on the element of surprise or subterfuge. If she failed or struggled in any way, her brother would act, using sheer force as the advantage between him and their intended prey.

This is how they continued their lives, not concerned with any other thoughts or emotions that could lead them astray. Ten years had passed since they last parted with Zephyr. What would have served as a sizeable fraction of the human lifespan was but a mere breath for the children. The memory of the time they spent with their father was as fresh as ever.

No matter how many years would pass, one thing was clear; they were nowhere near the goal they had been set out to accomplish. All this wandering was a symptom of the mourning they had engaged themselves in. If their sense of purpose was to be fulfilled, it would require conviction; it would require sacrifices.

"I will head East. Ariel, you must go West," Zedkiel said one day, trying not to let his emotions leak into his words. "Father assigned us a task."

A split; that was the conclusion they had arrived at. Despite the strength they had in each other's company, it did not bring them any closer to the task that Zephyr had trained them for. For that, they needed to part and make their way to either extreme of the human realm and amass influence, just as the Zephyr had commanded.

"Promise me..." Ariel nodded, her eyes downcast as she fought with her emotions. She knew Zedkiel was right. "Promise me we will reunite once this is over."

Zedkiel looked at his sister's dismal expression and tried his best to keep his sorrow under check as he replied. "I promise."

Ariel wiped away a stray tear and looked right into Zedkiel's eyes. "Take care of yourself, brother. I think it would be best if I return to our home, where we once held titles, and will recruit from our family. I will form allies that will further our cause and take full control over the Moon Banks across the continents."

Zedkiel nodded and placed a loving hand on her head. "Take care, my darling sister. I will travel East and acquire men of stature and nobility till then. We will meet back here with our armies, and Father will show himself to us."

Their task was relatively simple; they had been instructed to create empires of their own. With their training and a newfound purpose, it would be wholly possible. Zedkiel reminded his sister to only create two vampires. They would, of course, need to turn others to spread their influence and garner control. But, at the same time, he knew that anything over two would cause a problem for him to handle, and perhaps, it may even act as a betrayal of the covenant.

Ariel hugged her twin brother, trying hard not to hold on for too long and change her mind. She wouldn't part with sadness, she decided. And so, she shared the last of her laughter with her brother before she departed.

Leaving her sadness behind, Ariel headed toward the country of England, Castle Moon. Getting there was not a challenge for the young vampire. She traveled as fast as light, an act that even her senses had a hard time comprehending. In one moment, she would be on one end of the town. In the other, she would find herself on its outskirts. The journey would pass by so quickly that she would sometimes forget she had even started out. Ariel would often have to re-orient herself to her new surroundings, something that only improved with time and practice.

What was more impressive than her speed was the fact that it left no trace, neither sight nor sound. There was nary a whisper when she moved. The only hint of her existence would be the wind that broke as she sped by. But, by the time it could be observed, she was long gone. She could maneuver through wooded areas and towns undetected, as all vampires could.

The air trembled as Ariel raced toward a destination. She did not know where she was headed. All she knew was that she needed to be close to the nearest sign of civilization. It would not be long before she found it. It was a small town, still fresh in her memory. It sat at the edge of the woodlands, sprinkled with quaint log cabins, stone masonry, and the sickly-sweet smell of bluebells in full bloom.

Something about these surroundings trigged an impulse within Ariel. At the hour of twilight that she found herself in, old memories flooded her head in great waves of nostalgia and remembrance. As Ariel took a moment to take a sum of her senses, she understood why she was experiencing these feelings.

She had been here before.

Ariel stood still in the darkness, closing her eyes as her senses flooded with a memory. The scent of the woods was familiar. The town before smelled like home. There was a stream not far from where she stood, and her heightened senses picked up on the sound. It sounded the same as years ago when she and her brother had crossed these woods, trailing behind Zephyr like confused pups.

This town had been a haven for the twins' mother, before she had passed. It was not far from the castle and offered a respite from the duties of a queen. Although much had changed since Queen Ophelia had passed, the town seemed to carry the essence of her, still. If Ariel tried hard enough, she could almost imagine her mother's silhouette drifting through the trees.

Ariel slowed her pace as she made her way through, keeping in the shadows as she watched the quiet town. She passed by the bakery; she could tell that bread had been baking in its ovens a few hours ago. Ariel recalled the daisies her mother would put in her hair when the twins visited the town with her. And how Zedkiel would refuse to share the bread the queen would pass them.

The young vampire snapped out of her reverie at the sound of horse hoofs coming from not too far off. Ariel faded into the shadows, watching as a carriage passed by, ignorant of the quiet beast that hid amongst them, watching. The carriage went by, and the sound of wheels and horse hoofs against cobblestone faded into the distance. Ariel was reminded of the task at hand and how there was no time to waste.

Castle Moon was visible up ahead, its towers peaking above the dense foliage that was once meant to hide it. Ariel was there in the blink of an eye, with her destination in sight. Traveling went by quicker. She knew exactly where she wanted to be, so the young vampire closed her eyes and visualized the castle gates that were now closer than they had been in years.

Ariel opened her eyes and fought off a sad smile. There she was, before the castle's gates – and two disgruntled soldiers. They eyed her wearily, and Ariel wondered idly if the soldiers had eyed Zephyr sixty years ago in the same way when he had arrived to turn the twins toward their fate.

"Halt!" One of the guards called out, his hand already on the hilt of his sword. "Who stands there?"

Ariel took one step forward, letting the moonlight reveal her silhouette.

"Who are you?" The second guard inquired, his gaze traveling down the dark cloak she donned.

Ariel smiled, "I am Ariel, Princess of Castle Moon and daughter of the late King Edward Moon."

The guards at the gate shared a look of disbelief before chuckling, "Ariel Moon perished in the fire the night King Edward passed, young lady. The princess is dead."

The vampire nodded slowly, shaking her head at the guards' false but firm belief. When Ariel didn't budge, the guards stepped closer, their swords drawn.

"We cannot let an imposter pass," the first guard stated, his voice thick with menace.

"Even one as pretty as you," the other sneered.

Ariel clenched her jaw, all pretense dissipating as she sighed. She could break their limbs with ease if she wanted to. But she needed a peaceful way in.

"We know you're armed," the first one commented, ignoring his partner's lewd gaze and comments. "Surrender now, and we will let you live."

Ariel shook her head, "I did not travel so far to be denied an audience with the king, sir."

"Is that all you want?" the guard inquired, curious.

Ariel reached inside her cloak and pulled out one of the many blades concealed in her clothes. She set it down on the ground in a show of trust.

"An audience with the king," she repeated, spreading her hands in a show of harmlessness.

***

The guards had opened the iron gates for Ariel but escorted her to some living quarters not far from the castle. They would come to get her in the morning, and the stranger could have her audience with the king after the sun was up.

Ariel wanted to be on the king's good side, so she cooperated.

At noon the following morning, the same men returned to take her to the castle. As Ariel walked across the courtyard, she could feel the gaze of every guard on her. Her senses could pick up on the stench that permeated their uniforms and armor. She noticed the archers on the rooftops and made a mental note of where each was positioned. Whispers passed among the guards as she neared the entrance of Castle Moon. It was clear to her that the king had been warned about her presence.

Her assumptions were proven true when the doors to the castle slowly opened to reveal a squadron of fifty royal guards that were to escort her to the king. She smirked. Her younger brother clearly feared her already and thought that fifty men would be enough to render her harmless.

The throne room looked different from what Ariel remembered. It was more opulent, with large velvet curtains draping every window and a jewel-encrusted throne made of solid gold.

An advisor stood beside King Sebastian with his arms clasped behind his back. "Who stands here before the King?"

Ariel smiled, her crimson eyes glittering, "It is I, the former princess of the Late King Edward Moon."

King Sebastian had aged well in the years that stretched out since Edward's passing. His eyes still had that innocent sparkle that Ariel remembered, but there was little else that remained the same. She had seen him as a boy, and now he sat before her as an aged king with wrinkles that spoke of the battles he had fought.

Sebastian's eyes lit up, his curious gaze rampant with confusion, "Say again?" his voice came out raspy. "Who are you?"

"Look at me, brother." Ariel smiled, "I am the daughter of the late King Edward. Do I not look familiar?"

The King sat up straighter, his confusion obvious, "Is that really you, sister?"

"I go by Ariel Eleazar now, Sebastian. Your brother and I were taken from this castle years ago, on the night Father died. We sent you to your room to protect you." The vampire kept her voice soft, consoling the brother who looked so much older than her now. "The darkness that entered this castle claimed us as his own children and gave us new names."

"Eugene-" Sebastian began.

"Goes by Lord Zedkiel now." Ariel smiled, "Do not grieve us, Seb. We are proud of who we have become."

"It has been sixty years now." Sebastian's gaze turned glassy, his lips drawn in a frown as his past and present clashed violently. "What brings you back home, young princess?"

Ariel smiled at the term but then stuck out her chin and straightened her shoulders in an attempt at seriousness. It was time to set her plan in motion.

"I am no longer the sister you knew, Seb. As a child of darkness, I have aims of my own. I need my family to bring some of them to fruition, and for that, I would like your permission to take one of your daughters to extend the royal bloodline. She will be under my protection and will be my daughter of darkness."

The King's body jerked as he straightened up on his throne, his bony hands gripping the arms of his throne tightly, "What makes you think I will simply hand over my daughter to you? To further your plans of darkness?" His eyes pierced through hers; he analyzed her demeanor. Before she could speak, he said, "You are so proud of your evil design – have you no remorse? No regret?"

Ariel shook her head, pitying her brother. She said, "Sebastian, your brother and I were fated for this. Our lineage is blessed with power, which made Zedkiel and I such great fighters. Your firstborn will have that same strength, that same ability. She is destined for this."

"She is the heir to this kingdom!" Sebastian's voice boomed.

"You bear no sons, Your Majesty. Your name will die with you. Your daughter will be married off to a man she will not love, and the kingdom will disappear not long after your demise. Allow me to help you, Seb. She will become immortal – your name will live forever."

The throne room descended into silence.

"What if I refuse?" the king asked.

Ariel's lips turned up in a cruel smile. "Then I will take her. Kicking, screaming, crying." The vampire looked down at her hand, casually glancing at her nails. She continued, "I came to you to ask nicely. If you refuse, brother, then there is no force, no royal guard that can stand in my way."

"Ariel," Sebastian sounded tired all of a sudden, "As King, I cannot simply hand over my daughter. I will ask my daughters to volunteer. I cannot force one of them into a fate such as this; I cannot be so cruel to them."

Ariel was surprised at the love the king had for his daughters. "That will do. I will wait in the guest chambers for your response." She turned around and felt the footsteps of several guards trail after her. "I know my way," she said rather rudely.

The guards stopped at her tone of voice, watching helplessly as the strange woman left the throne room. She walked the castle's halls as if they were hers.

***

King Sebastian leaned forward; his elbows were placed on his knees as he rested his face against his clasped hands. How could he hand over his own children to the same fate his siblings had seen? How could Ariel demand one of his daughters with such ease? Had she not felt any pain when she was taken?

He heard the door to the throne room swing shut, the sound announcing that Ariel's threat was not to be taken lightly.

As Ariel made her way up the spiral staircase that led to the upper chambers of the castle, she picked up on an intoxicating floral scent. The vampire closed her eyes, her nostrils flaring as she took a deep breath, feeling the scent flood her senses. Ariel reached the top of the staircase in time to see a young lady rush toward the staircase on the opposite side of the hallway.

Ariel stepped into the hallway as if pulled in by the scent. The girl had long, golden bronze hair that curled at her shoulders and fell to her hips. She was petite, her delicate arms tracing the banister as she started walking down the steps.

The young vampire couldn't pull her gaze away from her, and she watched as the girl, who could only be one of Sebastian's daughters, disappeared below.

Ariel knew in that moment that was the daughter she had asked for. And the princess would be hers whether Sebastian permitted it or not.

Never before had the Princess of Darkness looked so baffled and enamored in her entire span as a vampire. Ariel's gaze became distant, replaying the bouncing curls, the fall of her dress, and how it hugged her slender hips.

***

Princess Alvira descended the spiral staircase that led to her father's throne room. The rumors had quickly made their way to the king's daughters. Alvira was the first to learn of it, she had heard her chambermaid talking to one of the other servants moments ago, and her first thought was to check up on her father.

She approached him, curtseying briefly before walking up the steps and sitting down before him on her haunches. To anyone else, it would have seemed awkward and inappropriate for a princess to disregard decorum with such ease. The ease with which she sat before the king spoke volumes of the love she had for her father, and she balanced formality and affection well.

"Father, are you okay?" her voice was soft.

"Yes, my dear," he smiled weakly before asking, "Where is your younger sister?"

"She is in her bedroom, preparing to bathe, I believe."

"So late in the afternoon?" Sebastian asked. "It's almost supper time."

Alvira shook her head, eager to get straight to the point, "Father, I heard that we have a guest. Your sister, my late aunt?"

The king's shoulders drooped. "Yes, we do. She will join us for supper."

Alvira saw that he was distraught and asked no further questions. But how does someone return from the dead? Were the girls to dine with a ghost that evening?

Castle Moon did not see guests quite frequently, and the arrival of the King's sister was no small affair. The castle was alive with activity, the servants and cooks rushing about, eager to prepare a feast that would impress the lost princess.

The king's daughters donned their finest evening gowns for supper. Princess Alvira and Dierra wore identical dresses. Each wore a stunning off-white dress; the silken fabric glittered in the candlelight, and the color of the dresses seemed to reflect off the diamonds on their neck, making them glow. The dresses hugged the girls' slender frames, the skirts widening at the waist for a more flattering silhouette. Their shoulders were bare, save for the stray curls that had escaped their tied hair and grazed their neck.

The Great Hall was filled with noble guests from all over the kingdom. The girls knew that every gaze was fixated on them, but they carried the weight of such attention with grace.

The clinking of glass announced that it was time for everyone to take their place at the table. The nobles sat first, followed by the princesses, and then finally, King Sebastian. One seat beside the king remained empty, and it was clear to everyone that it was reserved for the King's sister, the lost princess.

The light din of conversation halted as the doors to the great hall opened once more to reveal Ariel Eleazar in all her beauty. She wore a black gown that hugged every curve on her body. The neckline was deep and flattering, with net sleeves and a net bodice that bordered on risque.

The vampire felt every gaze on her pale skin, but she approached her seat beside the king and took her seat gracefully. It was clear that everyone was staring at the young woman who claimed to be the lost princess. But no one said a word.

Sebastian cleared his throat, raising his glass with a forced smile, "Please, let us begin our feast."

Servers filled the cups with mead, and each guest's plate was a sight to behold. The meals were cooked by the finest chefs in all of Europe.

Alvira had been enraptured by the strange woman and the confidence with which she sat beside her father. "Good evening, my dear aunt," she addressed her politely, feeling odd about calling someone who looked so young her aunt.

Ariel smiled back, and she could feel Sebastian stiffen beside her. "Hello dear, you look delightful this evening." She gestured with her hand, "Your sister as well."

The girls thanked her in unison. Dierra returned to her meal, disconcerted by how Ariel looked at them.

"Great Aunt, what brings you back to Castle Moon?" she tried.

Alvira would question Dierra why she was being so rude to their guest later on. But as the elder daughter, it was her duty to entertain the guests.

"I'm here on business, my darling."

Alvira nodded, looking away from Ariel's enrapturing gaze. She blushed.

"What is it?" Ariel asked with a smile.

"Oh," Alvira stuttered, "You look quite well, Aunt. I heard you were older than father, but—" the princess trailed off.

Ariel laughed, "I suppose that comes with being a lost princess, doesn't it? There are all sorts of strange things happening out there."

"Uh," King Moon kept his voice low, "Ariel, my beloved sister, thank you, and welcome back home to Castle Moon. I cannot express how strange and wonderful it is to have you back. But I also know you will not be staying long."

Sebastian looked at his daughters and dropped all pretense of civility and politeness. "My sister wants to dethrone one of my daughters, relieving her of her royal duties as Princess of Castle Moon." He spoke quickly and quietly so as not to alert the guests at their table, but he addressed his girls directly, "In all my years as king, I have never heard of such a proposition, and I would never have agreed to give away one of my daughters to such a dark figure as she. But I have no choice in the matter."

The sisters exchanged a worried look. Dierra stared at Ariel, anger imminent.

"I have no choice, my loves." The King's voice quivered, "I have agreed – albeit reluctantly to give my eldest daughter Alvira to Princess Ariel. As a gift. For the sake of the peace and safety of the kingdom."

Alvira's hand began to quiver. She dropped the fork that had been gripped tightly in her hand moments ago. "Father! What are you talking about? What do you mean?" she glanced at Ariel, who held a glass of wine to her lips and seemed unbothered by what transpired before her. Her crimson eyes were set on Alvira.

"Why must I go with her? I cannot. I will not stand for this, Father."

Ariel leaned forward and placed her hand on Alvira's wrist. Her grip was gentle, but the princess felt rooted to the spot as the vampire whispered, "My dear, it is best that you come with me. Or I would have no choice but to slaughter your family and the guests in these very halls."

The vampire enjoyed how the young girl stiffened and shivered.

"I will give you time to enjoy the last days of your mortality. And after three moons have risen, you will become my child on the night of the third moonrise."

Alvira made a disgusted face. "Slaughter?" she taunted. "There is an army leave with you."

Ariel shook her head and sighed. "I didn't want it to come to this."

The Princess of Darkness rose, and in the blink of an eye, she had darted to the end of the vast hall. She held a guardsman by the neck and twisted it, baring her fangs and sinking her teeth into his skin, swiftly draining him of his blood.

The hall erupted in chaos as guests screamed at the horror before them.

Ariel dropped the guard; her lips stained red. "SILENCE," Her voice boomed. "No harm will come to anyone. Remain seated."

Ariel walked back to her seat leisurely, watching as the guests settled. She took her place beside her brother once more, a single drop of blood leaving a trail down her chin as it threatened to drop onto her plate.

"What are you?" Alvira gasped. "What kind of monster would do such a thing?"

Ariel wiped away the blood with a napkin, "I am what you call a vampire, my dear. I am the very first of our kind. About sixty years ago, I stood in that very throne room with my brother Eugene and watched as the King of Darkness drained our father and approached us soon after." The vampire looked Alvira in the eyes, making sure that the princess would not break eye contact. "Your father was a child at the time, and although he rushed in to help us, we sent him away to protect him. Eugene and I had no choice but to kneel before him lest he wipe out the entire kingdom.

He was gentle with us, but he turned us into children of the night, like him. He gave us our names. Lord Zedkiel and I are the first of this kind. We follow our father, Lord Zephyr, to the end of the world, for he has given us immortality and, with it, the powers of the unnatural."

Sebastian sighed. "It was a night to remember. I was a young boy, eager to become a squire the next year. I had rushed into the throne room after my siblings, ready to help. But the beast before me was no match for a child, and Ariel saved me. I owe her my life, regardless of who she is now. I owe her this kingdom and the life I have lived. This is why I agreed to surrender a daughter so dear to me to someone who claims to be a daughter of darkness and my late, forgotten sister – Europe Moon."

Alvira took a deep breath, "Father, I understand. But I am not ready to hand over my life to my aunt. What she is, is an abomination to humankind. I refuse to leave with her. Please reconsider this – I am heir to your throne, and my children will be the next rulers of this kingdom. I will bear a son that will carry forth your name."

Ariel sighed, "If not you, then your sister Dierra will have to take your place. I will not leave empty-handed." At the princess's shocked expression, the vampire raised an eyebrow, "Or are you both so headstrong that you would rather an entire kingdom perish in your stead?"

Dierra gasped, her eyes welling up.

"Besides," Ariel continued, "You need not worry about such things. Time will cease to exist for you once you become immortal. Castle Moon will be but a vague memory for you. And what do the four walls of this meager castle offer if you can have the whole world at your fingertips? The powers of the unnatural world would flow through your veins."

Alvira glanced down at her hands, defeated. "I ... will accompany you, aunt – but only because you threaten to take my sister and this kingdom in its place."

King Sebastian's eyes were glassy with unshed tears, "It is decided then. You will leave with Ariel in three days. Prepare for your departure."

"After three moons, you will become immortal, child. So enjoy and celebrate your last days as a human." Ariel stood, patting Alvira's cheek, "Don't look so glum. This is a gift."

Alvira refused to look up.

"Come," Ariel commanded. "Let us take a walk in the gardens. It would be best if we spoke privately."

Ariel turned around and began walking away from the table, not waiting to see if the princess would follow. She knew she would.

Alvira joined her soon after, their footsteps echoing in the hallways.

"It's best if you air out your qualms and questions now, child. Get rid of this rage so that we can deal with this logically."

Alvira clenched her jaw, "I hate you. I hate what you've done. I loathe this predicament I'm in." Her curls bounced with her angry steps.

The vampire found it rather endearing.

Alvira continued, "I would much rather be married off to a fat, ungrateful, lazy excuse for a prince against my will than be part of your design."

Before the princess could say another word, Ariel had pinned her against the wall, her wrists clenched in the vampire's grip.

Alvira's eyes were wide with panic, her breathing heavy.

Ariel did nothing. The vampire simply held her against the wall, her body pressed against the princess, her eyes watching the wide brown irises that watched her in fear.

Ariel licked her lips. Alvira's eyes darted down to catch the movement. The princess looked up just as quickly as she had glanced down, but Ariel was already smiling at the girl.

The princess was blushing furiously as Ariel let go, laughing to herself.

"No, no, I don't think you would."

Their walk to the gardens was a quiet one. Alvira's thoughts were echoing in her head. She was torn between what she felt and what she knew was right. Something about her aunt Ariel was alluring to her. She knew Ariel was a monster, and still, the princess felt enchanted by her. She clenched and unclenched her fists, willing the nervousness to go away.

They reached the gardens, and Ariel led the princess to the maze at the heart of the lawns. Alvira watched in awe as the vampire navigated the maze with ease, making turns without a sliver of doubt gracing her features.

"How do you know where to go?" Alvira finally broke the silence.

"I grew up in this castle, princess. We used to play in this maze for ages. I know every curve, dead end, and escape these gardens have to offer."

Ariel glanced at Alvira, smiling at her briefly.

"Why me?" she asked as Ariel took another left turn.

The vampire nodded, satisfied that the princess was asking questions at last, "You are his firstborn. The magic within you is bound to be stronger. You're also of the same bloodline as I, which helps."

"Helps what, exactly?"

"Zedkiel and I were prophesied to be harbingers of greatness. When our father took us from this castle after turning us, we learned what true power was. We were blessed with powers beyond our greatest imaginations, and we were given our true purpose. Being of the same bloodline as us enhances the possibility of you accepting the transition more smoothly. You might be stronger than any other human I could have picked."

Alvira stayed silent, listening quietly to what her aunt had to say.

"This true purpose you speak of," the princess paused long enough to make Ariel look at her. "What is it?"

"As children of darkness, our true purpose is to serve Lord Zephyr. Lucifer cast him down to spend his years on earth as a solitary beast. But turning us into his kin grants him power. It frees him of the curse of loneliness. Our purpose is to raise an army in his name, to one day fight Lucifer."

Ariel slowed her pace, taking another turn so the princess and her would be alone at a dead end within the maze. Alvira almost bumped into her.

It was past midnight, and the duo had been walking and making small talk for hours. Alvira's hesitance had faded to some degree, and their conversation had been easy. The princess was full of questions, but Ariel felt the princess's apprehension disappear with every answer.

"Alvira," Ariel spoke gently, raising her hand to brush away the princess's hair from her face. "This isn't a punishment or a curse, my love. It's a blessing. A gift."

"Aunt, you must understand. When you say darkness, when you say people see you as a monster, when you drained a guard before our very eyes to prove a point – it scares me."

Ariel winced, "I... apologize for that."

"This conversation would have helped before the... dinner debacle," Alvira looked at her pointedly.

The vampire nodded sheepishly. Then, Alvira suddenly reached down to grab Ariel's hand. She lifted it to her lips briefly, planting a soft kiss. Ariel froze, her heart beating out of her chest.

She cleared her throat, "The morning sun is almost risen. I must go. But I will return here at the same time tomorrow. Be here to welcome me."

Alvira smiled shyly, "I will, goodnight."

***

On the second night, Alvira was already waiting for Ariel when she arrived. The vampire came directly to the gardens, aware of how whatever needed to be settled was not between the princess and her. Sebastian was no longer a significant part of her plan.

Alvira greeted Ariel with a brief embrace.

"You seem relaxed," Ariel noted, still breathless from the embrace.

"I am," Alvira laughed softly. "I've had time to think. Our conversation last night helped."

The vampire nodded.

"Come on, follow me. Beyond the maze today, we need some room."

Ariel led her away from the maze and into an open field a little distance away.

"What are we doing?" Alvira asked, standing beside Ariel as she shrugged off her robe, revealing her plain maroon tunic beneath.

Ariel rolled up her sleeves, "I wish to show you some of the gifts I wield, the powers you will inherit if you choose to join me."

Alvira watched in awe as Ariel raised her palms to the sky, her movements graceful as she closed her eyes, humming softly under her breath as she wielded the power of the moon. Alvira's jaw dropped open as she felt the moonlight grow dimmer. The princess glanced up in time to see the moon change shape, going from full to half gradually at Ariel's command. The vampire clenched her fist, turning it slowly.

"What-" Alvira froze, her thoughts halting in wonder and confusion. The moon seemed to grow larger in size. "Has it – have you brought it closer?"

Ariel laughed breathily, "Just by bringing the moon closer and changing the shape of the moon, I have affected the balance of nature. This can alter many things, like the tides, the temperature, the earth itself is impacted by this. When you have the power, you must be careful not to mess with the natural order of things. Our powers are limitless, but that does not mean you should abuse them. If people notice these abilities, we will be hunted instead of feared."

The vampire unclenched her fist, straightening up as she released the moon. "This demonstration would be enough to send sailors and traders into a frenzy," she said.

Alvira nodded. "I understand. No abusing our powers."

Ariel smirked at how the princess already seemed to have accepted her fate. The princess's confusion was charming, but so was her confidence. The shy young woman seemed more beautiful, with her brows furrowed in deep thought. She bit the inside of her cheek, pondering over her next questions.

Ariel demonstrated some of her other powers, and soon after, the two were sitting under a large oak tree. The vampire was lying on the grass, basking under the moonlight while Alvira absently played with her hair. Ariel tried not to shudder and focus on the princess's questions instead. But she could feel something shift in her. Alvira was intelligent and quick on her feet. She asked questions that Ariel had not anticipated, allowing her to look at her existence in a different light.

By the end of the second night, the princess was enamored, and the vampire infatuated. When they parted ways that night, Alvira embraced her once more, squeezing her tightly.

"I'll see you tomorrow?" she asked.

Ariel nodded, "If all goes well, princess," the vampire paused, taking in the girl's hopeful expression. "Tomorrow might be the night – if you're ready."

She could hear the princess's heartbeat; it was driving her absolutely mad. She picked up the nervousness in her aura and tried to give her an encouraging smile.

Alvira nodded, turning away to head back to the castle, leaving behind her intoxicating scent.

***

Before the third night, Alvira had made up her mind. She had visited her sister Dierra in her room for a teary farewell. The 17-year-old was furious, unsure as to why her sister had changed her mind so quickly and why she would never see her again.

"You don't have to do this for us, Vira," she pleaded. "You don't have to protect us."

Alvira paused in the doorway, "It's about more than just protecting you now, Di."

The princess said her goodbyes, packing her things as she prepared herself mentally to leave her home after only knowing the castle walls for twenty-two years. With a deep breath, she stepped outside, looking back briefly to memorize what Castle Moon looked like on the day she left.

Alvira entered the gardens, eager to see Ariel. But couldn't find her in the maze nor in the fields where they had been last night. Confused, she opened her mouth to call out to her. Suddenly, she heard the whisper of a familiar voice carried over to her by the wind. Entranced, the princess followed it to the middle of the garden. Beyond a curtain of vines, Alvira spotted a silhouette that could only be Ariel's.

Alvira pushed aside the vines, stepping into a clearing where a bed of flowers awaited her. Ariel lay on the bed, eyes closed as she enjoyed the moonlight on her skin, her bare flesh covered with rose petals.

The princess froze, her breath catching in her throat as she took in the sight of Ariel.

The vampire opened her eyes, motioning to Alvira to come closer and lie next to her on the bed.

Hesitant, the girl approached the bed. Her eyes shifted from the bed to her aunt and away again, feeling shy but curious at the same time.

"Come now, my love. You need not be shy. Remove your clothes and lay beside me – tonight, you will become immortal."

Alvira gulped, her hands shaking slightly as she removed her gown. Her heart was pounding, and she knew Ariel could hear it, she could sense everything she was feeling. She undressed completely, acutely aware of how the vampire's eyes trailed her slender frame.

Alvira sat down, turning to face Ariel. She took a shaky breath as she played with her hands, suddenly nervous.

Ariel inched closer and cupped her cheek softly. She held her until the princess looked into her eyes.

"Kiss me," Ariel whispered.

Alvira closed her eyes, her lips softly brushing against the vampire's. Alvira melted against Ariel, her mouth opening in a soft moan as Ariel deepened the kiss.

They pulled away, foreheads pressed together as they caught their breath.

"Will it hurt?" Alvira asked quietly, "Changing?"

Ariel smiled. "Trust me," she answered, gently pushing the princess onto the bed. The vampire kissed her again, passionately. Alvira arched up, asking for more. Ariel cradled the back of her head gently as she kissed her, trailing her other hand down her chest. She caressed Ariel's breast softly, smirking when the princess gasped, her nipples hardening against the touch.

Ariel broke away from the kiss, relishing how the princess moaned petulantly. The vampire kissed her collarbone, trailing soft pecks down her chest. Ariel moved lower, her breath brushing over soft skin. Alvira's breath hitched as Ariel's hand drifted lower. The princess bit her lip, biting down a moan, clenching her legs close together.

"Hush now, Alvira," Ariel whispered, her fingertips teasingly drumming at her naval. "Don't you trust me?"

Alvira looked down at her and nodded quickly, letting the vampire pry her legs open gently, her fingertips grazing her softly between the legs. Alvira gasped as she felt Ariel kiss her clitoris, her tongue starting to lick her passionately.

The princess cried out in pleasure, her back arching as her hands clenched the flowers beneath her. One of Alvira's hands found purchase in Ariel's hair, tugging softly as the vampire played with her clit.

Alvira tossed her head back, moaning as Ariel started to finger her, teasing the princess and bringing her to the edge of climax. Ariel watched the princess clench her fists and tense up. Laughing softly, Ariel slowed down just so she could watch the princess buck her hips in protest.

"Desperate, are we?"

"Please," she gasped, looking down at Alvira pleadingly.

Ariel bit her lip, unable to say no to those beautiful eyes and how badly they wanted her. Ariel picked up the pace, reveling in how Alvira gasped at the way her tongue played with her clit. She arched her back, feeling the pressure in her groin build.

Alvira clenched a fistful of Ariel's hair, groaning as she climaxed, her body shivering and twitching as it came down from its first high. Ariel wiped her chin with the back of her hand, coming back up to the princess's mouth. She smirked against her lips, laughing teasingly at how Alvira tried to catch her breath.

Ariel lay down next to her then, waiting for the curious girl to regain her breath and kiss her. The vampire guided her unsure hands to her vagina, encouraging her as Alvira touched her for the first time. Ariel closed her eyes, adoring the feel of the princess's touch. She nodded at her reassuringly, guiding her head between her legs. Ariel held her head in place, gasping and groaning as Alvira tasted her for the first time.

The vampire was writhing against her tongue, pleasantly surprised by how dedicated Alvira was to pleasing her. Moaning, the vampire finally grunted, "Enough."

She pulled away, grabbing Alvira by the arms and turning her on her stomach. Ariel pinned her down, leaving wet kisses down her back, licking the sweat off of the virgin's skin and going down to her buttocks. The vampire paid no mind to how the girl struggled against her grip or the way she moaned when she licked her. Ariel's senses were flooded by the scent, the feel of the princess. She could hear the girl's blood pumping through her veins. Half-mad with arousal, Ariel bared her teeth, feeling her fangs release as she bit down on her cheek.

Alvira screamed, her limbs struggling to escape from Ariel's grip. Ariel felt the venom release, sinking into the princess's skin. The vampire felt a part of her become connected to the girl as her blood began to change and match hers. Alvira was shaking hysterically, her body twitching as she changed, her blood shifting to become something more.

Ariel caressed her gently, running her hand down her back soothingly as the princess cried out in pain. She rose as Alvira's twitching slowed, dressing quickly and coming to the princess's side as she opened her eyes slowly.

Ariel held out her hand, helping the girl to her feet. Her face was flushed, despite being turned into a beast of the night mere moments ago. Alvira's face was streaked with tears, looking even more endearing to the vampire as she gave her a watery smile.

"You are now an immortal, Alvira. Your royal titles are no more. You will rise as Alvira Moon, daughter of Ariel Eleazar." Ariel tucked a strand of hair behind her ear, cupping her cheek, "I have given you the power to control the shade, the moon, the creatures of the night. You will always be stronger than the creatures you turn and create."

Alvira nodded solemnly, her blue irises now tinged purple. She knelt before her new master and mother of the night.

"You are my daughter now, Alvira. You need not call me Aunt Ariel any longer. I will have whereabouts of you when you are in danger, and you will feel connected to me in the same way. We will travel the world and turn more vampires for the army we must bring to Lord Zephyr."

Alvira looked up at her, her gaze reflecting the loyalty she felt to her master.

"Yes, Mother. I am ready to follow you to the end of the world."

Chapter 4
Forbidden

After Alvira's turning, Ariel and the princess decided to leave the immediate vicinity of Castle Moon. They planned to continue south, and along the way, Ariel would keep her eyes out for another potential vampire. She knew she was allowed to turn only two in her lifetime to preserve power and ensure there were no incidents where impulse or carelessness would lead to an unwilling, rebellious vampire.

It was wisest to hold out on that front. Perhaps, Alvira could turn another vampire that she deemed worthy, and the army's growth would remain slow but strong. If each vampire saved their second turning for a time more suited to the cause, Zephyr's army would only consist of the strongest vampires.

Ariel had come to the conclusion that stronger humans made for stronger vampires. Her royal bloodline helped, of course. But the Moon bloodline had been fated for this, and the magic that flowed within their veins was special. That was what granted Alvira such power too. As Ariel took the young princess under her wing, she soon learned that the delicate princess had far more to offer than her charm and good looks.

"Ariel, I understand that time is no object for us anymore – but how long must we train? How will we know we're ready?" she asked one day as they placed their belongings in the corner of the room where they would stay for the night.

Ariel smiled softly, "Your training has barely begun, my love. The first lesson Lord Zephyr taught us was patience. It has been mere days since your turning, and you are still learning how to detach from your worldly ties."

"What worldly ties?" she sounded petulant, "Have I not left the castle behind? My family?"

The vampire stepped closer to Alvira, laughing at the way the princess's breath caught even now, even after days of being so close to each other – so intimate.

"You left the castle because you listened to the reasons I gave you, Vira, but along with that, you were craving the adventure, the thrill that comes with being aloof from what binds us." Ariel cupped her cheek, "And I'm sure it is not lost on you how we are still not far from Castle Moon. We could travel at unimaginable speeds, cover immense distances, and yet here we are, staying at an inn less than three days away from your kingdom."

Alvira spun around, busying herself with the tie on her corset, "I didn't ask you to stay here, Mother."

"No, you didn't. But I know *you*." Ariel wrapped her hands around her waist, covering Alvira's hands with her own. "We are bonded now, princess." The vampire's hand drifted lower. "In more ways than one."

Alvira shook her head, "We don't have to stay here long. We can leave tomorrow if you like, where your father trained you."

Ariel hummed in response, "I'm glad you're focused on the next steps of our journey. But there's no real rush. We can take our time." She put her chin on Alvira's shoulder. "Perhaps it isn't all about you, Vira. Perhaps I also wished Father had stayed here a little longer, that I had a familiar place to return to after we trained."

***

The duo grew closer, but Ariel did not lose sight of what was truly important. The vampire focused on training the princess and was pleasantly surprised by how quickly she took to wielding a weapon. The vampire tried to ignore the way she felt whenever Alvira looked up at her with hope in her eyes, seeking her approval whenever she successfully executed a newly learned stance. But she could tell the princess was driven.

Alvira had accepted her change gracefully. She did not question the new demands her body had. When the vampire had held up a rabbit, she had sunk her fangs into its flesh easily, closing her eyes as she drank her fill.

They did not require much sleep as vampires, so nights were spent in deep conversation, answering any queries she had. Alvira's first hunt took place three months after her turning. They had lured a curious young man into the forest. When he had stumbled into the clearing, Alvira had welcomed him, entrancing the young man with her charm and beauty. Ariel noticed that the princess exhibited a quality that could only be another power.

Something about the way Alvira spoke could, at times, hypnotize another human. There was a certain, gentle timber she would use, and the other person would surrender themselves to her. Her first blood felt less like a hunt when she looked back on it after a while. The boy had bared his neck for her to drain, and she had drunk him dry with ease.

Alvira became more and more powerful, matching Ariel in speed and agility when it came to sword fighting. The princess took to archery as well, eager to learn how to fight. She kept expressing knowing how to defend herself, how to attack and win. It gave her the sort of high she could never imagine.

The vampire taught her not only to fight but she would teach her strategy too. If they were to conquer the South and build an army, it was vital that they studied how to handle difficult situations with tact. The answer need not always be violence or a human body lying empty at the back of an alley.

Alvira and Ariel did not venture too far from the Kingdom Moon, even during the princess's training. They would travel far to open fields to practice their powers, but the princess would like to return to a familiar space to rest.

They frequented many inns in the surrounding towns in the kingdom. But when one visit led to another in the same town, the innkeepers began to talk.

The women seemed too close to the villagers, with innkeepers and shopowners eyeing them warily the more they saw them.

"Do you think they're becoming hostile, Ariel?" the princess asked. She lay sprawled on their bed, a sheet barely covering her.

The vampire shrugged, "That is inevitable, princess. The people see that we spend our nights outside the safety of a home, and we spend our daylight hours locked in a room – together."

Ariel stood by the window, her cloak sliding off her shoulder.

"You think they're hostile because they see us together?"

"We don't behave like them," the vampire answered simply. "They do not like seeing us together, so intimate. We both look like young ladies of marriageable age and yet we do not even spare a glance to a passerby."

"Unless we aim to drink them," Alvira whispered, laughing lightly.

"They fear us because we do not act like the women they know or the women they like to see. We have no fear of them in our hearts, and that sort of brashness is bound to ruffle feathers."

"Does it bother you, Ariel?" Alvira sat up. "You sound disturbed."

"Of course not, darling. Just because we prefer the company of one another over that of men is no cause to worry," Ariel shrugged.

"Then what is it?"

The vampire gazed out of the window, her eyes set on the setting sun, "I recall Father telling us to lay low – to not draw attention."

Zephyr had wanted the vampires to remain in the shadows until the time was right. Until the army was ready. Until then, they were to be as quiet as they could, turning the tide slowly in his favor.

"But they don't dislike us because we're vampires," Alvira said.

"Their dislike and hostility mean nothing, Vira. But do we need to invite it?" Ariel asked. "Their norms mean nothing to us because the laws of their God do not apply to us. We are above it all."

"Precisely," the princess agreed. "To hell with the wandering weary eyes of all the strange men that think it's their business to tell us how to behave."

The rebellious rage in the princess's voice made Ariel smile. The princess's gaze had hardened her jaw set. She was determined to be with her.

The vampire chuckled softly, "Pay no mind to them, my little rebel." She crossed the floor to reach her beloved at the side of the bed. Ariel bent down to kiss her softly, her lips gently prying at Alvira's.

Ariel pulled away only when she knew the princess needed to breathe.

"Let's show them how little we care," Alvira panted.

Ariel laughed, letting the princess pull her down by her robe.

***

The people in the villages surrounding Castle Moon had grown restless. News traveled fast of the women who feared no God, who lived together and disappeared as soon as the sun set, returning only before the first rays of sunlight graced their streets.

Reports to the king did nothing. Sebastian was powerless against his sister, her hellish strength was a reminder of everything he wasn't, and his daughter had been sacrificed to the monster's cause. It had seemed to the king that in Alvira's final days at the castle, something in the girl had shifted, and she had looked forward to her nights out with her aunt.

It was embarrassing, to say the least, but he no longer had any control over Alvira. If Ariel had followed her design, his daughter was already lost to the darkness.

The king's inaction led to anger among the villagers. Their religion was their anchor, and to host women who so blatantly disregarded their Lord was a disgrace. One evening, the villagers had decided to meet outside the church, eager to discuss what to do with their uninvited guests.

"These women are here to do the work of the devil," one lady began. "They will spoil our children, teach them their devilish ways and steal them from us."

"They're disgracing the Lord!" another man joined in.

"The king will do nothing! We need to kick them out ourselves!" came another voice.

The innkeeper spoke up last, "I know where they are. I say we cast them out of our hometown, and if they perish in the process – so be it."

Cries of assent went up as rioters gathered, furious at the forbidden lovers that haunted their streets at night. They armed themselves with what little they had and decided to surround the inn where the women were staying.

It was almost dusk, and Ariel had risen from their bed, curious to see what the clamor was about. The vampire narrowed her eyes at the amassing numbers outside their inn. They stayed in a room on the first floor, and it was clear to her that the villagers below were chanting slogans against them, cursing them for their hellish designs.

"Vira?" Ariel called out.

The princess hummed in response, her eyes closed, her expression blissful.

"Vira!" Ariel repeated, her voice stern. "Get dressed. The villagers want us gone."

Alvira rose from the bed, brow furrowed.

"Get dressed!" she pressed, using her agility and speed to do the same. The vampire gathered their meager belongings, shaking her head and mumbling under her breath.

Alvira got dressed, staring at the view from their window.

"Are they truly so hateful?"

"You're so innocent, my love," Ariel placed a quick kiss on her forehead. "We must leave."

Alvira's gaze turned sad and fearful. She absently grabbed the bag Ariel held out to her.

"We need not steal away like thieves, Vira." Ariel soothed, stepping into the hallway. "We will leave from the entrance and face these rioters. We will look them in the eyes and tell them we do not fear their wrath, and we do not need their shelter."

Alvira nodded, taking Ariel's proffered hand. "We're far stronger than they could ever be. And we need not give up on each other for their sake."

Chapter 5
The Start of the Northern Region

As the Southern Region became home to Ariel, the Northern was not far off either. Ariel had Alvira, and they would turn more to suit their cause. Zedkiel had moved swiftly to the North. In the beginning, he would think of his sister often, doubting his abilities and recalling what his weaknesses were when he and Ariel trained together. What had given Zephyr the confidence that they were ready? Not just to be on their own but to head regions on alone as well.

Zedkiel still felt like a child sometimes. Though many years had passed, he still looked like the handsome young prince he was. He knew he caught the eye of humans, men and women alike, but none struck his fancy. His head was a muddle, his responsibility great, and his days lonesome.

Zephyr had separated the twins on purpose. He knew they worked well together, but their dependence on one another could be exploited. The King of Darkness had seen the doubt in Zedkiel's eyes on the very first night – and he knew the boy had to outgrow his sister's shadow.

Zedkiel sulked for a few months, but the journey northwards was fascinating. There were so many different dialects, languages, people, and places that struck his fancy—each different from the next. But there were always familiar undercurrents in every place he visited. Scents that would always ground him when his thoughts carried him too far.

The Prince of Darkness found himself in Russia. The cold climate suited him. His pale skin matched those around him. The people minded their own business too, which he liked the most. No one said anything about the young traveler in their Russian village, how he struggled to learn the language, or how he only stepped out at night and would return from the forests that surrounded the area.

But a young man like Zedkiel ought to enlist in the emperor's army. Zedkiel never stayed in a village too long, but there would still be the occasional hushed comment, the question about where he was from and why he wasn't in the emperor's army. Questions like these came from the concerned old lady who would sell him some fruit as he set off for another city at dusk.

Zedkiel would smile, saying he would get there eventually.

Perhaps the best person to turn would be someone from a royal lineage. The prince knew his sister had gone back to Castle Moon, to see if Sebastian was king, if he had children of his own that could help the cause.

And Zephyr had chosen them too. If they were to have a stronghold in the south, perhaps the Russian emperor would be the right person to turn to. And if he was too old, the young vampire thought, there might be a son or daughter he could lure into his trap.

A few months before Zedkiel decided to meet with the emperor, the young prince had a nightmare. Zedkiel hadn't had a drop of blood for almost a month. The winter months were unforgiving, and prey was scarce. The town that was his temporary abode had grown on him, and the locals knew his name. The young vampire had acquaintances, people he did not wish to drain to satiate his own monstrous appetite.

He had grown weak, and as he dozed off near dawn, the boy dreamt of Castle Moon. The watchtowers were ablaze, the city burning to the ground. Zedkiel ran through familiar streets, yelling for his sister and the father that turned him.

As he sped through the burning city, he turned a corner and almost trampled over something that collided against his knee. Zedkiel glanced down in time to see Zephyr sprawled on the cobblestone, his hand raised in a weak plea for help.

"Father!" Zedkiel fell to his knees, cradling Zephyr's head on his lap, "W-what happened?"

The King of Darkness closed his eyes, lips barely moving. "We lost." The vampire took a deep, shaky breath. "Your sister's army was strong – but we needed more."

"Ariel's army?" Zedkiel asked. "What about-"

"You were late, son." His voice was hoarse now, "We were alone."

The next morning, Zedkiel awoke, set his sights on Moscow, and wandered the forests less frequently. It did not matter that he was immortal now, and time was not something he worried about. But the sight of his father dying had shifted something in him. He knew he had to target royalty, and the emperor of Russia was just the sort of man for the job.

***

Moscow was impressive, the city sprawling with life despite the harsh weather. It was clear the city was the capital of the nation, even the outskirts of Moscow were home to the best amenities the country had to offer. The emperor was dedicated: harsh but fair. The nation thrived the most during the era of Akim Yaroslav, the Tsar of the time.

As Zedkiel familiarized himself with the city, he quickly learned that the Tsar's palace was heavily guarded, and getting an audience with the emperor was almost impossible. Citizens had to go through a rigorous process and several meetings with advisors first before their matter was presented before the emperor. Usually, the advisors would take care of matters themselves; Akim had trained them well.

At first, the young vampire felt stumped. How could he request an audience with a king like that? He recalled how

Zephyr had stolen into their castle in the dead of night and changed their lives forever. But his father's approach was one he did not agree with anymore. If Zephyr had trusted him enough to look after an entire region of his own, then perhaps his methods did not have to mirror the violence his father favored.

He had to impress Akim, that much he knew. If he enlisted in the army, it would take too long to get the Tsar's attention. His approach had to be more direct. A few weeks into his stay in Moscow, Zedkiel devised a plan.

He would walk into the Tsar's throne room in broad daylight. He would present the king with the sword owned by his highest-ranking general and ask for an audience with him. Zedkiel wanted to infiltrate the ranks and earn the emperor's respect before revealing his true intentions.

Getting the sword was easy enough. The young vampire had picked up whispers of General Lagasov, the man responsible for the king's safety. The general was a big, burly man with hair that was graying at the temples. Lagasov kept his hair in a bun, the jet-black hair streaked with white. His face told stories of the battles he had won, scars marring his cheeks.

Zedkiel had walked up to him, his fist over his heart as he said his salutations. First, praise for the Tsar, followed by a small remark about how he looked up to the general.

"What is a child like you doing at a pub like this?" he asked, his voice matching his menacing demeanor. He glanced at the barkeep. "Get him out of here."

"I came to convey my respect for you, Lagasov." The lack of regard in his voice earned Zedkiel a glare. "Before I crush you in battle."

At this, the Russian lost his composure. The general bellowed a laugh that could have shaken the earth. "You wish to fight me?" he shook his head, thumping his glass on the bar twice. "I'll give you points for gall."

"I wish to have an audience with the Tsar," Zedkiel began, unfazed by the insult. "And instead of presenting him your head on a platter, I wish to give him your sword."

Lagasov raised his brows in disbelief.

"You look down at me now, but I am showing you mercy, general." The menace in the young vampire's voice was hard to miss. "Fight me now, and you might live to see me stand where you stand today."

Lagasov threw his mug on the floor, and Zedkiel didn't flinch.

"At the Tsar's right hand," the Prince of Darkness finished.

The general rose, the bar stool scraping against the wooden floor. He placed a hand on his sword, preparing to draw it.

"I will slay you where you stand," the general bellowed.

Zedkiel smiled, a hand on his blade. Before Lagasov had even moved, the vampire brought his blade down on the general's left hand, slicing off a chunk of flesh. The general yelled in confusion, his dominant hand injured. Zedkiel kicked him behind the knee, bringing the general to his knees as he placed the tip of his blade under Lagasov's chin, "An audience."

The young vampire kicked his foot down on the discarded sword. He caught it with his other hand as it flew up. "With the Tsar."

Lagasov panted, his brows drawn in confusion. The floor was wet with the blood that spurt from the wound. Zedkiel licked his lips, baring his fangs at the intoxicating smell of blood.

His crimson eyes darkened, but he reminded himself who his real target was.

"You will accompany me and tell him how I took this sword from your very grip." Zedkiel lowered his sword, noting how his blade had cut the general. "And how I spared you."

Lagasov had done as Zedkiel asked, promising him an audience with the Tsar, Peter the Great. The young vampire had heard good things about him, about the power the Tsar held, and his dedication to expanding his empire and increasing his worth. Zedkiel had spent months traipsing through the Russian landscape, it had been vast and empty, and food had been scarce.

The vampire recalled one brutal winter when he had left the comfort of the small room at an inn in search of something to feed off of. He had gotten lost in a snowstorm, the weather frigid enough to even chill his immortal bones. Zedkiel had to cross the fence of a small ranch and drain two of the cows there. He had replenished his strength there, like a thief, crouching behind a barn as he slew the animals.

The Prince of Darkness had heard rumors about the Tsar. He knew that Peter the Great had done plenty to earn that title. The leader was determined and eager to leave his mark on the world and shift the ways of his people. He was a revolutionary, and the villagers spoke of him reverently. Zedkiel knew that Peter would be the right man to turn to his cause. The Tsar was royalty and powerful, and his strength of character would only amplify his powers more.

Lagasov promised him an audience with the king. In preparation for a meeting with a man of such stature, Zedkiel decided to change his attire. The vampire donned a black velvet cape draped lazily across one shoulder. A gold chain on his left shoulder kept the cape in place. The vampire wore a maroon silk shirt underneath. His attire made him look regal, his white skin a stark contrast to his clothes.

Lagasov eyed him up and down, "You clean up nicely."

"A meeting with the Tsar is no small matter," Zedkiel rolled his shoulders. "After all, I am to take over your position."

The Russian snarled, irritated.

The doors to the castle swung open, and Lagasov led him down a great corridor. Zedkiel held his head high, his crimson eyes set on the entrance to the great hall where Peter would see him.

The vampire was taken aback by the layout when they entered the hall. It was apparent that the Tsar had chosen to see him somewhere other than the throne room. The room was large, with heavy curtains draped over the tall windows. There were low sofas on all four sides, the seating punctuated by the occasional vase upon a pedestal. In the center of the room, the Tsar reclined upon a dewan, an unfinished game of chess set up on the table in front of him.

As the doors opened, Peter the Great opened an eye and arched a brow at the company his head of security had brought.

"Lagasov," his voice was smooth, monotone. "Who do we have here?"

"My name is Zedkiel Eleazar," the vampire began. He noticed how the Tsar looked from Lagasov to him and then back again. "I stand before you because I am here to take Lagasov's place."

The Tsar's lip twitched in a smile.

"Sire," Lagasov begrudgingly began. "This traveler has braved the storms of Russia to stand here before you. He's bested me in battle with the sole intent of catching your attention."

Peter the Great sat up, eyeing his head of security curiously.

Lagasov held up his bandaged arm sheepishly.

"Well, you have my attention, then."

"I wish to work closely with you, Your Highness." Zedkiel wasn't lying. His aim was to get close enough to the Tsar to turn him easily. "I have traveled far and have seen my fair share of battle. I wish to work with you."

"And take Lagasov's place?" Peter smiled.

"If you allow."

"Sit." Peter the Great gestured to the chair opposite his dewan. "Finish this game with me."

Zedkiel and Peter sat face to face, a game of chess between them. Zedkiel played black. He needed only a moment to get a grip on where the unfinished game stood. Odds were in the King's favor – but not all of them.

Their game lasted 45 minutes.

The Tsar moved his king another block toward the right. Zedkiel smiled, calmly placing his rook across from the white king.

"Checkmate."

The Tsar's eyebrows shot up. He paused before breaking into a hearty laugh. "Well done."

Peter the Great rose, and Zedkiel followed suit. The Tsar stood tall at 6 feet 8 inches and was pleasantly surprised to be standing eye to eye with the vampire. He held out his hand for Zedkiel to shake.

"You won't be taking Lagasov's place," he announced. The Tsar looked into Zedkiel's crimson eyes and saw the hunger therein. "I'd like you to work beside me. As my primary advisor."

The vampire beamed, "It would be an honor, Your Majesty."

Zedkiel's initial plan was to work with the Tsar and get close to him. Maybe he would find a window one month into working with him. The young vampire did not anticipate how much he would get along with Peter. The

Tsar trusted him more than he did anyone else in his cabinet, and he had been impressed by Zedkiel's eye for strategy. They ended up plotting battles and wars together as days turned to months and months to years.

The Prince of Darkness had many a window to bend close to Peter's neck, to sink his fangs into his skin and claim him for his army. But something held him back. He could bear to turn the Tsar. Peter continued to age while Zedkiel's skin remained free of any mark of time. They often joked about Zedkiel not being human, but the vampire never revealed the truth.

The truth was, the vampire had realized that Peter was more valuable to his people than he had imagined. If Zedkiel turned him now, the Tsar would abandon his current goals for those of the house of Eleazar. Humanity's progression would halt as a consequence.

Six years into their close companionship, Zedkiel and Peter had been sitting on a balcony in the palace, a bottle of vodka between them. The night was young, the moon bright and beautiful. Zedkiel's skin seemed ethereal in the moonlight, and the Tsar absentmindedly commented on it.

"Peter," Zedkiel began. "There's something I need to tell you."

His friend eyed him from over his tumbler. "Is it the secret to your youth? Does the gray in my hair bother you?" he joked.

"I am not who I say I am, Peter." The vampire sighed. "I have not been entirely truthful. I'm not even human."

Peter stayed silent, listening intently.

"I am what one may call a vampire. Not many of us are on Earth yet, but we shall be one day. I am the Prince of Darkness, son of Zephyr, the King of Darkness. He was an angel cast out by Lucifer, cursed to an eternity of lonely wandering as a monster no human would be a companion to. But he found us and turned us into vampires like him – beasts that feast on the blood of man. We have powers and strength beyond your wildest imaginations."

"You're immortal?" Peter interjected. "That explains so much."

Zedkiel laughed softly. "His purpose is to raise an army that would one day fight against Lucifer. He presumes Father is lonely and suffering. He will come down only when he thinks it is time for him to die. Lucifer believes his killing my father would be a show of mercy. But when he comes to Earth, there shall be a legion of vampires willing to fight in his name."

"It is a noble purpose, Zedkiel."

The vampire's brows arched higher, "It does not bother you that I am a beast? A monster that feasts on blood?"

Peter shrugged, "I am a monster that feasts on blood, Zedkiel. Think of the blood on my hands, the men I have killed, the people I am responsible for. We're not that different."

The vampire snorted in disbelief. "I came here to turn you to my cause all those years ago, Peter."

"And yet you did not. Why?"

"I care for you too much. The people of Russia need you more than my cause."

The Tsar hummed, amused. "I had seen the hunger in your eyes, my friend. Back then, I did not know what it was for."

"I don't aim to turn you even now, Peter. I value our companionship far more than that."

***

It was the year 1723, and Zedkiel had spent most of his time at Peter's right hand. He had supported the Tsar, fighting alongside him and helping him plot wars. Beyond the strategy and swordplay was genuine friendship, which the vampire valued immensely. Years had passed, and Peter the Great was now on his deathbed. As he coughed up blood, the vampire contemplated saving his friend's life by turning him.

The thought crossed his mind and was immediately replaced by visions of angry people and villagers outraged at how their beloved Tsar was now a beast. His legend would forever be tarnished. A part of him also knew that Peter would not be as strong of a vampire anymore, either. It would be best to let his friend find peace and rest. He had lived a long life and deserved the rest.

After Peter's death, Zedkiel left Russia. He had wasted enough time as it was. With his friend now gone, there was not much else the nation offered him. Zedkiel grieved the death of Peter the Great, leaving the land and heading East on horseback.

China greeted him with warmer weather and a culture so different from the Russians that it threw him off guard. Zedkiel took his time, learning how to interact with the people of the East. The oriental practices and culture were unique, ridden with myths, tales, and traditions. But the nation was caught in a war with the West. He knew that if he approached the locals as an Englishman, they would kill him.

The vampire donned the same garb as the locals, discarding his regal cape, and decided to pose as an immigrant from Russia.

Zedkiel had donned the garb of the Chinese people. Even then, he noticed how everyone gave him a second glance. Clearly, he was not a local, and his features were western, but his traditional clothing granted him some leeway and begrudging acceptance. At first, the Prince of Darkness was uncertain where he should go. He could look for another inn to stay at until he figured out his path.

The grief of losing Peter was still fresh, but it was a reminder that time was passing, and he had a job to do.

Zedkiel was still musing over his next course of action when he noticed a dark shadow flitting across an alley. Curious, he followed. The vampire stood at the mouth of the alley, but he could tell it was a dead end. Empty fruit crates lay scattered at the end, but no human was in sight. Zedkiel waited, looking around for signs of life. He felt something shift behind him. He whirled around but saw no one. The vampire's brow furrowed. Just then, Zedkiel saw the shadow on the wall in front of him flit across and jump onto another wall.

Confused, Zedkiel followed. The shadow jumped from wall to wall, leading Zedkiel away from the city. Zedkiel noticed the sparse landscape's small houses as he entered the outskirts. The shadow on the ground sped toward a small house with only one window that glowed orange as the sunset. Night was falling, and Zedkiel watched the shadow blend with the shadow cast by the small house.

Curious, the vampire got closer to the house. He peered through the small window that glowed from the flame of one large candle. Inside lay two weak children on a small mattress on the floor. Their parents sat cross-legged before them. The mother stirred something on a low stove on the ground. The parents looked exhausted, with dark circles under their eyes and worry prominent, while the children looked almost skeletal. The boy and the girl lay almost still, and Zedkiel had to squint to see if they were still breathing or not.

Zedkiel was too focused on getting a better look at the family inside when a voice addressed him. The vampire jumped at the sound.

"Your presence is known, Prince of Darkness. I know who you are."

Zedkiel looked at the figure that towered over him. The man was deathly pale, somehow looking even more dead than he. He was clad in all black, his robes gathering about him in a manner that hid the man's true form from anyone that saw him. He was quite handsome, Zedkiel noticed. The man's features were aristocratic, and his gaze an indifferent and cool tone of gray.

A glimmer caught the vampire's eye. The man had idly rolled the handle of a tall staff in his palm while Zedkiel had been eyeing him. At the end of the staff was a sharp, arced blade.

"You are the Grim Reaper." Realization dawned on him. "Angel of Death ... Father spoke of you."

"Right you are, prince. What are you doing here, vampire?"

Zedkiel put together the reaper's presence with the sickly children inside.

"You're about to take away their children," he stated. "Why?"

"They are ready to become Angel Knights for the Most High."

Zedkiel nodded, gears in his head turning as he put everything together. It was clear to him that the reaper stood there with a purpose beyond bringing death. These children were surely special if a divine power wanted them as angel knights.

"Not if I can help it," Zedkiel blurted, a little taken aback by his own gall. "These children will leave this house with me tonight. As children of the night."

"You dare interfere with the Most High's plan?" The reaper's voice had not gotten any louder, yet Zedkiel felt the hairs on his arm stand on end.

"I know of the greatness these two will accomplish, and I shall be the one to save them from their death." The Prince of Darkness seemed to be overtaken by a greater power, a grander knowledge that assured him these children would be the two he would turn.

Without waiting for a response from the reaper, Zedkiel went to the front of the house, throwing open the door just as the parents finished praying to their divine god. They took in the sight of a traveler dressed in traditional garb and knelt on the ground. Zedkiel smiled as they expressed their relief at receiving help from an angel to save their children from the brink of death.

Zedkiel motioned toward the father, telling him to come closer. After all, he had certain stipulations before he would save the children.

"If I save your children," Zedkiel began. "You will lose all claim to them."

The man was already in tears. "Please, save them. They are all we have. They are my heirs."

Zedkiel glanced at the twins; the boy's face was scrunched in pain.

"Old man, if I save your children from the reaper himself, they will no longer be yours. You may be the one responsible for their birth, but after I save them, they shall accompany me on their true journey. They will become mine to raise. They will live forever, but they shall be mine." Zedkiel searched his face for any hesitation. "Will you allow immortality to fall upon your children?"

The man glanced at his wife briefly, "Yes, please, just save them from death."

The woman finally spoke, "Wait... reconsider."

The vampire watched patiently as the woman gathered herself.

"This man will take away our children forever, my love. They would be as good as dead."

Her husband shook his head, "To see them pass away would be grief neither of us can bear. To know that our children are alive and taken care of, that must be enough. Save them."

The reaper chose then to make his appearance, "So, you pray to the Most High to save them—you pleaded to your Lord, and He sent me."

Zedkiel shook his head, "He offers your children the life of the realm beyond—the place where you shall go when you pass. It is another life, but it will be one that you cannot see. What I promise you is real. You shall be able to see them."

As the husband and wife glanced from one man to the other, it was clear that they felt safer with Zedkiel—the one who promised their children a worldly existence.

The reaper's face twisted in disgust, "I'm not going to fight you over two knights. But believe me, Vampire, the Most High will remember your treachery."

With those words, the reaper melted into the shadows, disappearing from the house. Zedkiel nodded at the parents, slowly making his way over to the twins that lay on the thin mattress. Zedkiel's ears could pick up on the faint heartbeats. He knew they were in immense pain.

Zedkiel took the girl's wrist first. Her eyes flew open just as his fangs pierced the thin skin. His eyes rolled up as he tasted a bit of her blood. He noticed her eyes glimmered in the strangest way. They were almost otherwordly. She cried out softly in pain, her eyes fluttering closed as the venom became a part of her.

The boy was next. Zedkiel lowered the blanket from his still form, grimacing at the sores that riddled the young boy's body. He lifted his wrist to his mouth as well, and as his fangs pierced the soft skin, the boy began to convulse. His mouth opened in a silent scream, but he was too weak to make any sound. As the venom entered his system, the convulsions first began to increase, but after a few moments, the boy lay still. The sores began to fade away from his skin, and within minutes, his skin became clear. The disease left the children's bodies, and when Zedkiel stood, he had a proud smile on his face.

When the children opened their eyes, now tinged crimson, something finally clicked for the Prince of Darkness. As he watched his children, he finally realized why Zephyr had done what he had when he turned him and Ariel. As that feeling sank in, he felt a ferocious urge to protect the twins, and he vowed never to leave them the way Zephyr had so long ago.

"Son," Zedkiel offered his hand to the boy, who took it gratefully and stood after months of being bedridden. "I name you Shadow Reaper—for the Reaper himself stared at your soul and saw the darkness within you. I see the fire in your gaze even now."

He extended his other hand to the girl.

"Daughter, I shall name you Star Reaper—for your eyes shined light on the darkness that stared you down. You are my children now—vampires that will live forever. Your old family will become a figment of the past that you will soon forget."

Shadow and Star looked at one another and then down at their bodies. For the first time in months, their bodies were not failing them. In fact, they felt stronger than they could ever remember feeling.

Star smiled up at him, "Thank you, mister."

"You can call me Father."

***

The children said their farewells. Although the goodbyes had been teary, both parents and children seemed content. The mother and father had seen a miracle unfold before them, and anyone who could bring their children from the brink of death the way Zedkiel had would surely protect them. The twins were also grateful. They felt different, more powerful. For the first time in their lives, the twins were not weak. They felt healthy, empowered, and, more importantly, strong.

As they walked toward the city, Shadow kept picking up his pace. He would speedily walk ahead of Zedkiel and Star and then return to them shortly after. Zedkiel laughed.

"Go on, test your limits then," he offered.

Star looked at him in awe, "You're going to let us run?"

"Of course. Did your parents not let you before?"

"We were always too sick—running would trigger coughing spells," Shadow told him.

Zedkiel patted Star on the head, "Go ahead."

The children raced ahead, surprised by their own agility and strength. Every new experience the children had only strengthened their loyalty to Zedkiel. He told them how they were destined to be great warriors in a war against Morningstar and how he planned on training them for the role. The prince impressed upon them the importance of maintaining a low profile and always being on the move. It was best not to let others know about their powers just yet—their numbers were far too few at the time.

Shadow showed great swiftness and a penchant for martial arts. He had trained in martial arts at a very young age before the illness had taken over his body, and he enjoyed it even more now. His powers granted him more flexibility, stamina, and agility.

Star, on the other hand, had different talents. She had felt surges of power coursing through her veins, and after a few strange accidents, she one day lifted a boulder three times her size. Her strength had taken everyone by surprise, but she loved it. As he trained the twins, Zedkiel's confidence grew—he knew he had chosen well for his purpose. And he knew this would anger the Most High and the Reaper.

"Children, we need to become even stronger," he began one day. "We have wandered earth like this long enough—we need to have a home of our own, far removed from mankind. A place where we can train in peace and where we can learn more about our dark powers. I have decided to head south, and you shall accompany me. There, we shall build our home."

Zedkiel and the twins moved southwards, exploring new cultures and countries but never settling. The children picked up new fighting techniques, different weapons, and different languages on their journey. The Prince of Darkness taught the children how to hunt, and on occasion, when a stubborn, arrogant human would cross their path, Zedkiel would let them hunt them down and drain them.

Human blood was a delicacy, but it was also a necessity. It renewed their strength in ways they couldn't imagine and was no less than a drug. The further south they moved, the harder it became to come by.

Zedkiel was moving them to Antarctica. The desolate, icy landscape was no place for man, which made it perfect for vampires. They were unaffected by the extreme climate, and the region gave them the privacy they needed as vampires.

In the lifeless land of Antarctica, Zedkiel Eleazar built his first castle. He built it as a home for vampires, a place where they could be safe. The prince of darkness always had a softer side to him, and the grand castle was his first attempt at creating a home after not having one for years. He had put a lot of thought into the castle—it was located somewhere away from the sun, of the Morning Star–and away from life so any and all vampires could stay there to utilize their full potential.

Here, at Castle Eleazar, time would be no object, and no vampire would ever be alone.

Zedkiel trained the twins, dedicating himself to their growth and improvement. He did not have to push the two very hard because the children were already driven and dedicated to the cause. They had known true weakness, and so they did not disregard or take the gifts they had been given for granted. He watched with fatherly pride as his children blossomed into great warriors.

At the castle, time felt nonexistent. The days blurred together, and Zedkiel lost track of how long he and the twins had been there. Shadow and Star grew stronger before him, and eventually, the day came when Zedkiel finally understood why Zephyr had sent him and Ariel on their own paths.

It had been a good day, full of laughter and playful teasing as the twins finished training. Zedkiel had summoned them to one of the castle's highest terraces, and there, as they gazed out at the icy wasteland, Zedkiel gave his children their true task.

"Children, I am proud of the warriors you have become. The powers you possess are far beyond what you can imagine. You train every day and push yourself further than you did the previous day, but even then, the true gravity of what you are capable of escapes you." He paused and looked at his son and daughter. "You must be careful. You cannot use your gifts to change the natural order of things. Our powers are limitless, and sometimes, you might feel compelled to abuse them."

Star and Shadow listened closely.

"No matter the circumstance, you cannot let any rage or frustration or arrogance compel you to abuse your powers. Promise me you will not misuse your new gifts." His gaze hardened. "A new Vampire Order is coming into existence. Our numbers will grow, and in order to not lose sight of our true purpose, we must ensure no power is misused."

Shadow spoke first. "I promise not to abuse my power, Father. Instead, I will pay forward what I have learned along with what I had been taught by the Grand Masters of martial arts in China. I will teach Star, and you, in exchange for the second chance you have given us."

Zedkiel smiled. "I appreciate the offer, son." He patted Shadow on his shoulder, amused by the serious determination on the boy's face. "Your training in the martial arts and what you have learned here will give you the power to control darkness and creatures of the night." Shadow's brow furrowed.

"Your speed and swiftness are your biggest advantage," Zedkiel explained. "Hiding in the darkness that is subject to your whims, you will indeed be a formidable opponent. No one would dare challenge you. Look within, and you shall find the depth of the darkness. Your true powers will awaken, for no light shall scare you away."

"Father, I ..." Shadow paused, biting his lip in doubt before he continued. "I have a proposal, and I hope you shall approve of it. I will indeed become formidable, but would you grant me permission to create an Assassin's Guild? I would train these assassins to eliminate any name you may ask of me. I shall turn only those I see fit, and they, in turn, shall do the same under my guidance. I will help grow our numbers."

Zedkiel nodded, impressed. "I permit you to create this guild. I see great things in your future, son. This guild will benefit our cause."

Star had been listening patiently, arms crossed as she waited her turn. But Shadow's suggestion had been impressive. "Brother, that is truly ingenious. I'm proud of you."

"Star," Zedkiel began fondly. "Your powers remind me of my sister, Ariel. You shall meet her soon with the gifts you possess. You have the ability to control time and space. The stars will be your beacon, for they will show you ways to develop your powers."

His daughter's eyes sparkled with possibility. "With time," he cut in before Star could say anything, almost reading her mind, "you cannot go back to the time before your change, but in the years to come, you will be able to relive this day if need be."

His daughter nodded eagerly. The family of three had trained for years until it was finally time for the twins to depart and expand the Vampire Order. Zedkiel stayed at Castle Eleazar and waited for his sister to find her way to this haven.

His children, now on their own journeys of greatness, traveled to Japan, where Shadow started by first building a dojo where he trained his sister. Shadow perfected his ninjutsu, teaching Star in the process.

As their training reached its peak, the siblings parted ways as well, understanding that it would be best to head in their own directions for the sake of their true goals and independence. Star traveled further south, toward Osaka, while her brother remained in Hokkaido.

Star began her solitary journey, alone for the first time in her life. At Osaka, she made a place for herself amongst the people swiftly. She had impressed the governor of the region and been hailed as a guest at Osaka Castle. There, Star Reaper resided, exploring the city and polishing her skills patiently. She knew she did not have to turn someone immediately. Star wanted to take her time and carefully select someone worthy of the noble cause her father had sent her upon.

During her time at Osaka, Star Reaper heard rumors of someone by the name of Dorothy Deathdealer. The name itself sounded powerful, but to most people, she was just a member of a nearby school for musical arts. She had moved to Japan not long ago and was studying music. She had been teaching children, especially young girls, how to master certain musical instruments and was becoming a household name.

Star Reaper was curious and did some digging on her own. Beyond the public eye, after inquiring into the darker, deeper underbelly of the city, Star learned that Miss Dorothy was also known for her skills with a blade. There was a certain swiftness with which she wielded her weapon.

Star Reaper was intrigued. Dorothy Deathdealer was clearly a woman who lived a double life and was skilled at balancing both. The young vampire sent word to Dorothy, posing as an admirer who would like to challenge her to a friendly duel.

Dorothy accepted, designating a spot for the duel the very next evening. Star arrived early, but Dorothy was there before her still. Star smirked. So the woman did not like to be one-upped. Dorothy turned to face her. Her long black hair was braided back, her dark eyes alive with the fire of a challenge.

"Dorothy," she introduced herself.

"Star Reaper," Star bowed lightly. She eyed the infamous blade that was strapped to Dorothy's side, the blade that she knew the woman had crafted herself and took great pains to sharpen. "Your admirer."

"And challenger." Dorothy smiled, circling her slowly. Star did the same, unaware of how they both circled each other like prey.

Star removed the formal cape draped around her shoulders to reveal her armor. It was designed by one of the greatest designers of the time.

Star had also acquired an exquisite katana so that they could be evenly matched in battle. Her katana's blade was thick yet sharp. She needed something that would stand the infamous blade that could cut through any steel. Dorothy nodded appreciatively.

Before Star could anticipate it, Dorothy had lunged forward with her blade drawn. Star immediately raised her own, parrying the blow. Dorothy's brow arched as the blades clashed together, almost evenly matched. The surprise didn't last long, and Deathdealer came at her with a series of blows—relentless attacks that Star matched in kind.

Dorothy had pushed Star to the edge of their predefined circle, and Star saw no window to push her back. The vampire's frustration kicked in and she became more aggressive, attempting to push her blade at the chink in Dorothy's armor in the split seconds between attacks.

Dorothy's movements were swift and accurate. Nothing Star threw at her caused the warrior to stumble. She was tempted to use some of her superhuman strength, but Star knew that would be unfair.

"Finally," Deathdealer panted between lunges. "A true opponent." Their movements were fluid, almost dance-like. The only music was the clash of their blades. "I can sense your strength and ability. But do you have what it takes to take me on?"

Star smirked. "You are an interesting character, Miss Deathdealer." She jumped back, spinning as she ducked and swung at Dorothy's legs. "I'll try my best to keep up with your swordsmanship."

Dorothy jumped, missing the attack by a hair's breadth. The women had not noticed the crowd that had gathered around them. They were so immersed in their duel that they lost track of time, constantly trying to push the other toward defeat. Locals had gathered about them, watching intently, hissing and cheering them on as they dueled.

Dorothy's sensei was in the crowd, along with some other masters. He was stoic and stood with his arms crossed, but his expression gave away his interest. He had not seen a warrior so well-versed in the ancient style of ninjutsu in years.

Star pretended to be fatigued. "You're good, but are you ready for me to unleash my true power?" she asked. Dorothy snorted.

"Let me make you an offer," Star dodged an attack, deflecting the blade casually. "If I beat you with less than a fraction of my full power, you will join me as my student." They continued their delicate dance. "And possibly my first child," Star finished, laughing as the words left her mouth.

"Your first child?" Dorothy chuckled. "I'm probably older than you, kid. What are you, sixteen?"

Star shrugged. "The gods have been kind."

"You haven't seen my full potential either, so I say bring it." Dorothy shrugged. "But if you happen to beat me, then I'll consider this funny little offer of yours."

Star nodded, opting to use her speed to put an end to the fight, which had gone on for too long already. Dorothy swung at Star, and she dodged out of the way. To Dorothy, it looked as if Star had not even moved, but all of a sudden, her blade had been pushed away. It was now pointing to the ground, and Star's katana was an inch away from her neck.

Dorothy's eyes narrowed, confusion evident. Star was declared the winner, and the crowd around them went wild. There were some in the crowd that were skeptical about the victory, having witnessed it themselves. The Old Masters conversed amongst themselves and decided to declare Star the victor of the match.

Dorothy frowned but bowed gracefully. She eyed Star carefully, wondering how she had moved so swiftly and how she had gotten so close so quickly. It was by far the greatest match she had ever been in.

The warrior left the arena, choosing to walk along a secluded alley as she replayed the battle in her head. Lost in thought of the battle she had lost, Deathdealer did not notice the knight of darkness trailing after her.

Star cornered Dorothy without her noticing. "Deathdealer."

Dorothy spun around, a hand on her katana. Star smiled. She was inches away from her. "So, do you see what I'm capable of?"

Dorothy puffed out her cheeks, irritated. "How did you beat me?" the warrior snapped contemptuously. "I was far superior to you in skill and in form."

"That may be true, but truthfully speaking," Star smirked. "I'm not human—and I admit you're the strongest human I have ever faced."

Dorothy's brow furrowed. "What are you then? How could you move so fast without anyone noticing?"

Star laughed. "You have a lot of questions, young one." Dorothy arched her eyebrow. "I'm far older than I look. I was changed into a vampire when I was a teen. Hence the youthful glow." Star smirked.

"Vampire," Dorothy tested out the word on her tongue. "What is that? Can I become one? How will it change me? Will I lose my beauty?"

Star wanted to laugh at the innocent and incessant questions. She took a step back. "Am I beautiful?" she asked.

"Yes," Dorothy answered without missing a beat. Star held back a chuckle.

“I can turn you into a vampire, yes. That will make you my kin—my child, so to speak. The transformation will hurt initially. The pain is quick, and the change is even quicker.” Star looked at her thoughtfully. “There is a curse that comes with becoming a vampire. No one can know of your existence. We’re not very keen on holy relics, and the morning star blinds us. We can bear it, but it drains us unless we’re well-fed.”

“Hiding in the shade forever?” Dorthy asked. “What about finding me a gentleman to settle down with, children, a family? I still want those things. I still want to be a girl.”

Star nodded, understanding. “This transformation comes with great compromise, Deathdealer. You will still be a girl. You can still have a family—just a different type of family. A forever family, with fellow vampires that will be immortal like you. Time will cease to matter, and your beauty will forever be yours. No blemishes, no wrinkled skin, youthful for all eternity.”

Dorothy looked away, turning the words over in her head, “This is... a lot. Are there any other... side effects?”

“There is one thing,” Star paused, waiting for the girl to turn and face her. “Food. You will no longer crave it. You can ingest it, but it will cease to satiate you. You will desire something pure, more potent than food.”

"What's more potent than food?" Dorothy laughed. "I don't want to starve as a vampire. That explains why you're so skinny, though."

"Blood. You will crave blood."

Dorothy made a face, scrunching up her nose. "That is the most disgusting thing I've ever heard."

"You can get by on animal blood if you like, but it doesn't have the same..." Star trailed off, rubbing her fingers together as she searched for the right word. "Kick," she finished.

"I don't like this one bit," Dorothy admitted. "This is a horrible curse. Why would anyone want to become like you? No offense."

Star waved a hand dismissively. "For me, it was simple. My brother and I were suffering from an illness that would have taken our lives. We had to choose between death and immortal living as stronger beings. Our father, Zedkiel, ruler of the northern region, granted us this immortality. He told us that long ago, his father, Lord Zephyr, Lord of the Legion, was once an angel created by God. Lord Zephyr's brother, Lucifer, was jealous and cursed him to Earth for being equal in power. Our Creator was cursed with the living flesh and forever banned from laying eyes upon his brother, the Morning Star."

The duo had started walking along the street, conversing casually as Star answered all of Dorothy's questions.

"Deep story," she replied curtly. "What's the motive? Are you exacting revenge against Lucifer? You guys need an army, right?"

Star nodded. Something glinted in Dorothy's eyes. "Meaning that there will be real-life battles," she mused. The thought of adventure seemed to excite her. "I'd like to join this Vampire Army and lead them to victory."

Star Reaper laughed. "You're something else, Deathdealer. I still can't quite figure out what goes through that head of yours."

Dorothy shrugged.

"Enjoy your last days as a human, Dorothy. Dine, celebrate, and spend time with the masters. I will come and find you myself. The change will be irreversible. You will be a vampire and my first child."

Dorothy made a face. "You make this sound so weird, creeping up on me and stuff. I don't like surprises, and Deathdealer doesn't either."

"Deathdealer?"

"My blade and my last name—I'm keeping both."

Star met Dorothy's blue eyes, fascinated. "You truly are different. Real bummer, though, about the name. I was thinking about renaming you." She kept her face serious as she tied to crack a joke with her. "I was thinking Fierce Reaper. That's cool, isn't it?"

Dorothy stuck out her tongue, and Star laughed, smiling at her. She hadn't met someone who had made her laugh like that in ages. Dorothy was bursting with life and humor, yet her name was Deathdealer. She taught music but knew her way around a katana. Dorothy was an amalgamation of opposites.

"I will honor it, and you're letting me keep my name, that is." Dorothy bowed. "I will see you soon, Mother."

Dorothy turned around.

"Please don't sneak up on me, or you might end up tasting my blade," she said nonchalantly as she walked away from Star, leaving a smile on her face.

***

A few days had passed, and Dorothy was having brunch with the old masters, enjoying her final days as a human. After the hearty meal, she returned to her dojo, where she harnessed her accuracy and speed using her blade. She kept finding herself thinking about Star's dark gaze and the promises she had made.

Every time Dorothy sank her teeth into her food, she couldn't help but think that food would stop bringing her joy in the same way soon enough. As she joked with the handsome new trainer at her master's old dojo, she realized she might never get to know him on a deeper level. She was going to choose a new life, a different life, full of adventure and... drinking blood?

The sun faded, and the moon began to rise. Dorothy closed the door to her dojo, her thoughts returning to her predicament. The sounds of howling dogs seemed to increase, getting louder and louder. Dorothy stood at her bedroom window, wondering what was causing such unrest.

Meanwhile, Star had slipped into the dojo. The excitement of finally turning Dorothy was getting to her. Star's fangs were already bared; she was ready to sink them into the young warrior.

Dorothy turned around, her hand at her blade.

"You're not changing me that easily, Star. You will have to earn my eternal loyalty."

Star grinned. "Not a problem. I did it once. I'll do it again."

Star charged at Dorothy, her speed making her almost invisible. Somehow, Dorothy had anticipated that move, and she swung her katana upwards the moment Star had finished her sentence. The blade connected with Star Reaper's arm, slicing it clean off.

Star barely glanced at it. Blood gushed from the wound but seemed to halt as soon as it started. Dorothy gaped at her as the skin scabbed over, turning black and then pink right before her.

"So you do bleed, somewhat," Dorothy muttered. "I can anticipate your moves already, Star. One battle was enough for me to learn how you fight. I can harm you even as a human."

"That really is quite impressive, which is why you will make for a fine vampire."

"If I get healing powers like yours...I would be invincible."

Star rushed at Dorothy again, but this time, she slowed down her pace by just a fraction. Dorothy's blade met thin air as she appeared behind the warrior, her fangs drawn. Star locked her arm around Dorothy's throat, holding her in a vice-like grip as Dorothy struggled against it.

Star was taller than Dorothy, which gave her the advantage she wanted. She tilted her head down, her nostrils flaring at the scent of her. Star could practically hear her blood pumping through her veins. Her teeth seemed to know exactly where to sink.

Dorothy moaned, her feet kicking out against the floor as Star's fangs broke the skin. Star's eyes were shining. Her senses heightened as she tasted Dorothy's blood.

Dorothy's eyes were closed, her breathing slow, and Star finished turning her.

"You're all mine now, Dorothy."

The warrior lay on the floor, sweating profusely as the change was completed. Dorothy was unaware of how she had curled up against Star, putting her head in her lap for comfort.

When her eyes finally fluttered open, the blue of her irises seemed darker, but her vision seemed clearer.

"Whoa," she whispered. Dorothy ran her tongue over her canines, feeling the sharp edge they now had to them. Her skin became paler, and her body temperature dropped below normal. She sat up, looking at Star, who smiled back at her affectionately. Dorothy still felt dazed. She scanned the room, and her gaze landed on the mirror at her vanity. The warrior approached it, surprised at how she felt stronger instead of weaker after a fight like that.

Her hair looked fuller, shinier somehow. Dorothy ran her fingers over her face, confused.

Star leaned against her bed, smug. "Well, well, well. Look who finally joined the ranks."

Dorothy spun around, a giggle bubbling up in her chest. “This feels amazing, Star.” She flexed her fingers. “My body doesn’t ache from any pain. I can see so clearly in the dark.”

“What did I tell you?” Star teased. “But you must lay low. If more common folk start finding out about us, they would be too afraid to see us for who we are. They will try to hunt us down.”

Dorothy nodded. Star had suggested training her, but Deathdealer said she wanted some time to herself to figure out her new powers. She was already a powerful human, and the heightened senses required some getting used to. The duo made a deal to meet once a week, and Star would check on Dorothy’s progress.

Star had been gifted with the ability to manipulate time to some extent. Dorothy, on the other hand, had the ability to leap forward and backward in time for brief moments, unlike Star, who could reverse time at will. The less pure the blood of the creator, the greater the likelihood that the new vampire would have lesser powers.

Since Star was created by one of the divines, Zedkiel, son of the father, she had powers of a grander magnitude. A vampire that would be born of two vampires would have powers of both parents if ever such a time came.

Dorothy and Star grew closer as they spent evenings together, where Star would answer more of her questions, recounting the short history of the vampires. The history was explained to her, and the rules of allegiance were taught.

After Dorothy's training had reached its zenith, Star Reaper decided it was time to return to her brother's dojo in Hokkaido. When they arrived, Star was in awe of how much the dojo had developed and improved in her absence. It had expanded greatly, and five large gardens that were part of the complex now. The dojo was a sprawling complex with wings designated for special kinds of training.

Star spotted a few warriors dressed in black clothes practicing their skills. Their agility was almost superhuman, and she realized that her brother had been quite busy. He had to have turned one of the warriors here, at least, and they, in turn, had done the same. Star found Shadow in the garden that was furthest from the entrance, meditating.

"Shadow," she called out, keeping her voice level so as not to disturb him. "I'm back."

"Indeed you are, Star. I had sensed your presence when you arrived in Hokkaido, but I wanted to be certain." Shadow rose from his perch near the pond. It was a beautiful garden with a small pond near the edge. Water gently tinkled down the rocks that lined the corner wall, collecting below. He turned around. "And who is your partner?"

Star beamed with pride, "This is Dorothy Deathdealer. My child–"

"Still weird," Dorothy cut in, grimacing at the title.

"She is an expert martial artist. She fights well and is a remarkable swordswoman. Her new abilities will make her a great warrior for our cause," Star continued. She smiled at Dorothy, doing nothing to hide her pride. Deathdealer was an exceptional fighter even before she had turned into a vampire, but the time they spent together had solidified their friendship, and Star had witnessed her growth herself.

Shadow looked her up and down, skeptical. "Let me be the judge of that. I don't think she will be able to join my Assassin's Guild."

Dorothy raised an eyebrow. "My apologies for speaking out of turn, but I didn't want to join your guild in the first place. I am a warrior and a fighter for this cause, Star." She looked at Star. "We didn't agree on my joining any guild. I will fight your brother, though. No harm in showing him what I am capable of, especially now."

Shadow nodded and walked off, signaling the girls to follow him inside. Star took in how beautiful the dojo had become. The light wood complimented the darker screens, and the lanterns and skylights were exquisitely designed, ornate and sturdy at the same time.

Shadow led them into a large, bare room that looked like it had not been used in a while. The weapons lining the wall suggested that the warriors sparred there. Shadow and Dorothy squared off in the middle of the room on the hardwood floor, preparing for a fight.

Shadow shrugged off his robe and stood up straight, level-headed and poised, not bothering to get into a fighting stance. Dorothy also took off her robe, revealing a thin linen tunic and dark pants underneath. She hung the robe on the door and placed her hand on her faithful blade, bending at the knees as she prepared to fight Shadow. She eyed his casual stance, trying to get a read on him before the fight began.

Shrugging, Dorothy charged at him, katana raised high. She came away, striking nothing but air.

Shadow smiled as he stepped aside, manipulating the light in the room and using a shadow on the ground to his advantage. He clenched his fists, and darkness descended. A shadow shifted in front of Dorothy, confusing her as to where he stood. She turned around just as he appeared behind Dorothy, tapping her shoulder.

"Your life could be over already if I wanted it." Shadow's voice was low and menacing.

Dorothy spun around, grunting with frustration as Shadow disappeared once more, the whisper of his blade making her spin around in confusion.

Dorothy laughed. "So you need your little magic tricks to fight me?"

"I can fight you however I please, Deathdealer," he snarled. "I just wanted to show you how useless it was to come at me with your full strength. You should never reveal all your strength in the first fight."

Dorothy threw her head back, trying to toss a stray strand of hair out of her face. "Bring it on, Shadow. You're all bark and no bite. Let me see what you've got."

The two charged at one another this time, thrusting their blades forward. The katanas clashed together, and the sound of the blades meeting echoed in the dojo. Shadow was smiling, pleased with the warrior his sister had chosen. She was keeping up with him.

"You're a good opponent, but you have not yet seen my full might," he warned, admiring her footwork.

"Enough with the teasing." Dorothy laughed. "Get to the point, Shadow. God, you and your sister are so similar."

Before Dorothy could charge again, Shadow disappeared out of sight. She had seen him move, but he had been so quick that her laughter died in her throat, her eyes widening when his katana nicked the bottom of her chin.

She froze. "I said no powers." Her voice came out in a whisper.

Shadow shrugged. “And I am a man of my word.” He lowered his katana. “I did not use my powers, Dorothy. If you weren’t so busy mocking me, you would know that.”

Dorothy lowered her blade as well, bowing slightly. “Sir, you are indeed a true champion.” Her brow furrowed as she mentally went over the battle. Their fight had been much like a dance. It was not all swordplay, either.

She had seen him dive away from her blade, twisting and striking out with his hand to subdue her fighting arm. “You are well-versed in the style of ninjutsu,” she said, trying to hide her admiration. “If I didn’t know any better, I would say it felt like you were the creator of the art.”

Shadow nodded. “I have trained for hundreds of years in this art. I know it like the back of my hand, and I have perfected the skills necessary to beat any opponent that thought they stood a chance against me. I am the Shadow, the art of ninjutsu.”

Dorothy went to get her robe. “But I imagine I have done enough to assure you that I am far superior to the men you have in your warriors’ guild.”

Shadow laughed. “You might be able to beat my best warrior in battle, I imagine.” He smirked at her. “With a little more training, of course.”

Dorothy eyed Star warily, who seemed to be enjoying this exchange far too much. “You both are equally infuriating. I hope you know that.”

Star Reaper and Shadow worked well together, and Shadow enjoyed his sister's company. Her partner, Dorothy, was a welcome addition to his dojo. He enjoyed training with her, and she had taken on his warriors with ease.

The trio worked together toward the mission Zedkiel had set them on. They knew they had to work tirelessly to increase their numbers until the day they were summoned to fight for Lord Zephyr. As vampires, they had to move frequently. Staying in the same place for more than five to ten years made the residents suspicious of the warriors that never aged.

They did not want to be seen as a threat, so they made sure to protect the towns they stayed in, as warriors should, and if they needed to feed, there was always the occasional troublemaker no one would miss.

Chapter 6
The Blood Gathering

It had started with the dreams. Zedkiel had spent his days in his stronghold in the north, waiting patiently for either his children to return to him or for Ariel to send word of her whereabouts. To vampires, centuries felt like years and years like months. What Zedkiel wasn't expecting were the dreams where he saw his father.

It was initially inconspicuous, just a voice in a dream, almost vision-like. But as time went on, Zephyr started appearing in Zedkiel's dreams, telling him to travel once more and to bring his progeny to the West, where he reigns as lord of the western region.

Zedkiel had been shaken the first time he saw his father in a dream, but after that, he began to welcome the sight of him. Seeing him refreshed the connection they had, and he felt emotional about the prospect of seeing him again.

In the dream, Zephyr was dressed in a regal black cloak. His shirt and trouser matched the dark fabric, making it hard to discern where one garment ended and the other began. He sat upon an iron throne, a sharp contrast to the pale interior of the castle from where he spoke.

"Where can I find you, Father?" Zedkiel had asked. "Is it time for the war?"

Zephyr had smiled. "You sound so much like the boy I had turned so long ago. Have you not grown?"

Zedkiel cast his gaze down, embarrassed. "I have, Father. Much has changed. Perhaps it is the sight of you that affects me so deeply. I seem to have regressed–"

Zephyr waved his hand dismissively. "No matter, my son. Come westward. You will know where to go because our connection binds us. Wherever you feel lost, cast your gaze about you and search for a shadow. It will be a small thing, bird-like. The shadow will take flight and guide you to me."

"You've trained the bats? The creatures I see in my dreams?"

"Yes, Zedkiel. Now," Zephyr's tone lost all lightness, "you must be quick. Time is of the essence. It is time we established the order."

Zedkiel froze. Life until now was a slow build to their true purpose. Zedkiel had lived a life of ease, and if Zephyr was now calling him and Ariel to establish the order, it meant their numbers had improved. They were no longer a handful of vampires. They were now a force to be reckoned with. And they would be ready for Lucifer when he came.

"Ariel–" he began.

"She's already on her way here, Zedkiel. Summon your children, and follow the shadows."

"Yes, Father."

***

Zedkiel had sent word to the twins, and they, in turn, summoned their progeny. The vampire had started his journey alone, but as he made his way to the western kingdom, he started to notice more and more familiar faces. He had sensed his children nearby, but soon, the odd new face became a frequent occurrence. It only took a nod to let him know that they were on his side, of his kind.

The vampires flitted through forests and towns, using the shadows to their advantage. They darted through cities, passing like a dark cloud, always too quick to be noticed and far too quick to be more than a sudden breeze to the average human.

Zephyr's castle was on top of a great cliff. The structure loomed over the steep hill it sat upon. The sound of crashing waves sounded almost like a whisper at that height. The castle was made of black stone, appearing almost like a silhouette even in the daylight. Fires blazed in the turrets, and banners hung from the walls. When Zedkiel arrived, he was shocked into silence. A sea of people seemed to drift towards the castle gates.

"Look how far we've come, children," he said to the twins.

"We always thought we were so few in number," Star commented, her voice an awed whisper.

"Father, you must join Lord Zephyr," Shadow said quickly. "You need to move through the crowd and meet him inside."

Zedkiel agreed, adjusting the dark emerald pin that glistened at his shoulder. His cloak fluttered in the breeze as he marched through the hundreds of thousands of vampires. They parted way as whispers of Zedkiel's arrival scattered through the crowd.

The Prince of Darkness walked through the open gates, eyes immediately going to the steps that led to the castle entrance. There, upon the platform before the giant doors to Lord Zephyr's castle, stood his father and, to Zephyr's right, Zedkiel's sister, Ariel.

Ariel pursed her lips in a failed attempt to mask her grin. Zedkiel laughed. "Ariel!"

The princess finally smiled, spreading her arms wide for an embrace. "You've grown, Zed."

"As have you, Ariel." He pulled away, "You look less miserable now."

Ariel hit his arm lightly. Zephyr cleared his throat, and the children turned to face him immediately. Zedkiel bowed before him, brimming with emotions. He had waited so long to be reunited with his family.

Zephyr put his arm on his son's shoulder, smiling. "You've done well. Your son and daughter have brought forth a legion of warriors."

"Father," Ariel said breathily, casting her gaze on the sea of people before them. "We are no longer alone. There are so many like us. We are too many for people to shun now."

"Still, we cannot afford to let humans know we walk amongst them," Zephyr said. "Already, they have legends and stories about us."

Zephyr raised his palm, and the hundreds of thousands of vampires fell silent. All conversation ceased as they all looked to their king for guidance.

"Tonight, we shall establish the vampire council. Once the council has been created, the Vampire Order will become a stronger force on this planet." Zephyr's voice carried over to the very end of the crowd. The vampires had powerful hearing. "Those of you who break the order's rules will be punished accordingly, and those who exploit their power for their own means or terrorize the human race will be stripped of their powers in a ceremony held in the courtyard of this very castle."

A murmur rippled through the crowd.

"I stand here today as your lord, The King of Darkness. And I shall always be your lord and your ruler. I will fight beside you on the day Lucifer returns, and I will be here for you to seek guidance from until the day of our great battle." He paused, taking in the sheer number of vampires before him. "We shall retreat to the recesses of the castle where the ceremony for the council shall begin. Until then, you are welcome to the castle. You may mingle amongst your kind and enjoy this reunion."

A cheer erupted from the crowd and increased in volume until it was deafening. The King of Darkness and his chosen children took a gracious bow and entered the castle. As the trio made their way down a dark staircase, Ariel finally spoke up.

"You said there would be five people on the vampire council, Father." Ariel sounded hurt. "Where are the other two?"

Zedkiel mirrored that hurt. They had believed they were Zephyr's only children.

"They are already in the war room," Zephyr answered. "I know exactly how you are feeling right now, children. Shelf your mistrust for now."

The siblings remained quiet, obediently following their father to the war room. Zedkiel held out his hand for

Ariel to take, who took it and squeezed it briefly before letting go.

Zedkiel's brow furrowed. *What was that about?*

Zephyr pushed open the ornate metal door and stepped through. Two figures, a man and a woman, rose from their places at the round table in the middle of the room. The twins took in the other two at the table but remained quiet. There was an emblem carved into the center of the table. It was a full moon and a beast with wide wings spread wide in the middle of it, stretching beyond the moon behind it.

"This is the crest of the house of Zephyr," The King of Darkness answered. He had seen the way the four vampires had eyed the carving. Zephyr motioned to the man on his left. "Children, this is Cain."

Cain nodded at the other three. He had a square jaw that was hidden beneath his neat, thick beard. His eyes were almost violet, and they stood out against his pale skin.

"The son of the first man," Zephyr said with pride. "And the first to turn after I was cast down from the heavens."

The King of Darkness placed his hand on Cain's shoulder. "He knew what it was like to be cast out from your kind, to be shamed and neglected. And I taught him how to make that his strength."

Cain smiled softly. "I would be nowhere without you, Father."

Zephyr extended a hand toward the woman. She was dressed in a plain white garment that hung about her, yet somehow, the silken fabric accentuated her figure. It was loosely cinched at the waist. There was another fabric draped over her arms. It seemed woolen, and it was embroidered with gold thread.

Her hair was straight and jet black, somehow making her porcelain skin glow. The woman met Ariel and Zedkiel's gazes, her eyes heavily kohled and green irises standing out.

"Uriel," she introduced herself. Her voice seemed to melt over their ears. It had a sleepy quality to it and went perfectly with her hooded gaze. "Empress of the Eastern region."

Zephyr smiled. "She is the leading vampire of the Eastern region. Don't let her demeanor fool you. She's swift with a sword." He looked at her, and Uriel smiled knowingly as if her swordplay was some inside joke.

Uriel looked ethereal and exotic at the same time. Her calm confidence was almost intimidating. The siblings had to admit that their father had chosen well. He introduced Ariel and Zedkiel and, with a gesture, motioned for everyone to sit down.

"This marks the beginning of the vampire race, my beloved children. We are the first of our kind and, therefore, the strongest. We must lead vampirekind to greatness. For us to thrive, there must be order. This ceremony, tonight, will mark the beginning of our empire."

The twins took their places at the table, and Zedkiel felt unnerved at the sight of someone else at Lord Zephyr's right hand. He tried to remind himself why he was here and what his true purpose was. They were all here as equals. Ariel continued to eye Uriel, curious about the ethereal woman at her father's side. Her brother had attachment issues, that much she had learned early on. Zedkiel's lips were pressed in a firm line. Cain nodded at Zedkiel, smirking as he recognized the fire in his eyes as well.

Zephyr smiled with pride, "Look how far we have come. I came to each of you when you needed me and helped turn you to your true destinies. Your power will forever remain unmatched by any vampire that comes after you." He took Ariel and Uriel's hands in his. "My children, you have made me proud. I see the throng of vampires outside, and I know that each of them is dedicated to our purpose. But now is the time for order. As we continue to grow, we must set down our laws, our rules for vampire kind so that we may be ready when the time to fight Lucifer comes."

"Is the order not already in place?" Ariel asked. "The laws you told us, the order we are to uphold – is that not it?"

"That is the gist of it, yes, but with our numbers growing as they have, it is highly unlikely that every vampire remembered the details of the order as you do. Immortality makes people do strange things, and it does stranger things to the memory," Cain spoke up.

Zedkiel bristled.

The eerie light in the chamber cast shadows on everyone's faces, but the vampires could see each other in perfect light.

"I can sense the tension, Zedkiel. We all can," Zephyr finally said. "Calm down, son. There are no enemies here."

The Prince of Darkness bowed his head, embarrassed.

"I wish to revise the rules of the Vampire Order, after which it shall be your responsibility to impart this knowledge to those you turn and have turned. We are far too scattered at this point in time, and I wish to split the vampires into groups and factions. The closer we are, the more we can keep each other in check. A rogue vampire is a dangerous thing. Ariel, will you tell us what you know of the order?"

"Of course, Father," Ariel smiled, meeting Uriel's gaze. The exotic woman enraptured her. "No vampire is to turn more than two humans. If this is done, the third will be far weaker than the first. If a vampire chooses a human that is fundamentally weak, there is always the possibility that their body will reject the blood resulting in immediate death. Second, when it comes to humans, if we choose to feed on humankind alone, it is vital we keep the procedure discreet. There are enough rumors and myths as it is, and we cannot afford discovery–humans fear what they cannot understand, and this fear will lead them to fight us or hunt us."

"But we can take them out easily," Cain snorted. "I never understood that bit."

"You can take out one or two. When a mob is closing in on you, and when they drive a silver sword through your chest, you will be the only one that gets taken out," Zedkiel quipped.

Ariel rolled her eyes, "Lying low is important. Blend in with humankind if you must, and feed at night. If a vampire kills another vampire, the kill may make them stronger. Similarly, if you turn a human that you have fallen for, remember that they can become formidable opponents. Power can corrupt a vampire. We're as susceptible to it as any human, if not more.

"The Vampire Order itself will consist of four regions, East, West, South, and North. Lord Zephyr will be the Lord of the Regions, of course; as leaders of every region, we will be held accountable for the mistakes made by other vampires in our jurisdiction. Turning another human being cannot be something that is done on a whim. You must think about whom you turn—do not let your desires guide you," Ariel finished, looking to the King of Darkness for approval.

Zephyr nodded, "Well done, Ariel. You've remembered most of it well. Zedkiel, my son, you are the leader of the Northern region, Ariel, you shall rule the South, as we had decided. Uriel shall govern the Eastern region, and Cain, you are to govern the West. However, I shall remain here, too, at the highest seat of the council, in the Western region.

"As we continue to grow as a race, we cannot let humankind get the best of us, and with the powers we are given, we must remember not to interfere with the natural order of things. Do not bend the universe to your whims, children. The repercussions will be great. A small shift in the fabric of space and time ripples throughout history and the future."

The four vampires nodded at the reminder. The responsibility on their shoulders was great, and they could not let the test of time and immortality dull the seriousness of their purpose.

"You have made me proud," Zedkiel said with a smile. "I was cast here as a wretched, cursed creature, but the legion of vampires outside is proof that what Lucifer granted me was no curse. He *will* come back to fight me. He *will* wish to visit me in what he calls my prison. Morningstar does not know that this prison is my empire, and my children shall avenge me."

The Lord of Darkness reached into his cloak and withdrew a small dagger. It was carved with the crest of the House of Zephyr, and he pressed it into his palm.

"This ceremony marks the start of our reign. We shall no longer remain scattered. Here, we unite, and we shall remain bound in this connection until the fates separate us," Zedkiel drew the tip of the blade against the inside of his left palm and handed the blade to Ariel. "We shall take a blood oath, as part of this ceremony, to vow our loyalty to the house of Zephyr."

Ariel pressed the dagger's tip into her palm, drew a sharp line on either palm that quickly pooled with blood, and handed the dagger to her brother. Zedkiel took Ariel's hand and pressed it over his open wound. Ariel gasped, closing her eyes as her breathing became heavy. Zedkiel did the same, passing his blade to Cain before joining hands with Ariel. The Prince of Darkness exhaled, closing his eyes as Cain followed suit. The first vampire took Zedkiel's hand just before he handed the blade to Uriel.

Uriel's sharp eyes took in the strange pained expressions on everyone's faces before she drew blood herself. She took Cain's hand and then Zephyr's and moaned softly. A wave of pain washed over her, an electric current that was too subtle to make her hand pull away from the sensation, but she felt connected to everyone else in a way she had never thought possible. Her vampire senses had blessed her with a deeper understanding of human actions and body language, but that hyperawareness was nothing compared to this connection.

Everyone's grip tightened as they felt their hearts ache with the pain Lord Zephyr had felt on the first night he had been cast out of heaven. The pain was unbearable, and the five vampires held on to each other as they waited for the pain to pass. Zephyr's agony was shared as the blood oath continued. Each of the vampires in the circle felt the utter hopelessness the Lord of Darkness had felt on his first night on earth, the harrowing loneliness and the debilitating weight of knowing there was no escape from eternity.

Zephyr exhaled. As he spoke, his eyes were still closed, "This blood oath binds us together even closer than before. It is a promise that we shall remain on the same side and will fight for the same purpose: Lucifer's destruction."

A hum of assent ran through the circle.

"The Vampire Order is to remain on earth until the end of time, eventually surpassing even mankind. We shall put an end to Lucifer's tyrannous ways and shall avenge the curse of the beast of the night."

Zephyr opened his eyes, and the rest of the order followed suit. The vampires reluctantly let go of each other's hands, but their connection felt strong even after they had broken the circle of the blood oath. The wounds on their hands closed up as smiles were exchanged. Lord Zephyr rose, and the four rulers rose with him. He smiled, satisfied.

"I have waited years for this feeling," he confessed.

"There's truly nothing like it," Uriel agreed. Her heavily accented voice was hard to place.

Ariel nodded, "Father, we have been bound from the day we became vampires, and our true purpose was never lost to us – but this oath, this gathering, has changed everything."

"We cannot see past this promise we have made," Zedkiel added.

Zephyr would deny it later, but Ariel was certain she had seen his eyes well up with emotion.

The Lord of Darkness cleared his throat, "Now, a feast awaits," he motioned toward the door. "The castle is ours. The vampires can feast as they please and mingle as they wish. At the end of the night, we shall disclose the rules of the order to this entire vampire legion.

He grabbed Ariel and Zedkiel by the shoulder, "I would love to meet your children," he nodded at Cain and Uriel too. "I wish to see whom you have chosen as the powerful vampires to succeed you."

Ariel grinned, "I can't wait for you to meet Alvira."

Zedkiel arched an eyebrow, "Who's Alvira?"

"You'll see."

"Come," Zedkiel led them out of the chamber. "Let the ceremony commence."

Chapter 7
Lovers' Spite

Zedkiel watched in awe as the ceremony commenced. Vampires from all over the globe had gathered for the first official vampire council meeting. The sheer number of vampires was overwhelming, but he felt moved to see just how much the empire had grown. When Zephyr had turned them, he would speak of this empire, but Zedkiel had always struggled to envision the throngs upon throngs of like-minded individuals.

He turned to ask Ariel something when he realized she was not by his side. The five of them had entered the great hall as a group, but everyone had quickly dispersed. Cain and Uriel had disappeared rather quickly, and Zedkiel was still reeling when he realized his sister was nowhere to be seen.

Banners hung from the ceiling, emblazoned with the Crest of Zephyr, and long tables were laden with food and drink. Zedkiel narrowed his eyes at the giant bowls of dark red liquid and was about to ask Zephyr what they were when he spotted Ariel. A beautiful young woman followed closely behind, and she gripped Ariel's hand firmly, excitement in her eyes.

Something about her nagged at him, but Zedkiel felt distracted by another sight shortly after. His twins, Star and Shadow, caught his gaze and waved at him. Shadow looked serious as ever, while Star had a playful smirk on her lips, her black-headed friend at her side. She nodded at Zedkiel in acknowledgment.

Zedkiel gestured for them to join him when Ariel broke through his reverie. “Hey Zed, I’d like you to meet Alvira.”

Alvira smiled at Zedkiel and held out her hand for him to shake.

Zedkiel eyed the distance between his sister and Ariel before he took her hand with a thin-lipped smile. “Zedkiel. Pleased to meet you.”

“Ariel’s told me so much about you, Zedkiel,” Alvira said, smiling politely. She had a beautiful smile, and her golden hair was tied in a neat, royal bun. Her features reminded him of someone familiar, but he couldn’t put his finger on it.

“I’m flattered,” he drawled. “But I haven’t had the same pleasure. Where are you from, originally?”

Alvira nodded. “Originally, I was Alvira Moon before your darling sister decided to whisk me off my feet.”

Zedkiel froze, and Ariel watched her brother’s expression gleefully. “Moon?” he asked.

“She’s Sebastian’s daughter!” Ariel said, laughing. “Would you believe it?”

His sister placed her hand on Alvira's bare shoulder, stroking gently with her thumb as she went on about how she had convinced the young princess to turn. Zedkiel's gaze darted from Ariel to Alvira, both of whom were engaged in another conversation already, and he felt something bubble up inside him.

"Keeping it in the family, are we?" he spat, surprised at how the words left his mouth.

Ariel's smile faded. "That's rich coming from you, *brother*."

Zedkiel's brow furrowed in confusion. Was this why Ariel had refused to return any of his embraces? Why her touch never lingered? Ariel wasn't being cold to him. She had *replaced* him.

Zedkiel pursed his lips. "I wasn't aware that you had moved on, sister."

Ariel laughed. "You're telling me you've done nothing but spend centuries in the north like some monk?"

Zedkiel felt his cheeks heat with embarrassment. He idly wondered if he even had the blood to feel something like that anymore.

"I turned two children and raised them, much like our father."

Ariel arched her brows. “You’re telling me you haven’t indulged yourself, even once? Never felt tempted by the odd, curious human?”

Zedkiel looked at Alvira, who seemed to be very uncomfortable being stuck in the middle of a conversation like this. He dully realized that Ariel had done the thing she had always done since they were kids. She’d moved on and left him behind, expecting him to catch up.

He had spent all those years thinking they needed no one else, that their bond was strong enough to bear any test of time. But Ariel had discarded her time with him with such ease. She had eyes only for Alvira now.

“No,” Zedkiel confessed proudly. “I never did.”

“Ariel, I’m going to go,” Alvira said uncomfortably.

Ariel stopped the princess by taking her hand in her own firmly. She grabbed the back of her neck and pulled her in for a chaste kiss before letting her go, relishing how her brother grimaced at the action.

“You’re pathetic, Zed,” Ariel finally snarled. “I kept thinking you would grow up, but you keep getting hung up on the strangest things.”

“So, none of what we had was real?” Zedkiel knew he sounded petulant, but he couldn’t take his eyes off Alvira. She was bowing politely before Zephyr now, holding out her hand as his father kissed it. She was charming, even from a distance. She was the one his sister had replaced him with.

Ariel rolled her eyes. "We were children, Zed. We were turned into beasts, and Zephyr left us nothing but each other. We turned to each other for comfort and support. We adored each other, yes, but you can't seriously have expected us to remain bonded like this forever? When our paths had been set poles apart?"

Zedkiel sighed. "I suppose I am the fool."

Ariel thumped him on the shoulder. "You needn't feel like that for too long. I'll give you a few moments to wallow. Then I wanna see your kids."

Zedkiel laughed sardonically before realizing his sister was serious. He nodded and waved over the twins, gesturing at them to join Zephyr and Ariel so he could introduce them. He shook his head, blaming himself for not noticing his sister's cold behavior toward him sooner.

He caught up with Zephyr and Ariel once more, nodding apologetically at Alvira as he joined the trio. The twins approached them soon after, bowing before Lord Zephyr and then introducing themselves.

"Twins, really?" Ariel laughed, shaking her hands with both of them, impressed by her brother's persistence.

"I suppose you can say I'm set in my ways," Zedkiel smiled, meeting Alvira's shy gaze.

"Oh, let him off, Ariel," Alvira said softly. She grinned at Zedkiel in a way that made him feel lightheaded, almost. Her eyes twinkled with mischief. She was definitely Ariel's type.

The twins looked from Zedkiel to Alvira and shared a secretive smile.

"Do you see the sparks going off between those two?" Dorothy asked Star, who quickly shushed her companion.

"Quiet!" She laughed. "We can all see it."

"It's odd," Shadow commented. "We've never seen Father like this with anyone. He shared his special bond with his sister with us before, but looking at them now, you'd think Princess Alvira and Father have a history."

"I bet they're gonna make some history," Dorothy muttered, earning a giggle from Star.

As the evening went on, the five leaders of the vampire council made their rounds, meeting with vampires who introduced themselves with their bloodline history. Zephyr approved of the choices made by every vampire, and he was particularly in awe of Shadow's Assassin's Guild. His children had chosen well for themselves and trained excellent warriors who would carry the mantle with honor.

Vampires had truly gathered from all over the globe. Uriel introduced a trio of veiled vampires who hailed from Egypt. They had been warriors before they had submitted to Uriel's command and had been eager to acquire more power.

"You can tell how far someone is from the bloodline just by looking at them," Cain commented. "The power that radiates from every vampire is different. You can always tell who is stronger than they look."

"It hasn't gotten too bad yet," Ariel agreed. "At the rate at which we're going, after a few more centuries, the only thing that will set the humans apart from us will be the fangs."

"What a pity," Uriel said. "Surely some of the powers will remain?"

"Only barely," Cain countered.

Ariel looked to Alvira for her opinion but found her engrossed in a conversation with Dorothy and Star. Zedkiel stood behind his children, watching their interaction with a soft smile on his face. He was proud of them.

Ariel felt a pang of guilt at how they had reunited after so long. It wasn't fair that their reunion was filled with jealousy and rage after years together. She made a note to apologize to him while the night was still young. After all, they were bound by more than blood. He was her brother, and no one knew her as well as he. Ariel decided to acknowledge how well he'd managed on his own. Zephyr was proud of him. Truly.

Her tense shoulders eased when Alvira said something to Zedkiel, and her brother laughed heartily in response. Perhaps it wouldn't be so bad if they all got along. It was clear to her that Princess Alvira had bonded with her uncle seamlessly.

When Ariel approached the group, she felt none of the tension between them, and she smiled thankfully at the princess. She would thank her personally, later that night, for her uncanny ability to ease any uncomfortable tensions between her and other people.

Alvira nodded. "I was just telling Zedkiel about Father," she said, easing her partner into the conversation. "He'd been so terrified of you when you visited!"

"Rightfully so," Zedkiel teased. "All she has to do is glare at me to get me in line."

"She does that to you too?!" Alvira asked.

After a while, Zedkiel took his leave. There would be another vampire council meeting in the morning, and he wished to be rested and prepared for it. He nodded, saying his goodbyes. Alvira hugged him.

"I'll see you outside in an hour?" she whispered in his ear.

Zedkiel pulled away from her embrace, his eyes widening. He hadn't known what to expect when Alvira had so candidly whispered in his ear. *What could she want from him?* The vampire had picked up the widened pupils in her red eyes, the soft undercurrent of a promise in her whisper. Zedkiel had looked at his sister, expecting to meet her angry gaze, but she was engrossed in a deep conversation with Dorothy Deathdealer.

Zedkiel waited for the feast to die down. Vampires retired to their quarters, and the castle's corridors emptied out. The vampire council resided in the western wing, with entire floors at their disposal. Zedkiel wanted his children to be on the same floor as well, and most vampires chose their kin to accompany them the way he had.

It was only when the moon's light had started to recede that the Prince of Darkness decided to head out to the courtyard. He had just stepped out when Alvira appeared from the shadows, flitting past the columns and pillars until she stood right in front of him, her hand firmly planted on his chest.

"Took you long enough," she breathed, a wicked smile on her face. "Were you scared, Zedkiel?"

Zedkiel glanced from Alivra's hand to her face. "What are you doing, princess? Where's Ariel?"

Alvira sighed and pushed him against the wall before stepping aside and leaning against the wall as well. "I was hoping you had picked up on the same things that I had, but it appears not. Ariel's with Uriel. The two had much to discuss."

"Uriel?" Zedkiel had noticed the twinge of jealousy. "You're worried she's interested in her?"

Alvira hummed. "Not as much interested as she is fascinated. The woman is quite enchanting, her voice like honey. She *is* exotic."

"What are you talking about, Alvira? Why did you call me out here?"

The vampire met his gaze head-on, her eyes searching his momentarily. "When we met, I felt something shift inside me. I was attracted to you, Zedkiel. I felt a connection. I thought it had to do with us being from the same bloodline and both being powerful vampires, but it's different..."

She trailed off, biting her bottom lip as she pondered over her next words. Zedkiel's gaze followed the movement, his heartbeat picking up. They both had the heightened senses to know that their hearts were beating fast. The anticipation hung in the air, thick.

"Go on," he pushed.

"Zedkiel, I was sure it was different when we touched. I felt something electric when we simply shook hands. When we started talking, I felt entranced by you. Enraptured."

The Prince of Darkness swallowed, recalling the events of the evening. He had noticed Alvira even before he had realized she was accompanying his sister. He had taken note of how elegant and beautiful she looked. Her quick wit and humor had amused him, and he had noticed he liked her.

But was he really all that Alvira was making him out to be? Did she truly mean these words when she was with Ariel?

"I can *hear* you think, Zed," she whined.

"What about Ariel?"

Her smile disappeared. "I don't know. I still love her, Zed. But I feel like, with her, I didn't have a choice. We're bonded, she *turned* me. Nothing can change that. But with you...."

"You have a choice?" Zedkiel finished her thought, surprised when she nodded.

"I know I'll probably hate myself for this later, but I can't let this pass me by." She took his hand in hers. "I need to know. I *feel* this attraction to you, Zedkiel. I want to pursue you. I want to choose you."

Zedkiel's chest rose and fell with every heavy breath. He could swear every vampire in the building could hear what blood was left in him, pounding violently.

Alvira lifted her hand and gently cupped his face. "Do you trust me?" she whispered.

Zedkiel nodded, his hands finding her waist, his lips parting ever so slightly.

They kissed. Alvira leaned into him as his hands wrapped around her hips. Zedkiel kissed her passionately, his eyes fluttering closed as he lost himself in the embrace. Their lips met and broke apart, only to meet again before they even pulled away. Alvira eventually put a hand on his chest, gently pushing him away.

Zedkiel's eyes had darkened.

"You were right," he panted. "There's definitely something here."

Alvira laughed. He grabbed Alvira by the wrists and spun her around, pinning her against the wall as he pinned her. "We should explore this."

Alvira gasped, smiling slyly at him, "Would you like to show me your quarters, Your Highness?"

Zedkiel nodded, breaking into a run with her hand still clasped in hers, both of them laughing breathily as they ran through the castle. Their silhouettes were a blur as the moon faded behind them, dawn about to break.

They made it to Zedkiel's room, and the Prince of Darkness locked it behind them. The sun would be up soon, and all the vampires would stay indoors, either sleeping or resting until the sun finally set again. The castle's wide windows had thick curtains that would block out all sunlight, but vampires were tuned to their own routines regardless.

Ariel and Uriel had spent the night in deep conversation. She had much to learn from the eastern princess. She was equal parts warrior and royalty, each story of hers unique and full of knowledge. Alvira had stuck around in the beginning, but a couple of hours after midnight, she told her she was going to find Zedkiel.

Ariel had looked at her incredulously. "Are you sure?"

Alvira beamed good-naturedly. "I know we got off on the wrong foot, but you saw how we interacted all evening. I want to make things right between us."

Uriel had smiled knowingly at that. Alvira ignored the sneer. "After all, we're family," she finished.

Ariel hummed. "I suppose you're right. He will be less insufferable if the two of you are on good terms."

"Exactly," Alvira agreed, bending down for a quick peck before she left the women to their conversation.

Uriel had waited for Alvira to leave, "How long–"

"Centuries," Ariel smiled. "It's one thing when you're a vampire, and they want to burn you at the stake, but it gets absolutely unbelievable when they find out you're in love with a woman."

Uriel smirked. "Funny what these humans are willing to kill for."

"But it made us stronger," Ariel had commented.

Uriel waved her hand dismissively, changing the topic.

***

Alvira stretched her arms above her head, smiling lazily at Zedkiel as she swung her legs off the bed.

The Prince of Darkness met her grin, adjusting the sheets over his hips. "What do you conclude, princess?"

Alvira swung her legs back on the bed, inching closer to the prince. She leaned forward on her hands. "I'd say the results seem promising, Zedkiel," Alvira smirked. "I'd need a few more days like this... just to be sure."

Zedkiel laughed heartily, his grip tightening on her wrist. "As you wish, m'lady."

Ariel let him hold her in place, even though they both knew she was strong enough to break free from his grip. They had made love well past noon and had spent the past couple of hours in deep conversation, swapping childhood stories and recounting how they had coped with being turned into vampires.

Zedkiel had been charmed by her. The young princess was full of life. For a blood-sucking beast, she was surprisingly empathetic and gentle. It was almost as if the darkness of her circumstance did not taint her shine. Her pale skin seemed to glow with the sort of warmth only mortals had, but Alvira had the fangs to show. Zedkiel found her endearing and intelligent, and he felt seen by her in a way his father and sister failed to see him. To her, he was good enough.

Alvira couldn't explain what it was about Zedkiel that pulled her to him. Perhaps she liked that in a room full of self-assured beasts, his doubtful, nervous countenance made him seem almost human. She knew he was just as powerful as Ariel, but he had no trouble with stepping into the shadows while someone else took the spotlight. He preferred to keep his power quiet, his intelligence undercover.

Zedkiel was the polar opposite of his sister, and that was what drew the princess to him. She liked that he was not as assertive as her partner. And maybe she could use some of that in her life. Alvira wanted to know Zedkiel, and she was lucky because he had no trouble opening up to her.

"Stay," Zedkiel said.

Alvira smiled, dabbing at her body with a damp washcloth. "I really must go, Zedkiel. Your sister will be wondering where I am, surely."

Zedkiel's face fell. "This cannot go on like this, Alvira. We cannot always meet in the shadows."

Alvira finished getting dressed, adjusting her cape about her shoulders. "Of course, we can." She made her way to him, cupping his face and kissing him deeply. "Let's have some *fun*, Zed, while we still can. There's bound to be a moment of sourness when this all comes to light, but until then, let us have this."

"And when this comes to light, what will happen then?"

"We'll cross that bridge when we come to it," she winked at him, turning around to leave.

Zedkiel fell back against the sheets as Alvira left him, an unexpected smile on his face. He rose from his bed and proceeded to get dressed. There was another council meeting to be had.

***

Alvira met Ariel in the courtyards shortly after leaving Zedkiel's room.

"How was your night?" Ariel asked, nonchalant as she extended her hand for her beloved to take.

"Good!" Alvira chirped. "Zedkiel and I have more in common than we thought. We had the best conversations."

Ariel hummed. "Yeah, you smell like him."

"I hugged him before I left," she said quickly.

Her partner raised a brow. "I... didn't question you," she snorted. "But I take it all's well between you two now? I didn't like the pointless tension. I could feel it between you two last night too."

"Oh," Alvira laughed. "It's all in the past, Ariel. We talked about our journeys as vampires. He's been quite lonely, you know. He didn't know what to expect when he saw you after so many years, but a part of him still remembered you as the girl you were when you left him."

Ariel squeezed Alvira's hand appreciatively. "I can understand that. I suppose it was unfair of me to be so cold to him. A part of me also remembered him as that whiny brother of mine. We're siblings," she shrugged. "Sometimes we bring out the worst in each other."

"And your time with Uriel?"

"Oh, wonderful. She's... something else," Ariel whispered.

"Should I be jealous?" Alvira teased.

"Of course not, my love. If anything, Uriel was getting tired of how much I rambled about you."

Alvira swallowed, avoiding her gaze. "She seems a bit disconnected – otherworldly almost."

Ariel nodded. "I wonder what she'll bring to the table. The council meeting today is to help iron things out between the regions and what we're supposed to do after we go back."

Alvira stopped short. "How soon do you think we'll be returning?"

"Tomorrow." Ariel laughed. "Don't look so worried. We can stay if you like."

Alvira looked away quickly, trying to laugh away the blatant panic in her eyes. She needed to talk to Zedkiel.

***

At the council meeting, Zedkiel met her as if last night was all but a blur to him. He had an easy, almost cold smile on his face as he greeted his sister. Zephyr was just pleased to see his children seemed to be getting along after last night. Cain was the only one who hadn't actively bonded with anyone, but he had the sort of personality that blended in with others easily.

Zephyr looked around the table, nodding as he drummed his fingers on the table, "Now, onto the next order of business—turning the vampire council into a global Vampire Order. One gathering of all vampires will not accomplish anything if they leave here and do as they please. You are responsible for your kin and your regions. If any vampire trespasses the laws we have set here, they will be brought to the council to be tried and punished."

"And who will be judge?" Cain questioned, turning everyone's attention to him. "Who will determine what happens to a rogue vampire? Who decides *what* a rogue vampire is, exactly? And what happens if we disagree about the punishment?"

Zedkiel clenched his jaw, irritated by Cain's blatant disrespect of Lord Zephyr. "Calm down," Ariel whispered. "He has a point."

"There's a reason this council has an odd number of members. If we disagree, the majority will decide. As to how we know who a trespasser is, anyone who breaks the rules we have put forth can be tried in this council," Zephyr answered calmly.

"Examples will need to be made," Uriel added, shrugging. "There can be no order without discipline. It is our duty to uphold it. The real question is what we will do to keep checks on each other, the most powerful of all vampires."

Zedkiel noticed the way Uriel eyed Cain as she spoke.

After the council meeting, most of the vampires went on their way, returning to their hometowns and countries. Cain and Uriel went on their way, too, with Cain saying he had other matters to tend to while Lord Zephyr held down the fort. Their missions were simple. They had to uphold peace in their regions while steadily increasing numbers and always remaining prepared for when Lord Zephyr would call upon them for the great battle.

Finally, it was only Lord Zephyr, Ariel, and Zedkiel left in the large fortress, with Alvira staying by Ariel's side during the day and visiting Zedkiel at night. The duo had grown closer with every passing day, with even Zephyr noticing how well Alvira and Zedkiel got along.

"They seem to really connect now, don't they?" Zephyr asked his daughter over dinner one day.

"It's a relief, though. Don't you remember how cold he was to her when we first met?" Ariel said, watching as her brother and lover laughed over something trivial. "It's good to see them getting along."

"That said, Ariel, I think you should keep an eye on them," Lord Zephyr's voice dropped to a whisper.

Ariel's gaze darted from her plate, catching Alvira in a hearty giggle. She placed her hand on Zedkiel's arm as her brother ducked his head in a rare display of laughter. "Keep an eye? What are you suggesting, Father?"

"A hint should be plenty, daughter." Zephyr shrugged, taking a sip from the goblet before him. "For your sake, I hope all they have between them is good humor."

Something about Zephyr's tone of voice sent a chill down Ariel's spine. The Princess of Darkness straightened up, watching as Alvira met her gaze from across the table. Alivra beamed at her lovingly, and Ariel responded in kind, her smile wavering only when her lover's gaze shifted to her brother's and became just a little more genuine.

Ariel's fork slammed loudly against the table, and Lord Zephyr placed a placating hand on her wrist.

"Not now. Not here."

***

Ariel's display of violence had gone unnoticed by the lovebirds, but the Princess of Darkness had let the seed of suspicion take root inside her. Her nostrils flared when Alvira passed by her, smelling distinctly like her brother.

She could have tackled her then and there, confronting her, but a scent was not enough. She needed more. Alvira had come into their room after dinner, fluttering about, unaware of the raging storm inside Ariel. She chirped happily, engrossed in conversation, blind to how her lover had been reduced to one-word answers and occasional hums.

"What do you think, Ariel?" Alvira turned around, her smile dropping all of a sudden. "My love? What's wrong?"

Alvira sat down beside Ariel quickly, cupping her face. She watched as Ariel grew stiffer under her touch.

"Ariel," she whispered, watching as the vampire met her gaze reluctantly. Alvira's chest rose and fell rapidly, panic taking over.

Ariel smiled cruelly, "What's the matter, princess?" her tone mocking her lover. "What's got you in such a panic?"

Alvira stuttered, swallowing quickly. "You seem upset, darling. What's happened?"

Ariel saw her lover's panicky eyes and smiled. "You tell me?"

She laughed nervously. "I don't know. I was just wondering if something had happened. You seem so quiet and stiff..."

"It's nothing." Ariel brushed her off, shrugging off Alvira's hands. "Come on, come to bed."

Alvira's hands dropped heavily against the mattress, and she nodded silently.

Ariel grabbed her wrist, pulling Alvira to her. She placed a hand on her throat, tightening menacingly. "Why's your heart in such a frenzy?"

Alvira looked away, masking her fear momentarily before smiling at her beloved, honey-sweet. "Because of you, sweetheart." Alvira leaned down to kiss Ariel.

Ariel kissed her back, her grip tightening on the sheets as she tried to mask her anger, holding out for just a few more moments.

***

Alvira left Ariel's side as quietly as she could, fixing the sheets behind her. She slipped on her shoes and left the door open just a crack, promising herself she'd be back before dawn. The princess left, leaving her lover sleeping behind her.

Ariel's eyes flew open, her chest tightening with newfound hatred as she rose from the bed, grabbing her treasured dagger as she stood. She followed Alvira through the empty hallways, hoping beyond hope that she wasn't going to where Zedkiel lay sleeping.

Alvira had wasted no time reaching Zedkiel. The hallways held no trace that anyone had passed through them moments ago. Ariel stood outside Zedkiel's door, her hand hesitating before the door, pretending she couldn't hear her brother on the other side, laughing with her beloved.

"Ariel asleep?" Zedkiel asked.

"She fell asleep two hours ago, but I waited just to be sure," Alvira smiled. "Now, we can't let the day escape us just like this, my love."

Zedkiel scrunched his nose. "I can still sense her on you."

Alvira laughed. "That shouldn't be new to you. It's not like you and her didn't–"

"Please don't talk about that." Zedkiel pinched the bridge of his nose, smiling despite the disgust he feigned. "Come on, come here. I've missed you."

Ariel couldn't bear it any longer. She heard the bed creak on the other side and kicked the door open. As it flew open, the vampire charged in, leaping at Zedkiel as she pushed Alvira away, holding her dagger to his throat.

"Traitor!" she screamed as Zedkiel fought off her grip.

"Ariel!" Alvira yelled, reaching forward to release Zedkiel from her grip.

Ariel spun around, pointing accusingly at her. "You!" she stalked toward her, eyes blazing with anger. "You did this! You betrayed me!"

Zedkiel stood, rolling off the bed as he reached for his blade.

"Don't touch a hair on her head, Ariel."

Ariel turned, "That's *rich* coming from you! Defending her like she was *yours*."

Zedkiel stood in front of Alvira, every bit the protector. "She might not have been before, but she is now."

Ariel looked at Alvira, appalled. "How could you?"

"Ariel ... I can.."

"Explain?" Ariel snorted. "How you were *entranced* by my brother? What does he have that I could not give you?"

"A choice!" Alvira snapped.

Ariel froze. "What?"

"I know all about how you turned her, Ariel," Zedkiel spoke up. "She feels that you gave her no choice when it came to being with you. Alvira *chose* me."

Ariel's eyes widened. "Was my *brother* the only person you could choose?"

Alvira's gaze dropped.

Ariel stalked up to Zedkiel, holding the blade up to his chin. "You *took* her from me."

Zedkiel smiled. "She *wanted* me. At least, that's what she kept telling me. Again, and again, and again–"

Ariel growled, lunging and swinging her blade at Zedkiel. Zedkiel leaned back, dodging the blow by a hair's breadth, but he had ducked too late. The blade had sliced his cheek, leaving a neat scar down his face.

Alvira lashed out, kicking the blade from Ariel's hands.

"You'll fight me for him?" Ariel laughed menacingly. "I can't believe the monster you've become."

Ariel lunged at her once-beloved, and Zedkiel stepped between them once more, grabbing Ariel's wrist before she could throttle her.

Ariel screamed in frustration, the tears finally escaping her eyes.

"What is going on here?" Zephyr's voice broke through the chaos.

"Exactly what you warned me against, Father," Ariel spat out, still in Zedkiel's vice-like grip. "They're traitors, both of them. Selfish *fools* who chase their lust before their loyalties. Your son was never worthy of being a vampire!"

"Let her go, Zedkiel," Zephyr said calmly. He looked to Alvira. "Leave my palace at once. You're not welcome here."

"Lord Zephyr–" she stuttered.

"The laws I laid down were clear enough, but it seems there was nothing there for the damage our loved ones would cause us. I will not have my children slaughter each other over something as trivial as what they call love. And I can't have you remain here to mislead them. Leave, before I decide to resort to something less kind."

Alvira looked pleadingly at Zedkiel, but the prince would not meet her gaze. The princess left, and Lord Zephyr waited until she had descended the steps before he spoke to his children.

"I used to think you were a coward, Zedkiel," Zephyr eyed his son warily. "But it turns out you are a selfish fool. You couldn't bear to see Ariel happy with someone other than you, and so you took what she loved most for yourself."

"Father, I did not go after her, she–"

Zephyr tutted. "Does it matter?"

The Lord of Darkness extended his hand toward his daughter, letting her stand in his embrace as he smoothed down her hair. "I can't let you kill him."

"He deserves it," Ariel said, sounding petulant.

"I suppose I should be glad your lands are so distant, then?" Zephyr said softly, letting his son stand there and wallow in his embarrassment and silence. Eventually, Ariel left the room, leaving her brother to his own devices. After that momentary lapse, she had returned to being cold and calculating, her voice businesslike as she discussed strategy with her father.

Zephyr noticed how her ears twitched at the sound of two sets of footsteps leaving the palace. She flinched as the door closed behind them.

After being betrayed by her brother and the princess, Ariel became quieter than usual. She spent a few more days in the western stronghold before returning to her region, eager to devote herself to something else. She kept watch over the region and the vampires there, a silent but deadly presence that everyone feared. Ariel was cautious. She knew she could still turn one more person, and whoever that to be must be someone loyal before anything else. Royalty and power perhaps did not mean as much as loyalty did to the Princess of Darkness now. Whomever her kin would become, they could not be as heartless as Alvira had been.

Her time at the western stronghold had given her an insight into the Chosen One – the First that Lord Zephyr turned to his cause: Cain. The mysterious first vampire had a cold and aloof demeanor, and although he spoke to Lord Zephyr with great respect, he seldom had much else to say. Ariel had observed him for a while and tried to curb her curiosity about the first vampire. Was it attraction? She mused but dismissed the thought quickly. Her experience with Alvira tempted her to make rash decisions. She tried to dismiss it, but she would see the dark-haired vampire lurking in the gardens on nights, lost in deep thought.

"I'm surprised you didn't pick up on it sooner," Cain said to her on one occasion. Ariel had been standing on the balcony, watching Cain on the castle grounds. Her thoughts had drifted, and before she knew it, Cain was beside her.

"Hmm?" Ariel hummed distractedly.

"Your brother..." he trailed off.

Ariel scrunched up her nose in disgust. "I was a blind fool, Cain," she paused. "You knew?"

"I see things," his tone suggested he knew more than he let on. "You pretend to have moved on, Ariel, but you're still here."

Ariel glanced at him, amused. "I can leave."

"I know you don't want to," Cain's voice was deep, a sonorous undertone to it as he spoke, slow and languid.

Ariel snorted, "If you know why I'm sticking around, why haven't you said anything yet?"

"I know you have questions that you don't wish to ask Zephyr. And I know you have concerns about me too. You want to sink your teeth into this mystery before you head back to your kingdom," he smirked at Ariel, and the Princess of Darkness watched his face shift in the shadows. "Forgive the pun."

Ariel rolled her eyes. "I know nothing about you, Cain. I'm curious – can you blame me?"

Ariel had only blinked, and Cain stood before her, his dark hair falling over his crimson eyes. He stood closer than she anticipated. He was a tall, hulking figure, well-built and broad-shouldered. He almost eclipsed Ariel's form. Her eyes darted up, and Cain almost smiled.

"Ask away," he said, his voice gruff.

***

The princess had taken to the first vampire. Cain and Ariel struck an unlikely friendship that did not progress beyond the odd midnight conversation and stroll. Ariel wondered what would happen if she expressed an interest in him, but his intimidating aura kept her at bay. But the friendship progressed, and memories of Cain followed when Ariel left to head her own region. The first vampire seemed above all worldly matters, refusing to divulge any information that Ariel wanted without sounding incredibly cryptic.

He had not told her who his first victim was and whether he had any kin. He had lived eons alone but shared nothing with her. He would share a vague memory when Ariel would least expect it, which would become all Ariel could think about.

"Do you have special plans for your region, Cain?" she asked, prepared to be met with silence.

Cain's voice sounded light when he answered, making Ariel glance briefly at him, wondering if she was imagining his grin.

"I do, actually," Cain trailed off. "Zephyr gave me the gift of being the first of this kind and trusts me enough to give the west over to me while he stays in the castle. I'll be damned if I don't turn this region into a force to be reckoned with."

There was a tremor in his voice that betrayed the excitement he felt. It was the most emotion she had seen him express in her short time at the western castle.

Ariel had set up a stronghold in the south, where vampires in her region could come to train, learn and recover from any injuries resulting from their conflicts with humans. As time progressed and vampire numbers grew, human curiosity was piqued. People started taking an interest in the humans coming out of their dark dens after dusk and lurking in the shadows. Myths and rumors spread as lore around vampires developed. The occasional human would try to hunt, injure or capture them, but only a few escape. They began to believe that vampires were immortal and impossible to kill, while others rumored that the only way to kill a vampire was by piercing them through the heart. Beyond that, regeneration came easy to them.

The regions flourished at their own pace, and alliances were formed. The north and south grew further apart. Zedkiel and Ariel never spoke after the last debacle at the castle, and Ariel proceeded to develop a kingdom her brother would be afraid of and Cain would be proud of.

A part of her wanted the first vampire to see her skills for what they truly were, recognize her power, and see her as more than Zephyr's kin.

The fire of an unspoken animosity grew to a flame as the rumors of a vampire killing one of his own kind at the border of the southern region gained traction. Ariel was furious, and a team of vampires was sent to the border to investigate. A vampire from the northern region had slain one of Ariel's vampires in a small dispute over a human victim.

When the Princess of Darkness' small legion arrived at the border to fight, Zedkiel had already sent an army of his own to 'take care' of the problem. The vampires clashed in a short-lived battle, and both sides suffered losses. With over seven vampires killed on either side, the news of the skirmish reached Zephyr, and a council meeting was called instantly.

The twins had arrived at the western stronghold accompanied by their best warriors, prepared to fight if necessary. Cain and Uriel had been present already and awaited Lord Zephyr's arrival. The four leaders descended into the chamber and took their seats, the room illuminated by a strange green light.

"Where's your concubine?" Ariel muttered as Zedkiel took his seat.

"Safe from your clutches," Zedkiel snapped.

"Enough, children," Uriel drawled, her voice like honey. Cain snorted at the comment while the twins both glared at the other two.

The door opened, and Lord Zephyr stepped into the eerie light. The king of darkness looked as if he had aged in the past few months.

"Do you know what you've done?" Zephyr's voice was shaking with barely controlled rage. "When one vampire slays another, they take on the powers of those they have slain. I should try your entire armies in this court, have them slaughtered for this disobedience. All over what?"

The Lord leaned over, his hands clutching the back of his throne. He stared at the twins, "A measly fight over *food*? Immortal beings cribbing over a pint of *blood?*"

Zephyr's voice grew louder, and Zedkiel seemed to shrink in his chair.

"The two of you had your own kind *slain* to settle a petty score – I should have you both stripped of your powers right now!" He yelled.

Cain's gaze darted toward Zephyr in surprise. He wondered if the Lord of darkness had that power and had chosen to conceal it until now.

"Father," Cain started, his voice low and placating. "They're children. Let them be. They will learn."

"You would have them slay others to settle a pointless score, Cain?" Zephyr spat.

"No, father – I would have them spared because they still have value, despite their petty blunders," he said lowly. "Keep them apart, but let us guide them."

Zephyr's gaze turned to Uriel, who was staring and Cain. He turned to face Uriel, who blinked and nodded suddenly as if on board with the idea after a split second of a silent conversation with the first vampire.

"Cain has a point, Zephyr. Your children have proven to be fussy and emotional. Cain and I are your best bet. Let us look after them."

"We're not babies that need to be looked after," Zedkiel snapped.

"You behave like them," Cain argued.

Ariel looked from Cain and Uriel to Lord Zephyr, bristling. Her feud with her brother had urged her to act irrationally, but she knew she had to pay the price. She could tell her father was inclined toward the idea Cain had presented, to be mentored by the other two while Lord Zephyr looked after the mission.

But something else troubled Ariel. She watched Uriel and Cain exchange another conspiratory glance and what she could have sworn was the ghost of a fleeting smile. There was a connection between the silent leaders that she had not seen before. They got along well, their movements and conversation fluid as they complimented each other. Ariel sat through her father's furious tirade, distracted.

She had not realized that the slaughter of another vampire would grant you their powers, and she had not realized that they had inadvertently given vampires of lowly status more power than they were worthy of. The crack in the foundation of her and Zedkiel's relationship could lead to something bigger. She could feel it.

The night went on, and the council meeting reached an end. Cain was to mentor Ariel, while Uriel took Zedkiel under her wing. The armies were dismissed, and Zephyr had sent the four leaders on their way. Ariel's fog of confusion did not leave her as Uriel and Cain said their farewells, exchanging something that had been pressed in their closed fists moments before.

She looked at Zedkiel and found him staring at her, hatred reflected in his gaze.

Chapter 8
The Rise of the Vampire Kingdom

The twins left with their respective mentors, each silent after being admonished so harshly. Their embarrassment was enough to put an immediate stop to the growing conflict among vampires for a little while. Factions of vampires formed all over the globe, reporting to their region leaders every now and then.

As their numbers grew, so did the fear that was associated with them. Humankind often spoke of the beasts of the night that would steal away their best warriors, that would drain their weak, and dump them at the base of ravines. The telltale mark of fangs on the throats of their fallen led to the notorious reputation of the vampires.

Ariel and Cain's bond finally developed into something akin to friendship. The First vampire appreciated her mettle and drive. She was fueled by revenge, which made her easier to manipulate. Cain trained the Princess of Darkness, though there was not much that needed improvement. War strategy was something that required more attention, but when it came to combat, Ariel was almost as skilled as he was.

Uriel and Zedkiel struggled for a bit. The exotic vampire was far too aloof and cold toward Zedkiel, who demanded attention. Zedkiel worked hard to earn her favor and her approval, but Uriel would not relent. She did not give him the time of day until he stopped behaving like a child. He was far too distracted by Alvira's presence – a vampire who was reckless and selfish. At times, to Uriel, it felt like the princess wished to show off Zedkiel. The prince of darkness was oblivious to how the princess used him to make herself seem superior – and she seemed jealous of Uriel as well.

The princess felt threatened by the ethereal-looking vampire and would hover on the rare occasion Uriel would train Zedkiel.

Most of the time, Uriel kept to herself. She would stay in her room or roam the courtyards of Zedkiel's palace. She wrote letters to Cain, confiding in him. The duo had stuck an unlikely friendship, and they bonded over their shared disdain for the twins. It seemed that they both favored Ariel over the brother, and Uriel often joked about swapping charges for a little while. Cain could do with some change, and Zedkiel needed straightening out.

Uriel and Zedkiel would go on excursions to other areas in the region, keeping up with the Shadow guild and helping iron out any issues that arose in sections of vampire settlements. The vampires followed a strict code, avoiding mankind as much as possible and finding discreet ways of finding humans that would fuel them. Mankind had grown weary and took measures to protect themselves against vampires.

Stories spread of humans defending themselves against vampires by stabbing them through the hearts with wooden stakes or decapitating them with silver weapons. Vampires had to assimilate and evolve. They had to take special caution to blend in with humans and scout their victims. Some would scout hospitals, finding their source of blood there, while others would take care to grab an orphan no one would miss.

The northern and southern regions operated independently for a while, with little to no conflict between the two as they remained almost completely cut off from one another. Zedkiel and Uriel kept the peace for a few years before returning to their regions. The rift between the siblings remained but had grown cold.

Zedkiel and Alvira ruled over the southern region together, with the princess becoming known as the princess of the south, though many knew that she had once been a northern princess, and rumors talked about how she had betrayed the northern leader and broke her heart.

The regions were left to the four leaders that Lord Zephyr had appointed. The leader himself had disappeared. Vampires would talk amongst themselves about where lord zephyr had gone. There were reports of him being sighted in every region after a few months would pass – but no one had interacted with the lord of darkness in years.

As Zephyr's absence became more and more prominent, vampires started talking amongst themselves about where the leader had gone. Would the council still operate with the same strength when two of the leaders were at each other's throats?

Though no one dared to suggest that the lord of darkness had disappeared, different schools of thought erupted amongst vampire factions. There were those who favored Lord Cain and wished that he would take Zephyr's place when the time came. Uriel's followers believed that she was the most capable council leader. The shadow guild was the last to have seen Lord Zephyr and had no cause to rumor that he had died or disappeared. It was clear to them that the lord of darkness had something else up his sleeve. Perhaps he wished to test his children. The vampire kingdom had been growing smoothly and evolving with the times. Dissent was only natural. They had faith in the Shadow Guild's unity and Zedkiel's power. The four regions functioned as four separate entities, each with its own culture and norms.

Ariel deserted her castle soon after Cain left. She roamed her region, finding her kind everywhere she went. The vampires respected her, and she did not feel her position was under any kind of threat. But the Princess of Darkness felt like something was missing.

She had the power and respect of her kind and an entire kingdom to rule. She was an effective leader but a lonely one. Cain clearly had interests elsewhere, she had insinuated at something more than mentorship more than once, but the elder vampire would simply fix her with a quiet stare that she would have to look away from. He would never deny anything, and Ariel knew he used her attraction toward him for his own favor. He would intimidate her or manipulate her, and she knew what he was doing as he did it, but Ariel felt compelled to give in to him. Something about his aura, menacing as it was, was irresistible to her.

In a wandering search for something *more*, Ariel stumbled back to the kingdom that was once her birthplace. It was where she was born as a mortal and then born again as a vampire. Castle Moon was now no more than a public attraction but a sad remnant of history, demolished and remodeled.

The bloodline had not continued. After Alvira left, there had been wars and many regime changes that Ariel had not bothered to keep up with. She stood before the open gates of the city with a wistful glimmer in her eyes.

"What brings you to Moon Village?"

Ariel had heard the footsteps approach her but chose to dismiss them. She sighed and turned around, coming face to face with a young man who could not have been older than twenty-five.

"I grew up here." She smiled sadly. "Just revisiting some old memories."

He had bright green eyes and a mop of messy, curly brown hair. He eyed her curiously.

"You're lying," he said simply.

Ariel laughed, looking up at the sky as she did so. "What makes you so sure?"

"*I* grew up here," he said pointedly. "And I'm not one to forget a face – especially one as beautiful as yours."

Ariel scoffed, amused at the boy's gall and stubbornness. "Maybe I was here before you were born."

The boy cocked his head sideways, eyeing her before shaking his head in refusal. "There's no way you're older than me."

"Maybe I just have one of those faces," Ariel shrugged.

"Caius," the boy introduced himself, holding out his hand. "Caius Moones."

Ariel met his gaze then, curious. "Moones? Like the village?"

He burst out laughing, a hearty, full sound. Ariel felt herself smile.

"Yes, and no," he stopped laughing to give her a long look. "Come on, let's go to some other place."

Ariel refused to budge.

Caius looked offended. "I'm not that sort of man, and you most definitely are not that sort of lady, madame..."

"Ariel," she laughed.

"Ariel," he said softly, shaking his head as he continued his sentence. "I was merely suggesting that we sit someplace warm. It's getting dark. Let's share a humble meal, and we'll talk about the village you claim to know."

"Hmm," Ariel pretended to think, already slipping her arm into his proffered one, walking past the threshold and entering the village that had changed so much over time.

The duo walked to an inn, and Caius signaled to someone behind the counter. He led Ariel to the dining area, helping her get seated. It was a small and simple place. The drapes were worn and shabby, the tables stained with well-use.

Caius sat down opposite Ariel, nodding at the lady who placed two mugs before them.

Ariel eyed the drink.

"A Moon Village special – surely you'd remember the drink?" Caius challenged.

Ariel smiled, lifting the mug to her lips and taking a sip of the hot beverage. It was a sweet potato broth that Ariel identified instantly because it was a village special that had been passed down for centuries. The taste was more vibrant than she remembered, but it was a popular village delicacy in the colder months. It would double as a meal because of how rich and heavy it was and would keep anyone who drank it warm, happy, and full.

"It's saltier than I remember. There's also a ... meaty undertone to it." Ariel said, "Sweet potato broth."

Caius narrowed his eyes, "The innkeeper puts ribs in the broth to add some more flavor to it – but you've passed the test. What's your story?"

Ariel grinned. "What's yours?"

"Ah, the *Moones* thing," he looked down, almost embarrassed. "It does have to do with the village."

"Oh?"

"If you trace my family tree, I'm the bastard son of a Roderick Moon. The last of the Royal Moon's that ran the village. The royal bloodline had long since scattered. I think my father was a governor's grandson," Caius shrugged.

Ariel nodded. "And what is it that you do, Bastard Son of Roderick Moon?"

Caius rolled his eyes, "I have a very respectable job as a village sentinel."

"That sounds made-up." Ariel laughed.

"Well, it isn't."

Ariel nodded, stifling her laughter as she provoked the boy. "So, you're stationed at the gates – but that's about it?"

Caius turned red. "I am also an excellent swordsman, I'll have you know."

"But you weren't at your post when I arrived, Caius," Ariel teased, enjoying her interaction with him more than she would like to admit.

Caius was at a loss for words. Defeated, the boy looked away. Ariel smiled.

"Y'know, I'm not half-bad with a sword either."

Caius met her gaze then, curious.

"Who *are* you?"

"Do you wanna spar?" Ariel asked.

Caius groaned, pulling at his hair in frustration. "Why do you sound like the woman of my dreams, Ariel?" he pouted, and Ariel tried to fight the flutter she felt in her stomach. "Tell me you won't break my heart?"

"I don't make promises I can't keep, Caius," Ariel grinned. *But I will break your skin when I sink my teeth into your neck,* she thought.

***

Cain leaned his head against the wall, eyes set on the midnight sky. "I'm serious, Uriel," he said quietly. "I can't do this forever."

Uriel watched him curiously. "What makes you say you'll be stuck here forever?"

Cain finally met her gaze. "We're immortal. And so is Zephyr. He expects us to be obedient little children forever – or at least until he gets what he wants."

"The fabled battle with Lucifer," Uriel finished.

Cain straightened up, facing her. "I'm not the only one who feels like this. The twins are useless because Zephyr *was* a father to them but not to us."

Uriel stayed silent, her eyes refusing to give away how she really felt. "Are you suggesting rebellion?" she asked.

Cain smiled. "Not as such, but I cannot simply be a pawn in his plans." He searched Uriel's eyes for some sort of affirmation but saw none. "You won't come with me, then?"

Uriel didn't turn away from him, but Cain almost felt her eyes lose the sincerity he saw in them moments ago. It was as if a veil had hidden her true intentions from him. All this time together, and he still couldn't get a read on her.

"I cannot afford to, Cain. One of us has to stay behind," she said matter-of-factly. "Can't let him suspect both of us."

Cain clenched his jaw, visibly annoyed. "You're just afraid to be uncomfortable," he snapped. Uriel shrugged.

"Your empire is far too precious to you," he continued.

Uriel seemed unaffected. "I've put some effort into it, yes. It does mean something to me, Cain. I can't just desert it so you can have your revenge."

Cain shook his head, walking away from her. Uriel had come to visit a few days ago, and the companions had enjoyed one another's silent company. Cain had planted the idea of a rebellion in her head the last time they met, and Uriel had been curious to see what he had in mind. She was a bit disappointed at first.

He was the strongest amongst the council and outranked them too. But Cain was only bitter about the fact that Zephyr had abandoned him but chose to stay with the twins. And then, the Lord of Darkness gave mere children the same position as him.

He had also started challenging the idea of the war itself, questioning whether or not Lucifer had really cursed Zephyr or what Zephyr had done to deserve such a fate. Whenever he had tried to broach the subject with Zephyr, the vampire would fall silent, shutting him down.

Uriel didn't doubt Cain's ability to wreak havoc, but she couldn't desert her empire for the sake of one man's revenge. He was passionate and would see his war through, but Uriel couldn't risk it. She preferred keeping her intentions and her grudges covert.

Cain walked away from her to cool off, and Uriel knew he would come find her when his rage dissipated.

The duo parted ways as Uriel retreated to the castle. Both vampires mistook the presence of another vampire in their midst as each other, blind to the eavesdropper in their midst. The vampire was crouched beneath a bridge in the courtyard, not far from where they had been discussing things. Cain walked ahead.

A shadow darted out from under the bridge, leaving the castle swiftly, a smile on his face as the gears turned in his head. Perhaps his days of glory weren't too far off.

***

Ariel grinned, pinning Caius to the ground. He chuckled, eyes darting to where his sword lay on the grass, discarded. "What was that you were saying about me?" Ariel challenged.

"I was only going easy on you, m'lady," Caius beamed, his smile fading quickly when Ariel dug her knee into his stomach. He started coughing.

Ariel watched him curiously. She had been enjoying his company more than she had expected to. He also happened to be a descendant of her bloodline, which was a welcome surprise. She relented, letting him recover as she towered over him. Ariel thrust her sword in his face so by the time he recovered, he would be staring at her blade in his face.

"'Tis an honor to be bested by you, Ariel," he said softly, pushing the blade aside with his hand. He grabbed her proffered hand and let himself be pulled to his feet.

They stood inches apart. Caius could feel her breath on his face. His gaze drifted to her lips and then to her eyes in a silent question.

Ariel took a step back. “I have something I need to tell you, Caius. I can’t do this to you without telling you first.”

Caius’s brow furrowed. “Don’t tell me you’re promised to another?”

Ariel laughed.

“You’re married!?” he half-shouted.

“No,” Ariel laughed again, stepping closer to him once more. She kissed him firmly, pressing her lips against his with a certainty she hadn’t felt in ages. She felt him melt against her, his lips parting as they deepened the kiss.

Ariel pulled away, enjoying how dazed he looked.

“Then?” he asked.

“I’m a vampire, Caius,” she said quietly, watching his expression remain the same. “A beast of the night? Princess of Darkness...”

She trailed off, not accustomed to how unaffected Caius was.

“That’s it?” he asked, catching Ariel off guard. “Tell me more.”

Ariel tucked a strand of hair behind her ear, “...Uh, I’m immortal, and I have been alive for much longer than you think. I used to live here before the castle was in ruins. I'm Ariel Eleazor – but I was once the–"

"The lost princess," Caius finished, putting two and two together. "You're beautiful."

Ariel smiled at how he blurted out the last bit. "Caius, I came here looking for something profound. Some *meaning* of sorts. And you caught me off guard. I have only spent this night with you, but there is something here that I cannot risk losing."

Caius blinked, his expression turning serious and losing the dazed look that covered his face. "Ariel, I'm just a mortal. Surely there are other people more worthy of a princess such as yourself."

"Who better than the bastard son of a once-removed distant cousin?" she teased.

Caius laughed, taking a step away from her. "I'm not sure how this will work, Ariel. I have spent my whole life here. Granted, I have nothing tying me down, but I couldn't imagine leaving this village."

"Perhaps you have stayed here so long in wait for me. Maybe destiny kept you here for us to meet," Ariel tried. She stepped closer, cradling his face in her hands. She slowly traced a finger across his jaw, running it down his neck. She put her hand on his neck, feeling him swallow. Ariel could hear the pounding of his heart against her hand. She heard his blood rushing through his veins.

"...What are you doing?" he asked, voice trembling ever so slightly.

"Do you trust me?" she looked up, meeting his terrified gaze.

Caius nodded. Ariel bared her fangs, her nostrils flaring as she breathed in his scent. She kissed his neck first, feeling his body tense and then relax against her. He moaned softly, not expecting the tender gesture from the girl who called herself a beast moments ago.

She waited for him to relax before sinking her teeth into his flesh. Caius gasped in pain, eyes flying open in surprise. Ariel drank, relishing his blood. The blood dripped down her chin, staining Caius's shirt. Ariel eased his limp body to the grass.

Caius felt the heat of the poison seep into him. Something spread through his body, the sensation almost like tendrils. He felt a chill envelop him, followed by excruciating pain. Caius's body convulsed, but Ariel refused to let go.

She kissed the open wound, fully aware that once the poison took effect, the wound would heal completely. She licked the blood from his neck, wiped her mouth shortly after, and sat down beside him.

Caius was unconscious, but his chest rose and fell steadily beside her. Ariel watched him quietly, noting how his warm skin had turned pale. She leaned over him, lifting his lip to glance at the fangs.

"What are you doing?" he asked, his mouth half open.

Ariel let go. "Just seeing if you're okay."

Caius sat up, leaning on one elbow. "What did you do to me?"

"You're like me now," she said. "I turned you. You're immortal too."

"Do I have to kill people now? The way people say you do?"

Ariel shook her head. "It's not all bloody violence, Caius. You don't have to kill people if you're not ready yet. You can survive on draining animals for now. I'll teach you everything you need to know."

Caius nodded slowly, rubbing the back of his head as he pondered what lay ahead of him now.

"Are you scared?" Ariel asked quietly, wondering if the boy regretted his decision.

Caius smiled softly. “Not when you’re with me.”

He grabbed Ariel by the back of her neck, pulling her closer so their lips could meet again.

Caesar entered the castle he had been lurking outside of for hours. He wondered if Cain would know he had been around, but it seemed that his father had been far too preoccupied with his own thoughts to notice him. Uriel had ascended to her quarters, their small spat having driven the two vampires apart temporarily. Which suited Caesar just fine.

He entered the main chamber and saw Cain sulking by the window.

“Cain?” He called out as he walked to him.

The vampire turned around, his eyebrows arched in surprise at the sight of him. “Caesar. When did you get here? I haven’t seen you in ages.”

Caesar smiled, his smile was charming as ever. “Just this evening. It’s been a while, I simply wanted to report some progress to you, father.”

Cain made a face. “I’d rather you just call me Cain.”

Caesar eyed him curiously as he took his place beside the first vampire. “Why is that? Lord Zephyr prefers his children call him father.”

"I am not Lord Zephyr," he snapped. "He has his own ideas about how to reign over the vampire race and I have my own. I turned you long before any of the others even knew the taste of blood. I'd rather consider you a companion and a friend than a son."

"A confidante?" Caesar tried.

Cain shrugged. "Sure. What reports do you bring from your end of the region?"

Caesar straightened up. "There's an undercurrent of unrest amongst the vampires, Cain. We cannot be expected to get rusty in wait for a war that won't happen."

Caesar watched Cain stiffen. He wondered if Cain would realize that Caesar was repeating his own words back to him. Instead, the brooding vampire smiled.

"They do say great minds think alike," Cain smirked. "I understand the vampires are restless, it's only natural. But what is there to do other than wait?"

"The only way to prevent any of us from losing what skill we have is to create chaos," Caesar said casually. "We create a war, incite battle, pluck out the weaklings, and get Lord Zephyr's attention all in one go."

Cain turned to Caesar, surprised. "How long have you been thinking about this?"

"Long enough," Caesar said curtly, with all the arrogance of a young prince. "I came here to let you know that our region seems to be thriving in comparison to the others. Our vampires are stronger and more capable. And there is one faction, in particular, one that is under my direct command, who could battle the likes of your siblings."

Cain nodded. "You're quite confident, Caesar."

"I have taken my training quite seriously, Cain," Caesar said solemnly. "I know what the stakes are. But I cannot let my training go to waste as a second-in-command. Am I to lead small factions until the end of time? Lucifer seems like a fabled war now, and what better way to ensure our superiority over mankind and other vampires than by taking over other regions, making sure there are no divisions? What if it all belongs to us?"

Cain laughed silently before grabbing Caesar's face. He tilted his chin upwards, studying the dark eyes of the first vampire he ever turned.

"I was like you once," Cain whispered. "I see the hunger in your eyes."

"It isn't merely hunger, Cain."

Cain let go. "I have seen my fair share of this pathetic game. If you feel like a pawn, rest assured I am no king," he shrugged. "But I will grant you this, Caesar – you can do as you please."

Caesar swallowed thickly, trying to understand what Cain meant.

The first vampire grabbed him by the shoulders and turned him slowly to face the throne. "I have been waiting for this day," Cain said.

Caesar watched Cain's expression turn to one of relief.

"This is yours, my son," he smiled. "You may take this throne."

Caesar's brow furrowed. "What do you mean? What about you?"

Cain clasped his hands behind his back as he walked Caesar to the throne. "I have a bone to pick with Zephyr, and I know he will not come out of the shadows quite yet."

He pushed Caesar onto the throne and walked behind it, his thin fingers traced his face and rested on his crown. "This kingdom is yours now."

"You won't just leave, will you?" Caesar asked, feigning worry. He hadn't realized things would turn in his favor so quickly. He had planned to convince Cain of his abilities and talk him out of deserting his throne.

Cain was just going to hand it to him? No questions asked.

Caesar felt the weight of Cain's hands lift from his forehead. He turned around, expecting to see Cain behind him.

But the vampire had vanished.

"Cain?" Caesar's voice echoed in the empty hall. His own questioning voice returned to him, and Caesar burst into laughter.

Uriel stood at the door of the throne room, her brows arched in amusement. Cain always was the reckless type. She turned around to leave – if Caesar was any bit like his father, war was not far off, and the eastern region needed her leader.

***

The war did not break out immediately, but there was a steady build-up to it. Ariel's region was the first under threat. Given that the Princess of Darkness had not been seen at her region's stronghold in years, Caesar was under the impression the princess had deserted her kind. Betrayed by her lovers, she had fallen into a depressed state, perhaps.

But he had been wrong. Ariel and Caius returned to the region before the first vampires fell at the border of the southern region. There had been a minor battle between fifteen vampires, seven of which were her own.

Two had survived and reported to her immediately.

Ariel eyed their injuries. Vampires were immortal, but the further down the bloodline you went, the slower healing became. She clenched her jaw at the sight of the arm that was obviously out of its socket. The other vampire leaned on her knee, bleeding steadily onto the marble floor.

"You're saying they *approached* you and attacked?" Ariel questioned.

The one with the dislocated arm spoke first. "We were stationed at the border, as per your command, your highness. We do not patrol the area because we do not need human attention, but our settlement is at our predetermined border. They approached us as fellow vampires, friendly vampires."

"We welcomed them in as Cain's soldiers, but the moment they entered our stronghold, the violence broke out," the other vampire spoke, her breathing labored.

"Without cause?" Ariel asked again, unable to mask her shock. "What is Cain doing?"

"It's not Cain, your highness," the first one spoke up again. "It's Caesar."

"Caesar?" Ariel tried. "Who on earth is he?"

"There were seven of us in the stronghold, and we managed to put up a fair fight. Six of his men were killed too," the first one continued. "We hadn't known that killing them would grant us power, m'lady – but this knowledge is impacting other vampires too. We interrogated one of Caesar's men after overpowering them."

"Is Cain all right?" Ariel asked, her mind buzzing with questions. Had Caesar somehow incapacitated Cain? Was Cain inciting war? Surely, he would attack Zedkiel before anyone else.

"Cain is gone," the second vampire said, pausing to spit out a mouthful of blood. "Caesar has the Western region under his control now – and he sent his vampires to us to initiate a steady shift of power."

Ariel stayed silent. She could not let her vampires know that the situation was beyond her grasp.

"This can mean only one thing – a hostile attack from any other vampire, regardless of who he is, cannot be tolerated. This means war," Ariel stood up. "I'll send word throughout the region, we prepare for battle against the Western region, regardless of who is on the throne."

"But the slaughter of vampires is against-" the first vampire began.

"Our stance is defensive – for now," Ariel turned her back on the vampires. "But that does not mean we will take every hit lying down."

"Yes, m'lady," the vampires agreed.

Ariel bit the inside of her cheek. She had no one to turn to but Caius, a vampire who was powerful and doted on her but had no idea how to fight a war. Her brother and Alvira were out of the question.

Ariel sighed, summoning the vampires she needed to spread the word over the region. She briefed them quickly, making sure that everyone knew that she had the situation under control. Her region would not succumb to the trivial scuffles from the West. But she needed allies.

"Devon," Ariel stopped the last vampire before he set off with the message. He was one of her more trusted warriors. She had overseen his training herself. "I need you to take a message to Uriel instead. Can you do that?"

Devon nodded. "Of course, my queen – what is it?"

"Tell Uriel to meet with me – tell her about the war that's broken out, and say," Ariel took a deep breath. "Tell her Ariel wishes to discuss the terms of an alliance."

Devon's eyes widened. There was a subtle nod that ensured he understood his orders, but Ariel could tell the vampire realized the situation was far more deadly than a group of rogue vampires from a bordering empire.

A great storm was brewing, and they had to set aside all their differences for it.

Ariel trained with Caius every day, trying her best to ensure that her partner was a capable warrior when the war demanded it. She called upon Lord Zephyr every day, hoping her father would grace them with his presence, but each day passed by without event. She needed to talk to someone about what Caesar was doing, but even Uriel hadn't responded yet.

A part of her knew she had to rise above what her brother and Alvira had done – after all, they were standing at the cusp of a war between vampires. The battle that they all prepared for seemed so far away, and Lucifer sounded more like a fable than ever. The real problem was the bloodbath among the vampires that awaited them. With everyone slaughtering each other, power dynamics would shift. If a lesser vampire killed a stronger one, they could easily alter the hierarchy they had all worked so hard to maintain.

Caius's presence was comforting. Ariel was grateful for his easygoing nature. He kept things light, managing to bring a smile to her face when all she could do was worry. He was new to this life, and still, he handled things with grace. Ariel leaned on him, relying on his steady presence. Caius would brush away her hair as she leaned over maps spread over the table, and he would stand by her side as she held meetings with the vampires she had trained over the years. There were unspoken ranks amongst them, determined by power. Devon was by far the strongest, he had been turned by Alvira as her first vampire, and he remained loyal to Ariel even after Alvira had deserted her kingdom.

The strategy meetings and training were endless, with a new dispatch of soldiers to keep a steady rotation of strong vampires at the borders to keep their kingdom strong and protected.

Finally, word from Uriel came. It came in the form of her gracing Ariel's kingdom with her presence. There was much fanfare to her arrival, and when the leader of the Eastern kingdom sat before her at dinner, Ariel spoke cautiously.

"I trust your journey went well?" she began guardedly.

"We can skip the formalities, Ariel," Uriel said, raising a flute of blood to her lips. "I apologize for the delay in my arrival. I needed to investigate the western kingdom on my own to see what was happening."

"And what of Cain?" the Princess of Darkness asked. "Is he all right?"

"He's missing," Uriel said flatly, ignoring the worry on Ariel's face. "He has disappeared willingly, princess, and he will not be found until he wishes to be found."

"Does he not care for his kingdom?"

Uriel smiled. "He finds the idea of it childish. Caesar was his son; he may as well have handed his kingdom over to him on a silver platter."

"But what do we do with him? He's threatening to overpower the rest of the empire."

"Don't be daft," she shook her head as if disappointed by Ariel's reaction. "He isn't strong enough to overpower us, but I will admit he is annoying. If he takes even one region under his control, it will be too much power than what any of us will be comfortable with. We need to maintain a unified front before the fool."

"You agree to ally with me, then?" Ariel asked.

"I will do more than that, princess. I know Zephyr values you too much – and you're smarter than your brother too, whom I've invited to join us, by the way."

"You – what?" Ariel spat.

"Be reasonable, Ariel," Uriel's voice seemed to drip honey even when she was criticizing her. "Your brother will understand that your temporary truce will only last as long as the battle. I hope you can keep your hands off of a dagger until then."

Ariel nodded curtly. "We just need to get rid of Caesar. If that means a full-blown war, then my army is ready."

"As is mine," Uriel responded. "If you can host us, our armies can unite against the Western region, and we can take the battle to them instead."

"We can overwhelm them, force Caesar into a corner."

"And kill him," Uriel said dismissively. She rose from the table as her meal concluded. "I'll save you the trouble of talking to Zedkiel – leave him to me."

"Thank you, Uriel," Ariel said earnestly. "Truly."

The queen of the eastern empire left with a curt nod, the palace staff rushing to escort the queen to her quarters.

"She seems nice," Caius offered with a small smile. "Chilly – but nice."

Ariel smiled, taking his hand under the table and giving it a firm squeeze.

Zedkiel and Alvira arrived the following night. Uriel received them with Ariel and Caius at her side. The siblings remained cold toward one another, but Zedkiel understood the gravity of the situation. They agreed to put aside their differences for the sake of the vampire kingdom.

The days stretched into weeks as the battle plans were pored over by the three leaders. Eventually, the day came for the soldiers to march into battle. Caius and Ariel led their army themselves. The princess wished to make a statement, and her power granted her the ease the overpower Caesar if needed. Uriel and Zedkiel stayed at the camp that was set up near the western border, with Alvira insisting she head the northern army to prove her capability.

The armies amassing at the western border had not gone unnoticed. Caesar had increased security, and shortly after, his army had started gathering at the border as well. The tension of battle was high, with either side waiting for the first body to drop.

Oddly enough, the first body to drop was Ariel's.

Dawn broke with the piercing, painful cry from the Princess's tent. The guttural cry sounded almost like it belonged to a dying animal. But the cry had been Caius's. He had gone to check up on her when she failed to rise for the first meeting of the day and had found his beloved slain.

Caius had been inconsolable. He was half-mad with grief and rage, threatening to behead whoever stood in the way of his hunt for the princess's killer. Uriel stood over Ariel's body, solemn.

"We send our armies out today," she announced. "Tell the men to prepare for war."

Zedkiel's shoulder shook silently as the tears escaped his eyes. He knew his sister had died without forgiving him for what had happened, and there was no way to make any amends. Uriel looked at him and fought off the urge to shout at him.

"I will be on the battlefield – in Ariel's stead," Uriel said pointedly. "Now is not the time for your tears, Zedkiel. If Caesar has anything to do with her death, then you should be on the battlefield too. We cannot stand for the slaughter of our council."

Caius stood at the very front of the armies, a space beside him bare, as if in remembrance of his beloved. His face was expressionless, his eyes dead.

He led the charge valiantly, and bodies fell on either side. A bloodbath ensued, and vampires met their ends swiftly amongst the clash of swords and daggers. Alvira took an equal part in the battle, her powers stronger than anyone remembered. Zedkiel seemed taken aback by her sheer strength but decided that she, too, drew from her rage at Ariel's death.

The battle was over in minutes. Caesar's numbers had depleted quickly, and there had been a call for a truce.

"Devon," Caius called out to the one vampire that had fought as valiantly as he and defended Caius like a brother. "Hold the line – the Council and I must see to Caesar and make him pay for what he has done."

Devon nodded, his eyes giving away the pain he felt. “Do not spare him.”

Caius smiled weakly. “Wouldn’t dream of it.”

***

Uriel, Zedkiel, Alvira, and Caius stood in Caesar’s court. The young king looked shaken.

“I see that it was unwise to instigate the war,” he began. “The council has swiftly put me in my place.”

“The council hasn’t even started,” Uriel said, her honeyed voice taking on a sharp edge no one had ever heard before. “You have murdered Ariel Eleazor – and have taken the Western kingdom when it was not yours to take.”

Caesar looked confused. “Ariel’s dead?”

“Don’t pretend!” Caius shouted, letting Zedkiel hold him from lunging at the smug king. “We know what you did.”

Caesar shook his head. “I haven’t left my palace – anyone can vouch for that.”

“Be that as it may, but you sent forward someone to do the job for you,” Zedkiel accused. “You have an equal part to play in this.”

Caesar rose from his throne. “I am innocent!”

Uriel bristled, her gaze resting briefly on Alvira, who had remained silent so far. She shook her head. "Your reign was brief, Caesar. We hope you enjoyed it while it lasted."

Uriel turned on her heel, motioning Zedkiel and Alvira to follow her out of the throne room.

"Caius, make sure we can hear his screams at the palace gates," Uriel said over her shoulder. "Destroy him."

Chapter 9
Human Evolution

Caius took care of Caesar, and when he emerged from the palace holding his severed head, the battle had effectively ceased. Ariel was given the funeral she was worthy of. Her body was cremated, and all the armies had gathered in support. It was a silent affair that ended before the break of dawn.

Caius stood beside the flames, silent and tearful. Zedkiel stood a little distance away, with Alvira holding tightly onto him. The vampire army mourned the loss of a great leader.

As the last of the embers died out, a dark shadow eclipsed the dying moonlight. All eyes turned to the massive silhouette. The shadow regained its form, and Lord Zephyr revealed himself. He looked from Zedkiel to Uriel, eyes dark in question.

"It was Caesar," Uriel said.

Lord Zephyr cast his gaze over the ring of vampires closest to the flame. Zephyr scrunched his nose in disgust. "No, it wasn't."

Caius whipped around. "What is that supposed to mean? Do you know who did it?"

Zephyr stared at Zedkiel curiously. "I have my suspicions, but Caesar was simply a fool with a penchant for power. Nothing more."

Uriel stepped up. "Good riddance regardless. We had to do away with that essentialist anyway. His desire for a 'pure' vampire creed was ridiculous."

Zephyr nodded. "The council must work more vigilantly to restore balance. Caius and Alvira, you were Ariel's kin. You must look after her kingdom and ensure these scuffles are stomped out before they threaten any other kingdom."

Zephyr stared at the dying flames, and his eyes welled with tears. The Princess of Darkness was amongst his first children. She showed promise and was a capable vampire. He'd had great plans for her. It was unfortunate for a species so immortal to be victim to a death like this. Whoever had taken her life now held her power. It wouldn't take long to figure out who that was.

The slightest show of unnatural power would lead to their discovery, and Zephyr would make sure to put an end to the killer the moment he found out. Zephyr took Uriel into confidence, letting her know she had to keep her eyes peeled for someone who had gained an unnatural amount of power.

The first vampire war had come to a close, and the hierarchy of power had clearly been upset by that. Many vampires had climbed up the social ladder in a manner, their newfound powers granting them respect and higher rank.

Such fights and scuffles among vampirekind would be natural now. The council had to guide the remaining vampires to ensure that the vampire kingdom did nothing but strive towards their ultimate goal.

As the vampire kingdom evolved, so did the humans that lived among them. Mankind had progressed well over time, and their ancient ways of living had given way to an industrial revolution. Their technology granted them swift development, and the vampire race evolved with them.

The myths and rumors had given way to "reason," leaving behind only a small faction of people who believed vampires existed. Most of mankind looked at the idea of bloodsucking beasts as entirely fictitious. The believers had cults of their own, with some stupid enough to invite vampires into their lives, not knowing that if they were unfit to be vampires, they would become food for the very beings they had incited.

Human creativity knew no bounds. They developed new ways of defending themselves. Their weapons grew more interesting, but vampirekind was quick to adapt. They had come up with silver bullets as a defense mechanism as well. The curious human mind was also eager to study vampire blood.

Zedkiel had to send in two groups after a few humans captured some of his vampires in an attempt to experiment on them. Zedkiel's men later reported that the captured vampires had been bound to a table with straps made of silver, and the humans tried to draw blood in an attempt to study their kind.

It was clear to the humans that vampires were superior in many ways. Their strength, agility, stamina, and lack of a need for sleep made them enviable, and humans refused to rest until they had studied every intricacy of vampire nature. The genetic makeup of vampires fascinated them immensely, and mankind could not rest until they had a few answers of their own.

After fifteen years of failed captures, one man succeeded. A scientist by the name of Arthur Morgan had captured three vampires on his own. To adapt to mankind, a lot of vampires pretended to live regular lives. Many had jobs and earned money, leading inconspicuous lives.

Arthur Morgan had identified three vampires in his midst. He had invited them over, on the pretense of watching a football game together. Upon their arrival, he promptly lured them into a basement with walls lined with silver.

By the time anyone had bothered to investigate, there had been three vampire casualties, and Arthur Morgan had extracted many vials of vampire blood and gathered enough DNA and details to fuel his research for many years to come.

Uriel was the first to be alarmed. She had called a council meeting, and everyone except Alvira had arrived.

"Where is your beloved?" Caius asked Zedkiel as they sat down.

"Alvira does as she wishes, Caius. You, of all people, should know that already. She comes and goes as she pleases, beloved in the northern kingdom and popping by the south whenever she wishes, as joint ruler."

Uriel smirked. "You seem bothered by that, Zedkiel."

Zedkiel looked up at Uriel from over his chalice, eyes cold and unfeeling.

"Trouble in paradise?" Lord Zephyr asked as he entered. His presence was followed by a wave of deadly silence. "Well, Uriel?" Zephyr asked. "What seems to be the issue at hand?"

"This happened in an area that falls under my jurisdiction, but the matter at hand is grave enough for us all to be wary. A human has captured and killed three vampires for the purpose of his own research. He is working on what he calls a strengthening serum."

Caius nodded. "I've heard whispers of this too. It seems we're too late, and the first of the serums has already been developed."

Uriel's expression was grave. "The serum took five years of polishing. It has reached a stage that now calls for a human trial. Arthur Morgan has created a council of his own with three other scientists."

"What does this serum grant them?" Zedkiel asked.

"Superhuman powers," Caius said. "Speed, agility, strength."

"So, no different from their performance enhancers?" Lord Zephyr asked. "Their athletes use those, don't they?"

"But this sort of drug will go undetected, granting them far more power than we'd like," Caius said.

"And most importantly, Zephyr, this will reduce their fear of us," Uriel said pointedly. "Our next battle is not against our own kind or your mortal enemy. Once humans see the benefits this serum grants them, we will no longer be feared, mythological creatures."

"We will become a commodity. The hunted becomes the prey. They'll harvest us," Caius warned.

Zephyr's eyes darkened. "Then we cannot waste any more time. We must find Arthur Morgan."

"And destroy whatever storage he has." Zedkiel nodded.

Knowledge of the serum's development had been alarming for the council. Zephyr expressed his concern over how bold humans had become. If Arthur Morgan was allowed to keep researching vampire blood as he wished, it wouldn't be long before he became one of the most powerful human beings alive. The business would grant him immeasurable wealth, and the serum would become an infinite source of money and strength.

Caius had been the first to suggest a spy. Morgan would be quick to pick up on the presence of a vampire in his midst, so they would need a human being to gather intel.

"This is preposterous. How could you even suggest trusting a human with this?" Zedkiel shouted.

"You must learn to evolve with the times, Zedkiel. Your time in the castle has made you rusty. I am merely suggesting sending a human to work with Morgan and learn what it is he's doing. Provide us with a way in," Caius explained.

"In exchange for what?" Uriel was curious.

"We'll promise them whatever they desire, which in our case is better than the serum itself," Caius said suggestively, looking to Lord Zephyr for support.

"You wish to bribe them with the promise of turning them?" he asked.

"We don't have to do it if we do not think they're worthy. We could easily dispose of them once we have what we need," Caius shrugged. "Once we have what we need, we can send hunters to dispose of the serums before they begin large-scale production. Right now, all we know is that the serums exist, they've started human trials – and thus far, there's been no major hiccup. Morgan has every reason to begin production."

"Then it's decided," Uriel added in support. "The idea of a spy is not too bad. If we can have the promise of loyalty, that is."

Caius took a deep breath. "I'm willing to take that risk. I'll find someone worth sending in. If this fails, I give you all the permission to dispose of me. Have my head if you want to."

Lord Zephyr arched a brow. "You have so much faith in your plan?"

"I have faith in human desperation, Lord Zephyr."

The council moved forward with the plan, allowing Caius to infiltrate the region and find someone worth turning into a spy. Uriel was not surprised when he settled for a college graduate who had just finished her degree in biochemistry. She was naïve and beautiful. A blonde-haired, petite little thing named Annalise. She had been enamored by Caius's charms, and when she learned about who he really was, her curiosity got the better of her.

Caius played every bit of the damaged romantic part, sharing his tale of woe and exaggerating the danger to his kind. Annalise was eager to help in any way she could, and if that meant interning for Arthur Morgan and earning his favor, that's what she would do.

Uriel and Zedkiel, on the other hand, prepared an army of their best hunters. Star and Shadow were amongst those chosen to break into Morgan's facility when the time came. But until then, the hunters trained diligently. Preparing for the worst of what Morgan had in store for them. The storage facility had not been lined with silver because Morgan had, so far, gone undiscovered by the vampires, and so he didn't feel threatened by them yet.

Morgan's confidence was the only thing that worked to their advantage. Other than that, they had to figure out how to break into a high-security facility and get rid of the vials. They had to destroy the vials before production began. Which, according to the intel Annalise had provided, was due to start in a week.

The super serum's human trials had been successful. Once the serum was injected into the subjects, they fell into a coma with steady vitals and awakened after three days after flatlining. The subjects were then put through a series of endurance trials to see the difference in their stamina, agility, and strength. Strangely enough, the subjects reported a higher craving for raw meat, preferring freshly slaughtered meat that had not been cleaned, drained, or frozen.

Morgan refused to acknowledge their bloodlust a first, but the subjects became demanding and uncooperative until they had been fed properly. The scientist resorted first to deer blood, but later on, struck a deal with a blood bank to keep his "neovampires" fed.

Annalise had been interning with Morgan for almost a month before he showed a romantic interest in the girl. She went with it, leading him on in exchange for information. The scientist relished the attention she gave him, and her naivete helped boost his ego.

She promptly reported everything back to Caius, who mobilized the hunters for their first mission. Morgan would be taking Annalise out for dinner to a restaurant on the outskirts of the city. It would give the hunters ample time to break into the facility and access the vials. They would first break into Morgan's house to get the necessary identification cards. Once they had their way in, they would proceed to the facility and break into storage.

Annalise had provided Caius with detailed blueprints of the building. The council commenced the mission, with Zedkiel, Caius, Uriel, and Lord Zephyr all present in the vicinity to keep watch over the mission as it progressed.

Their ability to move as shadows saved them much time, and breaking into storage required little effort.

"Boss, are we emptying it out or destroying them?" Dorothy asked.

"We take some, we leave some," Star muttered, fighting off a full-body shudder at the sight of so much harvested vampire blood. "Destroy the vials and –"

Star was looking around, casting her gaze for something to pour into the vials. Shadow clicked his tongue, catching her attention. He gestured giant canister with a toxic label on it.

"Perfect."

Two of the chosen hunters left with four containers of the vials. Uriel had suggested they take these samples to study on their own while Star, Shadow, and Dorothy got to work on contaminating and damaging the rest of the serums.

Within an hour and a half, their mission was complete.

The hunters reported their success, and Caius was quick to text Annalise of it. She promptly answered the call, feigning worry and letting Morgan know she had to leave. An excuse left her lips easily, and she left the dinner with a satisfied look about her.

"Looks like your head stays on your shoulders for now," Zedkiel teased.

"You did well, Caius," Lord Zephyr praised. "I'm glad Ariel chose you."

Caius nodded, the memory of his beloved still fresh in his mind. His thoughts wandered briefly—the memory of Zephyr telling them that Caesar had not killed her flashed in his memory.

He shook his head, returning to the moment and meeting Uriel's knowing gaze. The biggest of their concerns was behind them – the serums had been dealt with.

***

Arthur Morgan returned from dinner with Annalise, distracted. He wondered if he should have offered to drop her off at the hospital where her aunt was supposedly breathing her last. He sat down heavily on the sofa, thoughts wandering.

"Hello, Arthur."

Morgan stiffened. The voice belonged to a woman; it was eerily familiar. Morgan turned around slowly.

The woman sat at his dining table, twirling a small dagger in her hand. He recognized her as one of the first people to consent to his trials. They had a brief fling afterward, but Arthur was quick to dismiss her later on.

"Carmen," Arthur greeted. "To what do I owe the honor?"

"What's the matter, Morgan? I can hear your heart thumping all the way over here," she stood, ambling towards him slowly. "Is that fear? Or are you just excited to see me?"

She bent down, trailing a nail down his cheek. "Feeling ... unsafe?"

Arthur laughed shakily.

"You should be concerned, you know," Carmen said casually as she stood. "Your house isn't as secure as you think it is. Neither is that lab of yours."

Arthur stood then, turning to face her. "What about my lab?"

She shrugged. "Let's just say you should go take a look."

"Carmen – what did you do?"

Carmen smiled a Cheshire cat smile. "I didn't do anything, Arthur – but my, do you have friends in odd places."

Arthur pushed her aside as he walked past her, storming out of his house and getting into his car. "If you have anything to do with this – I'll kill you."

Carmen leaned against his door, waving at him cheerfully as he sped past.

Arthur Morgan reached his lab and rushed through the double doors, breezing through the corridors and down to the basement where the serum was stored. He slammed his fist against the light switch and froze.

His lab had been trashed. Broken vials of serum lay littered on the floor, spoiled by the acid that was mixed with it. The lab reeked with the stink of acid. Cases were missing, while the rest of his equipment lay either damaged or broken. Morgan felt the lump in his throat tighten.

He felt her presence this time.

Morgan turned around slowly. "I gave you this power," he seethed. "I can take it away."

Carmen glanced down at the accusatory finger he had placed on her chest and pushed it away. "I didn't do this, Morgan. I'm just the messenger."

"Who for?" he spat.

Carmen leaned forward, and Arthur's nostrils flared at her overwhelming, heady, floral scent.

"I work for myself, tiger. You know that already." She grinned. "All I'm saying is, I saw someone go in and out of your lab. They went in empty-handed and left with your precious serum in their hands. I stopped by and saw this, and I figured you should know."

Arthur's shoulders slumped in defeat. "It's all gone," he sighed, leaning against the doorframe.

Carmen tutted, not liking this side of him. He looked so pathetic and torn. So desperate.

"All gone?" she asked.

"Don't be a bitch," he shook his head, thumping his head against the doorframe again and closing his eyes.

She rolled her eyes. "One would think a scientist like you would have the sense to not put all his eggs in one basket."

Arthur's eyes flew open.

"That's it," he whispered. "Carmen, that's it!"

He fisted her shirt and pulled her to him, planting a kiss on her lips before running up three flights of stairs and barging through the testing room.

"Where is it?" he panted, rushing over to where the machine was prepped for the next morning's test. There, inside a small compartment, sat the serum, encased in a vial that would feed the serum directly into the IV.

Morgan snatched the vial and held it up to the light. "This is it. This is all I need."

***

Caius burst through the doors, demanding an audience with Lord Zephyr.

"What's got you in such a tiff, Caius?" Zedkiel asked from his perch in the council's room.

"We missed one vial," he spat, getting everyone's attention with those four words.

Zedkiel looked from Uriel to Lord Zephyr.

"It's...just one vial, Caius," he said dumbly.

Caius's gaze cut to him, communicating exactly how foolish he thought Zedkiel was. "Even one vial is enough for him to replicate what he desires. He called up Annalise, eager to share how he thought he had lost everything, only to fatefully find *one* vial."

"Can she get it from him? Drop it by 'accident'?" Uriel quipped.

Caius shook his head. "The formula has survived. Annalise says he's rushing into production faster than ever before. Now that he knows he has an enemy who wants him to stop, he's more eager."

"We can send in our hunters to scare him, send a message, steal what's left?" Zedkiel tried helplessly.

Caius snorted. “We need to accept that Arthur Morgan has created something we did not want him to create. The next step is to face his army.”

“Army?” Lord Zephyr inquired.

“There are more than three dozen registered neovampires now, and he’s putting out more and more every day. Humans are eager to develop powers that make them anything but human, so they’re stronger and have virtually no weaknesses,” Caius reported. “The least we can do is combat them by brute force alone.”

“What do you mean by no weaknesses?” Uriel asked. “Surely, if they’re using our blood, they have our problems?”

Caius shook his head. “That’s the thing, daylight won’t harm them, Neither will silver. That just leaves us with cutting off their heads to make sure they don’t regenerate what we take from them. They’re quick on their feet too. But it’s possible we have one advantage still.”

“Which is?” Lord Zephyr asked.

“We’ve been training for a war, Lord Zephyr. Us against Lucifer, but until that happens, we have shadow warriors. We have powerful hunters. We can use our forces to deal with this nuisance first. In order to get rid of these neovampires, we must declare war.”

Uriel nodded in agreement as silence prevailed in the room.

"Your Highness, I do not mean to ruffle any feathers by disregarding the chain of command or suggesting war when you think otherwise. I understand that doing this means coming to light and finally leaning into the myths that rumor about our existence. I do not take this lightly," Caius followed with an afterthought.

Zephyr's lips twitched up momentarily. "You remind me of Ariel every day, Caius, and you have earned your place as ruler of your kingdom. You have as much of a right to speak as any of the other council members."

Zedkiel bristled.

"If, for the betterment of vampire kind, we must declare war, then that is how it shall be," Lord Zephyr announced. "We must prepare for battle."

***

The plan was to get word to all vampires and tell them to move into the region where the concentration of neovampires was the strongest. Once they infiltrated the region, they would use what intelligence they had to flag down neovampires and recruit them into a cult. The vampires would all share the same story, of how they were the purer breed, and neovampires could do well with an initiation that brought them into the fold and made them part of the greater vampire organization.

It would take time, but wars could no longer be fought in the traditional sense. Lord Zephyr knew they had to change with the times, and that meant luring the neovampires into one place and using their own strengths against them. Humans would give anything to become part of groups that give them a sense of belonging, and so the clubs became more and more exclusive.

"When you stormed into the council room and demanded we declare war, this is not what I had in mind," Uriel said, lifting a glass to her lips as she took a swig of her drink.

"I'll admit I didn't think we'd spend so many days in dark bars watching neovampires and vampires grinding on each other," Caius grimaced, averting his eyes from a couple in the corner of the bar.

"It's all part of the show, right?" she said. "Have to sell it to them before we go in for the kill."

"I want to kill myself at this point," Zedkiel groaned, throwing his head back. "I'm so tired of doing parlor tricks for these children."

"Where's Alvira?" Uriel asked. "She was supposed to show them how she can manipulate the moon."

Zedkiel shrugged. "Alvira's...different now. Ever since Ariel...she's become distant and absent. She's always off someplace else."

Uriel bit the inside of her cheek, distracted. "What happens once we eliminate them?"

"We go kill Morgan." Zedkiel shrugged.

"We can't have them join us as we've promised because of their sworn loyalty to their sci-fi father," Caius shrugged. "The only mercy we can promise them is a swift death. They're a scourge."

"Sometimes I really wish we had chosen something more sophisticated than a bar," Uriel sighed, downing the rest of her drink.

Caius observed the room, and as his eyes scanned familiar faces, he knew it would be a good night to begin the extermination. That's why Zedkiel and Uriel joined him tonight. He nodded at Dorothy, who stood by the door.

She slid the locks in place, swiftly signaling to the other vampires in the room to guard all potential exits.

The shift in the room was subtle but palpable. The vampires were in position. Caius finished the rest of his drink and pushed himself away from the bar. The dull thumping of the music continued, and in the lull between two songs, weapons were drawn.

Caius wielded Ariel's dagger, while Zedkiel preferred a longsword. Uriel preferred getting her hands dirty. On Caius's signal, violence broke out. Blades slashed through the air, turning the dance floor into a bloodbath. Bodies littered the floor, and the screams were dampened by the music that played far too loud for any human to suspect foul play.

"No, no," a woman wailed. "Please!"

A vampire towered over her, his bloodied fist at the ready. Dorothy eyed the hesitation in the vampire's face and cut in. She pulled her knife from the throat of a neo and swung around to swiftly snap the woman's neck.

She looked up at the vampire. His name was Christian, he was her second convert.

"What was that?" she panted.

".... I liked her," he muttered, looking away from her fallen corpse.

"Well, too bad."

Chapter 10
Rebirth of Vampires

The council's strategic elimination of the neovampires had been extremely effective. Almost all of those who had been living in the shadows had been wiped out. Every trace of their existence had been eradicated, leaving only ashes and rubble behind.

Arthur Morgan had escaped underground. After the slaughter, he knew that someone, or something powerful wanted him gone. The loss had pushed him off the edge. Everything he had worked on had been wiped out. He kept scouring what was left of his data again and again, hoping something would pop out at him, some solution, a way to salvage all he had worked for.

Carmen had also managed to survive the purge, going underground with Morgan the moment she recognized one of the vampires who had been present at Morgan's lab during the theft.

She struggled when it came to picking a side. Carmen knew the vampires wouldn't accept her because her existence deemed her an abomination, but she didn't want Morgan creating more neovampires either. She didn't like to admit it, but she liked Morgan. He had become obsessed with the serum, and as one of the last remaining neovampires, he needed her.

"You understand what's happened, don't you?" she asked him one day. She sat on the rotating stool in his lab, watching his sleep-deprived hands begin to tremble.

"All my work was stolen from me, Carmen. They took the serum and destroyed it, and when it survived, they took my creation, *my* vampires, and killed them like the heathens they are."

Carmen nodded. "And you know who they are, right?"

He finally looked up at her. "The vampires, I assume. They felt threatened by me, by what I created."

She felt a pang of pity for him. "What's the plan now, Arthur? It's over. Put an end to this madness."

He started shaking his head, refusing. "No. No, I'm not finished, Carmen. There's a *board of directors*."

She snorted.

"There's a board of directors, and we have seen what the neovampires were like. If I had another week, another *day*, I could have created the perfect serum for us."

Carmen stopped twirling the empty test tube in her hand. "What?"

Morgan nodded, his red-rimmed eyes only adding to how manic he looked. "What did you think? That I would make a little neovampire army and be done with it? We *all* want what you have. I was polishing the serum, making it stronger, better, so we could become like you, more superior."

She had been staring at the small semi-permanent needle mark in her arm. Morgan had taken vials and vials of her blood to see if he could replicate the serum once it was all gone. He would keep mumbling to himself, muttering how it was impure.

Carmen felt disgusted.

"I'm going to create the perfect serum," Morgan said. "And I'm going to use it against those filthy vampires."

***

After two months of hiding from the vampires that so desperately wanted to kill him, Arthur Morgan had his eureka moment. He had been petting his German shepherd, distracted by his own thoughts. His distant gaze fixated on his dog's ears, and his wandering thoughts traveled to wolves.

He shook his head, the thought was ridiculous.

"What?" Carmen asked.

"Huh?"

"What were you thinking about?" She offered him a glass of water.

"It's a stupid idea, don't worry about it."

"Come on, let's hear it."

Morgan bit the inside of his cheek. "It's just a thought, so don't laugh, okay?"

Carmen nodded.

"What if we used a combination of neovampire and wolf DNA?" he started. "If vampires are real, maybe the idea of werewolves isn't too far off? I'm not expecting anyone to turn into a wolf or anything, but what if we combined them both?"

"It's not...entirely insane," she admitted. "I can see it working. I don't know how you'll combine the two, but that's the whole...science thing. So, you figure that out."

"You think I should go for it?"

Carmen looked at the glimmer in his eyes, and for some reason, she couldn't find it in herself to say no. She knew it would mean he would return to his maniacal self, obsessed with creating the perfect serum, and she would become nothing but a guinea pig for him.

She couldn't explain why she stuck around to look after his sorry ass after the neovampire slaughter, and she didn't know why she still stayed when he told her he had planned to become a more superior being after perfecting his serum just so he could rule over them. For some reason, her eyes brimmed with tears when she nodded.

"Yeah." She blinked away the tears. "Yeah, you should."

***

Annalise still worked for Morgan, but he had become suspicious of her. His interest in her romantically had dwindled. But she was still a valuable asset. Caius didn't have the heart to dispose of her yet, and he had made his case with Uriel. Arthur Morgan was still alive out there, and as long as he lived, she would be an asset.

It was six months before the name Arthur Morgan came up again.

A vampire had burst through the doors of the council, cradling the body of a young girl. He collapsed on the floor of the courtroom, his sobbing uncontrollable.

"Who did this?" Uriel rose from her seat and joined the man on the floor. One glimpse at the girl showed that she was a vampire. Her fangs were still bared. The blood loss had been minimal, but something, some sort of beast, had torn into her. Her insides were exposed.

"They're back," he wailed. "They're back and it's ten times worse!"

"Who's back?" Zedkiel inquired.

"The neos. It looked just like them!" he cried. "I thought I had found a neovampire, and Claire and I were going to take care of them like we had a couple of others a while back."

"You're a hunter?" Caius asked. The vampires had been split into a number of groups based on skill, and the neovampire hunters were the best at what they did.

"Yes, sir." He nodded. "Something's changed. This one was stronger. Different even."

"Give us more details...?" Uriel trailed off, raising her eyebrows for him to give her his name.

"Raiden," he replied. "He saw us coming before we even knew where he was. They're faster."

"Faster, how?"

"They heal, your highness. None of our attacks seemed to land, and the ones that did had no impact. It barely bled before the skin healed up again."

"Did you succeed in killing him?" Lord Zephyr asked.

He looked down at his sister's bloodied, mangled body. "No, sir."

The council exchanged worried glances.

"We need to know more," Zedkiel said.

Raiden was dismissed after his sister was given a proper send-off. The cremated body of the young vampire blazed brightly in the heart of the forest, and the council members stood around the pyre.

"We need to find Morgan, and kill him," Zedkiel said.

"Before we do any of that, we need to get Cain and Alvira. They must be brought back into the fold. Now is no time for childish tantrums," Caius said.

Uriel sighed. "I haven't been able to get a read on Cain in ages. Ever since he disappeared, he's been completely off the radar. We needed him in the last war, and we need him now. Tantrum or no tantrum, he was the best strategist we had...after Ariel."

"Zedkiel, what of Alvira?" Lord Zephyr asked.

The prince of darkness's eyes shifted in embarrassment. "She had developed a small faction of her own in the kingdom. She's been training young vampires, mostly females, polishing their skills."

Uriel and Caius's eyebrows shot up in surprise.

"Will she be joining us with this little army of hers for the impending war?" Uriel asked.

"I...can't say. Ariel's death changed her. She's different now."

"Crazier?" Caius snorted. Zedkiel glared at him. "Lord Zephyr, you might have more of an impact on her. She doesn't respect the rest of the council, but she must listen to you," Caius suggested, looking away from Zedkiel, fighting off his smirk. He thrived off of getting under Zed's skin.

Lord Zephyr agreed. "If these neovampires cannot be bested by our hunters, there's little than can weaken them. But they must have a weakness. We need to find it . And for that, we need everyone on the same page."

Chapter 11
The Dark War

Uriel and Caius had searched tirelessly for Cain, but it was clear the first vampire did not wish to be found. Alvira had proven to be a much easier target. She had been easy to locate, and once she realized the threat to vampirekind, she did not hesitate to offer her services. No one commented on her own miniature army and how her vampires revered her beyond compare. They did her bidding, and Alvira thrived off of it.

As the vampires assembled and formulated one united front, tensions were rising in Arthur Morgan's lab. His success with this serum had granted him immense power, but at the same time, he grew more protective of the formula and more suspicious of everyone around him. Annalise no longer charmed him, and instead, he was wary of her keen interest.

Eventually, he offered her the rare opportunity to become one with his army. He dangled the vial of the deep red liquid before her, eyes wide and manic.

"Is this not what you want, Annalise?"

She stepped back. "W-what do you mean?"

"If you're so curious about what it's like to be a neovampire, why don't you become one?"

Annalise smiled, hoping he wouldn't be able to detect the undercurrent of tension in her voice. "I – I don't want to become a neovamp, Arthur. I'm just eager to learn."

Morgan rolled his eyes. "You've been playing the part of my eager little student long enough now. I think you're ready for the practical exercise."

She shook her head and backed up against the shelf. "I don't think I want to change. I like who I am right now."

"You don't wish to be stronger?" he tilted his head. "More powerful? Immortal?"

Annalise shook her head again. "I think there's something to be said about the flawed nature of humankind."

"So you would readily reject perfection?" he cackled, finally stepping away from her. "My, my, Annalise. You sure are a curious little thing."

She watched him place the vial back in the case and exhaled heavily.

"I need you to be ready for our meeting tomorrow," he said, back to his normal business-like self. "If we lock this deal, the mass production will commence, and every athlete, every high school graduate, every other one of us will be begging to transform."

Annalise nodded, taking mental notes to share with Caius in the evening.

"And then we can wipe out these 'purebreds' once and for all. They begged for a war the moment they took away my research, the minute they slaughtered innocent neos. And you know what they say about revenge, don't you?"

"It's best served cold?" she tried awkwardly.

"Precisely, my dear. They won't know what hit them."

***

Things did move faster than any of the vampires could anticipate. In the human world, the neovampire drug had become a worldwide success. Their numbers were growing every day, and vampirekind was reduced to either pretending to be neos if they lived in the mortal world or returning to the sprawling castles in each region, away from human settlement.

Arthur Morgan's success had turned him into a messiah for neos and humans alike, with people lining up to receive the miracle drug that would make them more powerful than they could ever imagine. But every neo came out of the lab with only one purpose in mind: killing vampire kind.

Morgan would not rest until every single vampire had been slaughtered, much like how they had slain his kin not long ago. Despite his power and position, there was very little he knew about who ruled over the vampires and what the names of his real enemies were.

Despite all the efforts both parties had put into their preparation for war, neither saw it coming. There was no day, no building up of tension or tipping point that led to the dark war. But vampires had severely underestimated their enemy. The neovampire had no weakness except for one that Alvira had stumbled upon.

She had captured a neovampire, curious to experiment on this new kind of vampire to see if there was more power she could gain from this species. The moment her teeth connected with the neovampire's throat, the creature began to writhe in agony, his screams ending only when his heart finally gave out, unable to handle the first drop of pure vampire blood in its own bloodstream.

The only weakness, it seemed, was pure vampire blood. But how could one expose the neos to that blood without getting close? The council's war strategies couldn't address the issue but settled for one technique.

Decapitation was always the way to go. And if vampires fell on the battlefield, the bloodshed might slow down the neovampires a little bit.

***

The night was dark, the air heavy with the scent of blood. In the heart of the vampire kingdom, tension was building. The neovampires had been growing in numbers and strength, and the threat was imminent.

The neovampires saw themselves as the future of vampirekind, and they were not afraid to fight for their place. It all started with a small skirmish, a disagreement between a neovampire and a purebred. The neovampire had been insulted by the purebred, and they came to blows. It should have been a small matter, but it escalated quickly. The moment the neovampire learned the woman before him was a purebred, he wasted no time in summoning his companions.

From the shadows, the darkness that the vampire had claimed as their solace for eons, came the neovampires. Flitting about the darkness and shadows with immense speed, surrounding the vampire.

She had called for help, she had tried to flee, running for safety to the only place she knew would shelter her. The northern kingdom.

The neovampires saw this as an opportunity to prove their superiority, and they launched a full-scale attack. Growing like a dark cloud on her tail, they followed her to the gates of Zedkiel's castle.

Needless to say, no one had anticipated that the neos would discover their home—this safe haven that Zedkiel had worked so hard to create. It had been where most of Shadow and Star's warriors resided. They were amongst the strongest.

But even they could not have faced off the neos alone. Caught off guard, they struggled to defend themselves. They were outnumbered and outmatched.

As the neovampires continued to gain ground, they were joined by human kingdoms that had been terrorized by the vampire kingdom for centuries. As the armies grew and numbers amassed, the vampires quickly learned that they were not only facing the neovampires but the very humans they had terrified for centuries.

They had only discovered the northern stronghold, and word traveled fast. Vampires fled to the nearest outpost, sending word to the rest of the kingdoms, letting them know what was transpiring in the northern castle.

The battle waged on as reinforcements rushed to the rescue. Alvira's army was in the lead, and Uriel and Caius were the first to note the ease with which she rushed into battle. There was no hesitation in her demeanor, and she charged forward ruthlessly.

"Has she always been this strong?" Caius asked.

Uriel stayed silent, eyes narrowed as she observed the familiar style with which she fought, an echo of the princess, Ariel.

"Keep an eye on her," Uriel muttered, diverting her attention to the bloodbath that awaited them. Millions of lives were lost in the ensuing battles. The neovampires were relentless, and they showed no mercy to their enemies.

Caius led his battalion forward, and the armies clashed in a violent burst of clanging swords and daggers, claws and screaming. Their heightened senses granted them little advantage, as chaos erupted everywhere, the battle only confused the senses.

In the heart of the battlefield, six neovampires stood tall, their sleek forms glistening in the moonlight, while the four vampires bared their fangs and snarled in anger, backs pressed against each other, keeping an eye on the enemy.

The neovampires moved in a blur of speed, attacking the vampires with incredible force. The vampires met them head-on, matching their speed and strength with deadly precision.

The first neo leapt toward the closest vampire, slashing at his chest with razor-sharp claws. The purebred vampire countered with a swift kick, sending the neo stumbling backward. With lightning-fast reflexes, the vampire lunged forward, sinking his fangs deep into the neovampire's neck.

The hissing and writhing began, with the enemy snarling in agony. Confused as to what had shifted, the fight around the writhing neo halted momentarily, granting the vampires the upper hand, but only momentarily.

The neos snapped out of their confused trance quickly enough, and one launched an attack from behind. The vampire spun around, meeting the neovampire's assault with a swift punch to the jaw. The neovampire fell to the ground, dazed, as the purebred vampire moved in for the kill.

Meanwhile, two neos had teamed up against a single vampire. He was a hunter and was putting up more of a fight than the other vampires. His agility granted them more of a challenge. The neovampires circled their opponent, taunting him. The hunter smiled, refusing to be intimidated as he fought back with a ferocity born of desperation.

As the neos closed in, one of Alvira’s vampires unleashed a powerful blast of energy from her palms, knocking the neovampires off their feet. Before they could recover, the hunter charged forward, plunging his claws deep into their chests.

The battle ended in retreat, with vampires fleeing the moment they could afford to. The neos left the field languidly, celebrating their first victory. They had faced losses too, but it was evident from the corpses in the castle courtyard that the vampires had suffered the brunt of the battle.

Lord Zephyr stared at the carnage before him, pensive. The northern castle was deserted, rivers of blood ran over the courtyards and corridors, glistening in the fading moonlight. Uriel, Caius, Zedkiel and Alvira, all were present. Silent as they took in the sight.

"We were arrogant," Uriel broke the silence. "A part of us always believed we would be on the winning side."

Lord Zephyr's voice was thick with emotion. "We have never lost so much of our kin before."

"They have the potential to wipe us out, Zephyr," Uriel said matter-of-factly. "Something must be done."

"We must protect what's left of our kind," Caius agreed.

Zephyr reached out and put a hand on Zedkiel's shoulder. The prince of darkness had been silent and stoic, tears ran down his face endlessly, but he did not say a word. He grieved for the kin he lost, for the home he had worked so hard to create. It was supposed to be a safe haven.

"Come with me to the western kingdom, son," Lord Zephyr said. "We will rebuild. This is not the end."

Zedkiel blinked, and met his gaze. "I feel like a traitor, Father. How can I live when the people of my kingdom lay down their lives for this cause? Am I to leave them here to rot?"

“We must retreat, Zedkiel. We need to go underground as long as we can. The shadows of the land will protect us.”

Alvira took a step toward Zedkiel, hoping to comfort him. She froze when he recoiled from her, eyes widening in surprise. Alvira scoffed but looked away. She hadn’t been expecting coldness from him, especially in the midst of such loss. She turned her embarrassed gaze to Caius, who seemed to look past her as well. Embarrassed, Alvira stood by Uriel, put in her place by the prince’s reaction.

Alvira realized she deserved the cold shoulder. After all, she had been so distant from them for so long. There was bound to be some tension. Even the perpetually indifferent Uriel seemed to emanate dislike for her.

***

Lord Zephyr stood on the balcony of the castle, staring out at the landscape below. Alvira had set fire to the battlefield below, turning the ground into a pyre. His mind was consumed by the war he had been raging for centuries and the toll it had taken on his kind. They had come so far, grown so much. And now he watched as years of effort were laid to waste.

He watched the flickering flames in the distance and couldn't help but reflect on the loss of his progeny. So many of his children had fallen in battle, their centuries of development lost in the blink of an eye. Zephyr couldn't help but wonder if their sacrifice had been in vain.

He knew that the days of open warfare were over. His kind was no longer strong enough to fight in the open, and they had been forced to retreat into the shadows. He couldn't help but feel a sense of sadness as he thought about the future of his kind.

As he turned to leave the balcony, Zephyr knew that the war was far from over. He knew that his kind would continue to fight, continue to survive, no matter what the cost. But as he walked through the empty halls of his castle, he couldn't help but wonder if there was another way. A way to coexist with the neovampires, to find peace in the darkness.

But for now, all he could do was wait and hope that his kind would survive the trials that lay ahead. Caius had been standing behind him, and as he turned, he met Lord Zephyr's gaze.

"Your Highness," his eyes blazed with unbridled hatred. "Alvira is the strongest amongst us."

"Don't be preposterous," Zephyr scoffed, trying to walk past him.

Caius held out his hand, stopping Zephyr in his tracks. "No – Your Highness, you misunderstand me. Alvira is the strongest amongst us," he repeated. "Stronger than Ariel had been. Uriel and I watched her on the battlefield today."

Zephyr's brow furrowed. "And?"

"Alvira slaughtered Ariel in cold blood," Caius said. "I swear upon her grave. It must be her."

Chapter 12
The Extinction of the Vampire Race

After everything Zephyr had done and witnessed, Caius' baseless claim didn't seem too outrageous. Once, Ariel and Alvira had been close, but the days of their mutual affection were long gone. Despite the growing differences between them, nothing was more valued by him than his kin. The Princess of Darkness had been amongst his strongest warriors. No force of nature could stand against her. He had trained and raised her so, himself.

Zephyr had turned a blind eye to these power struggles, taking them as nothing more than mere childish squabbles, but he should have known better. He knew better than anyone else how these petty disputes and sibling rivalry could turn ugly. These battles had gone too far. The threat from the external forces was too great to ignore the strife within. Something had to be done about Alvira, but there was something else that needed to be taken care of.

Zephyr stood alone in the council room with his back to the ornate doors. The king of darkness was lost in his remorseful thoughts. The neovampires had turned far more audacious since their recent victory. Almost every evening, the children of darkness were slaughtered in cold blood. They were brought to his door drained of every drop of blood – the blood they had acquired from human vessels.

It had never occurred to him that he could possibly ever struggle in a war against anyone other than his equal. *Where did I go wrong?* After much contemplation, he decided secrecy was what his army lacked and needed. He was the king of darkness, after all.

"Father, you called upon me," Zedkiel spoke in an uncertain voice. Lord Zephyr had already expressed his desires, but the prince of darkness couldn't help but disagree with his decision. Though he understood the need to seek shelter in the shadows, the fire of vengeance burnt bright in his chest.

Without turning around, Zephyr drew a chair for his son while he remained standing. "Sit."

"We must find somewhere to hide soon; it's our only option. The survival of my progeny is on the line." Wistfully, Zephyr stared ahead at what remained of his children following the battle – only a soot-covered courtyard.

"I understand." Zedkiel felt defeated. Without arguing, he buried his face in his hands. After all the carnage he had seen, he was wise enough to realize his fate if he refused to yield.

"My son, you must know we will not go into hiding like a bunch of cowards. Surrender has never been an option for us. Remember, we're purebred, and nothing can stand in the way of our victory. Today, vanity has been our downfall, but so will it be our rise." Zephyr used his cunning to fuel the flames of revenge, but Zedkiel was no stranger to his manipulative tactics.

"So you say, father, but without any means to retaliate, how will we win this war? We have not only lost our children to these low-life beings, but also the toughest amongst us." Zedkiel shut his eyes, recalling the confusion he had felt as chaos erupted around him in the middle of the battleground. Never had he thought a day would come when he'd feel powerless before mere human beings dozed with some chemical.

"That's what Alvira and Caius will be tasked to find. It is your responsibility to look for a hideout before the final battle ensues." Zedkiel's eyes lit up at the last words. There still remained hope for his race. If they could all unite again for a single purpose, they could terminate all threats once and for all.

"The final battle?" Zedkiel asked with a smile that looked more like a sneer. "Father, let me fight in this battle. I've seen enough bloodshed. My thirst will not be quenched by blood anymore – not until I've avenged my kin."

This was precisely why Lord Zephyr had decided to separate the prince from Alvira. "Do as you're told. You'll be called upon when the time comes. Don't you worry, son; this time, victory will be ours."

From the beginning of time, Zephyr had only known to prey on the weaker beings. Neither had he ever hidden from a predator, nor had he ever felt the need to. He had always led the battalion with a smile on his pale face and hunger in his crimson eyes. He was the ruler of darkness. There was no way he could stand and watch his breed imitated, mocked, and ruled by another. He knew he wouldn't stand a chance before Lucifer if his progeny cowered before these weaker beings.

Although retreat was made necessary, he couldn't do so before striking fear in the hearts of the mortals. Once the despair of the defeat faded, Zephyr made up his mind. He had to formulate a plan to get his power back.

Zephyr knew neovampires advanced in their abilities and strengths. Every new batch of their serum added to their powers and made them less vulnerable. Word had it, they had succeeded in altering the genetic makeup of some human beings. If that turned out to be true, the neovampires wouldn't need Arthur Morgan's formula. Moreover, their offspring would inherit their advanced abilities.

Months passed in preparation for the last battle. While Caius traveled distances around and beneath the earth's surface to locate a perfect hideout, Alvira and Caius stalked the night in search of answers and prey. With luck, Caius had discovered just the place in the far north—a land covered with glaciers as old as the vampire himself. The cold and dark of the frozen ocean would serve as the best refuge if need called for it.

Although the vampires had joined hands to fight their common enemy, Alvira was too smart to miss the sideways glances from Caius. She never missed his lurking shadow, the shuffle of his shoes, or his futile attempts at eavesdropping. She knew the king of darkness was on to her, and she was just another pawn in his game of vengeance. Alvira was far too valuable of an asset to be compromised just yet.

Quite expectedly, Alvira had come up with the best strategy to fight the neovampires. Instead of blindly waging war, the warrior suggested isolating the neos from their pack. When the opportunity was ripe, the vampires hunted down their prey one by one. The neovampires had the advantage of faster healing abilities, miracles of science, and endurance to sunlight, but the vampires had years of experience over them.

Alone and terrified, they were no match for the ages-old vampires. Though their numbers dwindled significantly, the vampires feared the emergence of a new creature – a new race that never strayed from the pack.

Though it had only been witnessed by one of them, word had gotten around. No one knew if the tale was true, but vampires dreaded it just the same. When the full moon appeared against the black sky, a child of darkness had concealed himself in the shadows of the forest. Neither his darkness nor his strength was able to save him from the beast that prowled. His throat was ripped open with furred claws before his scream could send the ripples of his shrieks through the terrifying night.

When the mutilated corpse of a vampire was found, a state of visceral hysteria started reigning over the children of the night. The fear of the unknown, or the neowerevampires as they were being called, had spread even faster than their population. Some recounted tales of a prowling beast in the dark with twice the agility of vampires. Others had a far scarier theory: the new creatures had developed a resistance to the only venom that could poison them – the vampire's blood.

Everyone seemed to agree with the fact that vampires stood no chance against them. Whatever the neowerevampires' newfound abilities were, their emergence threatened the existence of vampires like never before. Consequently, many populations had already packed their bags and decided to migrate to colder, isolated regions. The King of Darkness had formulated this plan in the first place; however, with his pride wounded, he had strayed from his original decision.

Zephyr's resolve faltered when he received the humiliating message. It happened a few days after the first attack from the neowerevampires. A hooded figure appeared at the gate of his castle. Though he was holding up a bloodied corpse of a child, he requested an audience with Lord Zephyr.

Intrigued, the King of Darkness had invited him into the walls of his castle. From his perspective, the sketchy foreigner posed no threat. A foolish lamb might have stumbled into the lion's den. He also entertained the possibility of acquiring information from him about the neowerevampires.

Despite being cornered by several vampires, Zephyr's guest betrayed not a trace of fear. Lowering the corpse at Zephyr's feet, he revealed his furry claws and large, yellow fangs. Before his son could rip the neowerevampire's throat apart, Zephyr shot him a wary look.

"You mongrel, what is the meaning of this? Do you know who I am? Do you realize who you stand before?" Zephyr's voice came out in a low, warning growl.

"The King of Darkness, I presume. I have a message for you, Lord Zephyr." While Zephyr eyed him dangerously, the guest continued with the same air of ease, "You shall be driven from your home as you were shunned out of heaven."

This time, Zedkiel didn't need to intervene, for Zephyr slaughtered his guest before he had a chance to finish letting out his provocative laughter. His scarlet eyes turned darker as he registered what he had done. The disgraceful creature paid only a small price for the disrespect.

Zephyr didn't learn much about the new race besides their powerlessness in the face of the first vampire – something Zephyr had already suspected but needed confirmation of. He watched wistfully as the dismembered messenger bled all over his carpet.

"Clean up this mess," he said, turning towards his strongest warrior, the disdain palpable in his voice. As his eyes drifted in Alvira's direction, he felt her silent rebellion, but she bowed her head in obedience lest she suffer his wrath.

Previously, Zephyr's cunning mind kept him from being overruled by fleeting emotions of pride or rage. Pride had always been Lucifer's undoing, not his. However, with the prospect of defeat at the hands of mere mortals inching closer, Zephyr found his sanity hanging precariously by a fragile thread.

With this new turn of events, even Zedkiel had come to accept defeat – temporarily, of course. Though he ached every day with bloodlust and vengeance, he contained himself. He reminded himself that they must bide their time. After all, the vampire race had done that since the start of time. No one argued with the urgency or the necessity of the migration. Well, besides the King of Darkness.

Zephyr's pride had been wounded. His thirst for vengeance was so strong, it consumed all his senses. Centuries of preparations had gone to waste, and for what? Lucifer had cursed him to terrorize mortals for eternity. Though he had accepted his fate, Zephyr could never accept defeat. His obsession blinded him from making any sensible decisions.

He went as far as to send Uriel's warriors on a suicide mission to acquire information on the new race. When the entire army was slain, the indifferent empress had had enough and finally called everyone in for a meeting.

Predictably, neither Star and Shadow nor Cain turned up at the council meeting. The fortress was surrounded on all sides by the enemies. Only Caius, Alvira, Zedkiel, and Uriel still stood by Zephyr's side, but they remained on the stakeout for an escape route. Never before had a council meeting been called by anyone other than the lord himself. A tense atmosphere sank across the hall as everyone gathered in silence.

"About time, children. We need to devise a plan to take our power back – show these mortals who they're dealing with." Although Zephyr was in uncharacteristically lively spirits, Caius exchanged a nervous look with Uriel. They knew talking sense into the lord was going to be so much more difficult than they originally thought.

Turning towards Zedkiel, Zephyr continued, "Son, you'll partner up with Caius to investigate the source of transformation. It can be taken care of if it's a serum. A bite, however..." He trailed off, lost in thought.

Momentarily, everyone in the hall shared an apprehensive look, but no one dared to voice their thoughts. Eventually, Uriel ventured to break the charged silence. "Zephyr, we're fighting a futile war. There's no chance of survival if we don't get out of here soon. Our enemies are closing in on us, and we have no resources, no armies, and no defense."

Uriel was met with the response she expected. "*Our? Our* chance of survival?"

"I mean the vampire race." Heaven forbid she offend the King of Darkness by questioning his invincibility.

"That is where you're mistaken, Uriel. Our race is superior. Those mutts don't stand a chance against us."

When Zedkiel saw Uriel wasn't getting anywhere with her argument, he weighed in. "I agree with Uriel, Father. We all do. This was our plan all along. Of course, if you're still convinced fighting is the right course of action, we will stand by your–"

"No, we won't. Say it like it is, Zedkiel," Alvira cut off the prince mid-sentence, months of pent-up frustration spilling out in a fit of rage. "Zephyr, you're obsessed with your plots and schemes of revenge. You're so obsessed, you've lost sight of your vision, and we won't continue laying down our lives for your purpose."

A heavy silence followed Alvira's frustrated speech. Before she could exit the hall, Zephyr grabbed her throat, effortlessly lifting her against the wall. Although his sharp fingernails dug into her skin, drawing blood, the warrior refused to flinch. Zephyr watched from the corner of his eye as Caius and Uriel left the hall.

Zephyr could feel it. The princess had grown stronger, far stronger, since his daughter's demise. Reluctantly, he let her go. As everyone left, Zephyr realized that isolating him had been Lucifer's plan all along.

Chapter 13
Rise of Lightstar

His vast territories were impregnable. Had they not been, no one in their sane minds would've ever trodden upon his barren lands, the ash-covered ground, and the air that reeked of decay. If there were any foolish enough to dare, the evil one had several means to take care of them. Either they were lured in by the promise of fleeting rewards or considered worthy of his audience, which was a rare occurrence in itself.

Not to imply, the evil one remained secluded in his tower in a desolate land, for the numbers of his army grew quite equally with their strength. Every soldier, trained and *nurtured* by the evil one, held him in awe. Their blind loyalty remained unwavering, despite their master's questionable ways. A powerful spell bound his soldiers to his will, desires, and motivations.

Unlike the King of the Darkness, the evil one didn't have to hunt through the nights to build an army. He didn't need to seek the weak, the abandoned, or the desperate. He had no need to go around the world, cherry-picking his prey. Neither did he need to fabricate lies to capture his prey, nor did he ever weave fragile webs to manipulate their minds. A single peek into his piercing eyes could bring anyone down to their knees. However, not everyone had the fortune—or misfortune (depending on the captive's perspective)—to succeed.

The lost souls stumbled into his territory of their own accord, and the strong ones always made it through all the tests of resilience. When their hearts bled unceasingly, their souls were tainted by the sufferings of the world. Thus, they embraced the pain. Cursing their fates, they sought out the evil one to write their own destiny. They walked through the gates of the castle and endured ages of torture, only to rise stronger and mightier than before, like a phoenix from the ashes.

Of course, the power-hungry souls also reached out to him. Their hearts were already so blackened with greed they could never sever their connection with the evil one. They felt the pull until their destiny led them to his castle eventually.

It was definitely the latter that led the mysterious woman to his territory. Her black mid-thigh dress did little to conceal her pale skin; however, the cloak compensated for it, covering her skin as well as her identity. At every turn, she was met with offensive creatures of inhumane strength wearing human skin. Some tried to dig their fangs into her neck, while others tried to claw out her throat. Some tried to catch her by surprise with a sneak attack, while others savored the hunt.

Of course, unbeknownst to those creatures, the woman had the latter attribute in common with them. Before they could put up a fight, their prey turned into a vicious predator before their eyes. However, there were some beasts who could've crushed her, yet they only engaged with her for not more than a few minutes. She was clearly a well-trained fighter with remarkable strength. Despite her abilities, she still seemed to struggle against quite a few of her opponents.

When she finally reached the castle, she was mildly irritated to find a cut in her dress. Any other woman would've thanked her lucky stars for having come out of that challenge alive, but not her, of course. The gloomy castle contrasted significantly with the lively atmosphere of her former home. Twelve massive towers on opposing sides were connected by thin walls of granite. Along the roof, the structures were lined with symmetrical crenelations.

The field outside was decked with ornate marble statues, fountains with intricate architecture, and gazebos. The castle had clearly stood the test of time, as evidenced by the cracked walls and the vines growing inside of them.

Before the woman could knock on the hefty metal doors, she was invited inside by a butler. "Good evening, ma'am. My lord awaits your arrival."

With her mood already so foul, she didn't bother to come up with a response. She knew she needed to put up a good performance before the one she sought so earnestly. Instead, she followed the butler silently down the dark passageways to the great hall. Her excitement grew with every step. Although she had a turn of heart only recently, her devotion was no less.

No tales could have prepared her for the man—no, the fallen angel—seated before her eyes. Her heart had stopped beating long ago, but she could've sworn it skipped a beat. All her elaborate plans escaped her mind as she stared into his dark, piercing eyes.

Lucifer Morningstar sat on his throne, radiating all the pride he was known for. A pompous, victorious smile was plastered across his handsome face. His luscious dark curls fell over his forehead, perfectly framing his chiseled face. "Princess Alvira, you took your time."

The spell broke as Alvira looked away. As she lowered her gaze, she couldn't tell if it was out of respect, defiance, or the inability to meet the sheer power of his stare. She could see a trace of resemblance her former master must've once shared with him. However, the curse had stripped Zephyr of all the radiant beauty Lucifer still possessed.

"My Lord, I met with some minuscule hurdles along the way," she replied confidently.

The Lightstar let out a malicious chuckle. Not many had the power to withstand the force of his army, much less break out of his piercing gaze. Although her unquenchable thirst for power drove her to him, he pulled the strings once his prey locked gaze with him.

"No matter. This time, your tardiness can come to pass, for your incredible strength pleases me. You'll become a valuable warrior, Princess Alvira." Alvira was already fighting to hold on to her will and senses, but a part of her wanted to let go. His words of approval sent a shiver down her spine. She understood how he had gathered legions of followers, willing to make his bid and sacrifice themselves for his approval, all from the comfort of shadows.

"My Lord, I'm honored my strength pleases you, but I must tell you, I bring more value than the mere strength of a great warrior," she replied, eager for more praise. A foreign force compelled her to submit herself to his services. Although she was aware of the compromise when she had sought him out, she resisted yielding her will, nonetheless.

"Of course! I know all about your wicked deeds and shameful sins. I know about all your lies, murders, and greed. Don't think for a moment you can fool me as you did that disgraceful being. Zephyr doesn't hold a candle to my might, my power, my superiority! I've been watching you from the shadows, and I'll continue to do so." Alvira shuddered in her spot as his piercing gaze bore into her eyes.

"Indeed, my Lord. I pledge my allegiance to you and no other. I'll serve you alone, fight for your purpose, and lay down my life if I must." As Alvira said her vows, she knew her words held no weight. They were meaningless, for she was bound to become The Lightstar's loyal servant the moment the unbridled yearning for power corrupted her heart.

Within a few days of her stay at Lucifer's castle, Alvira realized her role as his servant was unlike any she had assumed before. Despite sharing the egotistical temperament with her former master, Lucifer's ways and strategies couldn't be further from Zephyr's. Although she had recently joined his side, she was beyond surprised when Lucifer didn't extend his invitation for her to the council meetings. In fact, there were no council meetings held, to her knowledge.

Unlike Zephyr, Lucifer didn't reveal his motivations to anyone, much less to a turncoat. The secrecy might have been the key that gave him an edge over his brother. No one could betray Lucifer because he was too vainglorious to ever let anyone in. All she had been able to gather was the size of his army – that, too, only by chance. It was twice the strength and thrice the size of Zephyr's.

Neither his indifference nor his secrecy bothered Alvira as much as his absence. It was the most significant contrast she had observed between the brothers. Lord Zephyr could always be approached in the shadows. It was easy to reach him, sometimes, even irritatingly so. However, Alvira often found herself tormented by the divide between herself and her new master.

More often than not, he was away on his travels. To where? She could only guess. Previously, she was certain she would've lost her sanity to her master's cryptic ways. Even if she wasn't always involved in the vampires' wars, she had never been kept in the dark. Although this uncertainty bothered her to no end, she far more longed to feel the connection with the evil one. She yearned to have a single peek into his piercing eyes and craved his appreciation day and night.

Although her master was away, Alvira wasn't free to explore the dark secrets of his castle. Every night, she was given an assignment by Lucifer's messengers. Most assignments didn't significantly differ from her previous duties as a warrior. Sometimes, she was required to gather intel on her former allies, while other times, she was sent to assassinate without any rhyme or reason. However, these assignments also included some bizarre duties, such as monitoring an island for hours on end, collecting blood samples from various animals, and even killing a child.

When Alvira returned to her castle, save for Lucifer's other servants, she found it deserted nearly always. Since their first introduction, she had only caught a glimpse of her master twice. In his absence, Alvira felt like a fog was lifted from her mind. She could think straight, questioned her new position, and her sense of self-preservation returned. However, it was always accompanied by an intense, almost painful sense of restlessness. Her free will was as meaningless as her existence, for the powerful yearning debilitated her. No matter how hard she tried, she could not shake off the unquenchable thirst.

One night, Alvira was sent to hunt down a neowerevampire in the vicinity of the castle. Once again, the assignment was beyond her understanding. The neowerevampires were a threat to vampires' existence – Lucifer's biggest enemy. Why he chose to have one exterminated, she could only guess.

Alvira remained vigilant as she moved through the shadows across the rocky terrain. As these perplexing thoughts plagued her mind with doubts, she was nearly caught off guard when the four-pawed beast leapt at her. Composing herself, she immediately struck the side of the beast's neck with her claws outstretched.

The neowerevampire growled in pain and threw its entire weight over Alvira. She tried to dodge, but the beast's agility matched hers. Alvira cursed out loud as she heard a nasal bone crack. Ignoring the pain, Alvira used the heel of her palm to throw off the beast. The brute landed on his feet, shapeshifting into a young man of athletic build. Besides a few scratches on his neck, he looked perfectly in shape.

"Princess, you're not fighting up to your reputation." He sneered mockingly at the warrior. Alvira was short-tempered. The pompous remark would've cost the brute his head, but her senses were overpowered. As she felt the magnetic pull amplified, she knew her master was nearby. Lucifer had returned home. From miles away, she could hear the echoes of his laughter bouncing off the walls of his impregnable castle.

The realization was accompanied by a sense of rush akin to that of adrenaline. She felt the need to return – to see her master for herself. After days of unease, she felt rejuvenated. As the feeling built, her opponent appeared as insignificant as a fly to her. She couldn't draw out the fight any longer. The amplified power must have emanated from her, for the neowerevampire's provocative smirk was replaced by a look of alarm.

Before he could make a run for it, Alvira's fangs were already sinking into his neck. "You're lucky I'm in a hurry."

***

To Alvira's disappointment, when she returned to the castle, the evil one was nowhere in sight. The great hall was deserted. Although no one occupied the majestic throne, Alvira couldn't shake off the gravity, pulling her into her new home. Other servants, butlers, and soldiers reflected back a similar glazed look in their eyes.

Alvira followed the magnetic pull, which led her to her master's study. The door was ajar, and she could hear two different voices carrying from the inside. Both sounded unfamiliar, yet she felt a hint of recognition in one of them.

"Arthur, I have to say, I'm satisfied with the results," it drawled. Alvira felt a shiver run down her spine, and she knew the voice, although unfamiliar, belonged to the Lightstar. As she found herself eavesdropping, she felt shame and terror in equal measures. However, no matter how hard she tried to move, she remained frozen in her spot.

"Mr. Alastair, it is an honor to work with you. I can't express how grateful I am! If not for you, I could never have recovered from that setback. Thank you for funding my research." Alvira detected awe and admiration in the voice, similar to her own. She couldn't help but gasp as the pieces came together.

"Pardon me, Arthur. I think we have a visitor. You can come in now, Princess Alvira," Lucifer raised his voice to address the warrior.

As Alvira stepped through the door, she shared the look of surprise on Arthur Morgan's face. However, the source of her astonishment contrasted significantly with the scientist's.

Lucifer Morningstar sat before her, wearing an altogether different skin, with his hair a shade of pale blonde; his features less handsome, yet still alluring, but his eyes were the same – as dark as the midnight sky.

"M – my Lord?" Alvira couldn't help but stutter.

"Princess Alvira, meet Arthur Morgan, the greatest scientist known to humanity," Lucifer filled in the silence.

As he flashed her a sinister grin, everything clicked into place. Of course, Lucifer Morningstar led the humans to experiment on the wolves and vampires. Of course, they stood a chance against the pureblood vampires in the first place because they had Zephyr's ultimate rival by their side. *No, they've always been a pawn in the fallen angel's game,* Alvira corrected herself.

Alvira realized the evil one must have been roaming the earth for ages, disguising himself as anyone he wished to be. She wondered how many times he must have appeared before the vampires' eyes, watching them every step of the way. They were lulled into a false sense of security while Lucifer Morningstar had always been steps ahead. Human beings had never posed a threat to the vampires' extinction. The war had always been between the two equally powerful angels – Zephyr and Lucifer.

Chapter 14
The Dawn of the Death Dealer

The sun had yet to rise when Lucifer spotted the morning star twinkling bright in the dark sky. As his sharp eyes admired the sight, his chest swelled with pride, and a sinister smile creeped on his face. There was no being, and certainly no object or heavenly body, worthy of his praise; however, the sparkling star reflected back his own beauty.

The calm of the night was pierced by the sound of his thrilled laughter. *The time has come at last!* For eons, he had kept himself concealed in the shadows. He was driven to a barren land while his lowly brother paraded through the land. He roamed the earth, stripped of the riches and luxuries, but he always kept faith. He had faith in only one purpose – to wipe off the existence of the only being as powerful as himself. The moment had come to exact his vengeance, for he could not have been more in power while his brother could not have been more stripped of it.

Zephyr was left empty-handed, isolated, and desperate. Even his loyal children had started joining the Lightbringer's side. They had abandoned the only purpose they had been created for. Lucifer couldn't fault them, for it was smart to choose the victor's side. However, he believed his victory had been predetermined from the moment the lowly creature had chosen his battle with the mightiest of the angels.

Although Lucifer had built an army large enough to annihilate his enemy, he refused to rest. As the vampires fed on blood, the evil one nurtured himself with his vainglorious musings. Every conquest added to his pride, so he continued his search for power. Subjecting his enemy to an honorable defeat wouldn't do. Lucifer wanted to punish Zephyr for likening his own disgraceful existence to a deity as majestic as himself. He wanted to bring his brother down to his knees – to see him grovel at his feet and beg for mercy.

Since the start of time, humans had served to quench Zephyr's thirst for blood. It was about time they satiated the mightier brother's hunger for power. Such thoughts occupied his mind as he prepared himself to meet with Randolf Linwood. Assuming his identity as Alistair, he attired himself in a three-piece gray suit. Lucifer looked more like a well-groomed business mogul than a fallen angel set on destroying the world.

Randolf Linwood was an aristocrat who had risen to prominence via Lucifer's support. The man was of no consequence to Lucifer. However, the gentleman was a member of the United Nations Security Council, and that's all that Lucifer was interested in.

"Mr. Linwood will see you in a minute," the secretary informed Lucifer. She had an awe-struck look on her face, but the Lightbringer didn't spare her a glance. He was far more focused on his resolve, trying not to blow up the office. It was beyond his understanding how a mere lowly human could dare to keep him waiting.

Instead of responding, Lucifer walked straight to where he expected to find the buffoon. Without knocking, he barged into Linwood's office and found him speaking over the phone. He stood up abruptly, registering the presence of the man standing before him. As he met Lucifer's angry glare, a shiver went down his spine.

"Randolf, I presume, we agreed to meet at eight." Although Lucifer's voice was laced with contempt, it wasn't met with the typical response.

"I apologize, Mr. Alistair. I wasn't made aware of your arrival. Jenna must have made a mistake." Mr. Linwood didn't seem bothered by the rude greeting. Instead, he asked his benefactor to take a seat. "How was your flight?"

Lucifer's dark eyes flashed with anger. Had his pride not been wounded, the master of deceit had all the charm. As a matter of fact, he took immense pleasure in fooling these half-witted men. "Randalf, you know how I loathe engaging in such trivial matters. I would rather you report me on the proposal I made."

"About that. It doesn't look good, Mr. Alistair," Linwood responded, feigning confidence. "It's not a matter of money. Legalizing the serum was next to impossible, to begin with. Making it mandatory? Out of question."

It took everything in Lucifer not to crack Linwood's skull open. "I traveled all the way to hear this? To hear that you've failed?"

Linwood swallowed hard, but his shivering hands betrayed his terror. "Please, try to understand, Mr. Alistair. No government in their right mind would agree! Inject the entire army with a dangerous serum? It's extremely risky."

Lucifer couldn't help but laugh at the human's petty fears and double standards. "A dangerous serum? You humans have been playing with fire since the beginning of time."

The odd choice of words didn't go past Linwood's notice, but he was too occupied trying to reason with the monster. "We don't know the side effects. We don't know how long the supernatural abilities would last. People want to get a taste of danger, but no one would want to spend their entire life like this."

"Randalf, you can't possibly have possibly forgotten about the pureblood vampires."

"They're nearly wiped out of existence. There's no need to continue the production anymore."

"Have you lost your mind, human?" Linwood couldn't help but raise his eyebrows, but Lucifer paid no heed. "Arthur Morgan has already started mass production of the serum. You gave me your word, Randalf. What's holding you back?"

Linwood tried to look away, but his eyes were transfixed on Lucifer's. Ever since he first collaborated with Lucifer, he had felt like he had made a deal with the devil. No matter how hard he tried to walk away, he was always reeled back in. He valued his life too much to speak his mind, but the truth was he just didn't have it in himself to pull the strings. He didn't want to live in a world where children would rip out each other's throats in the playground. He didn't want to live in a world ruled by monsters.

The serum had brought far more destruction than world peace. Previously, the vampires were creatures of the night and mythological tales. Though they took lives, they only hunted through the night. They didn't dare reveal their existence to the humans for fear of their own survival. However, the invention of serum had fueled a war in which humans didn't stand a chance.

"Give me a few days, Mr. Alistair. I'll see what I can do," Linwood said uncertainly.

At Linwood's response, Lucifer decided to change tack. The Lightbringer could resort to threats, to violence, but his pride didn't allow him. Instead, he assumed another role – the role of the man he was pretending to be. “Vampires and humans can’t coexist, and they have certainly not been wiped out. Their father, the King of Darkness lives, while his children are being slaughtered by us. Don’t you realize, Randalf? Unlike us, they have no feelings, they don’t bleed like us, and their hearts don’t beat like ours do. The King of Darkness will not rest until he has conquered the world. They are nothing but blood-hungry monsters. Remember, we’re fighting for the greater good.”

As Linwood nodded his head, Lucifer knew he had already won.

***

Zephyr didn’t have it in him to burn with rage anyone. The storm inside his chest had calmed down, leaving only destruction in its wake. The greatest vampire had deteriorated into a shell of his former self. All his manipulative schemes, his cunning tactics, his charming influence had been replaced by pathetic desperation. His vengeful thoughts reigned over his common sense. Of course, this despair and surrender wasn’t void of reason, for he was left with no alternative.

Each and every one of Zephyr’s allies had switched sides, save for his valued family. For what it was worth, the King of Darkness was glad to travel in isolation. Large groups brought on far more attention and danger than was necessary. Although the vampire could take on any beast, the same couldn't be said about the rest of his children. Every pureblood vampire slaughtered before his eyes was a wound to his pride.

As Zedkiel knocked on the door, he was prepared to be met by the sight of Zephyr's hollow eyes. Although they had been forced out of their home for days now, the mighty vampire had barely spoken a word. Zedkiel could only envision the state of his father's mind. The vampire had put too much into a single purpose, only to have all his efforts crushed by mere mortal forces. Zedkiel found it unwise to break the truth before his father under such circumstances, but he wasn't left with a choice. Every moment they wasted crying over split milk, their lives were endangered even more so.

Before Zedkiel could open his mouth to reveal the truth, Zephyr decided to break the silence. "Have you sent word to the rest of them?" He couldn't help but ask for the sixth time within a week.

Despite the stark reality, he couldn't give up on the lingering glimmer of hope. Eons of preparation had gone down the drain, just turned to ashes before his eyes. *There ought to be an army powerful enough to fight back – to get back on my feet!* It was beyond his understanding how all his armies could've been wiped out when his entire time on earth had been spent building them.

"I have," Zedkiel answered. His sharp eyes turned gentle as he registered the look of desperation on his father's face. "They're just looking out for themselves as you've taught them to. Father, they haven't abandoned your cause."

"Abandoned my cause? Know your place, you scum! I don't need your sympathies!" Zephyr's roar echoed through the thin wall of their humble guesthouse. With one swift motion, he slashed the worn-out couch with his claws. The first vampire knew better than to lose his temper over something as trivial as pride. However, his despair had gotten the better of him.

Everything about the run-down guesthouse disgusted him to his core. The greasy furniture, the worn-out bed, and the lingering stench of sweat were no less than a personal offense to him. However, for the sake of safety, the vampires had to travel extremely cautiously. The enemy seemed to be aware of the vampires' elite lifestyle and were hunting them down in five-star hotels, their homes, and even in public restrooms. The neos were everywhere, patrolling and hunting – systematically wiping out the vampires' entire race. Besides a desolate, run-down guesthouse, no place was safe for the vampires anymore.

The commotion alerted Uriel. As she joined the cramped space, she exchanged a nervous glance with Zedkiel. However, the King of Darkness paid her no heed.

"Father, I meant no disrespect, but you need to come to terms with the reality." Zedkiel clenched his jaw in frustration, yet he managed to keep his temper in check. These outbursts were getting more frequent by the day. Uriel had warned him, but he continued to stand by the vampire's side. "There's something I need to tell you. It's not good," he cautioned.

For a moment, Zephyr looked like he would lash out again. Although his eyes burnt with unbridled rage, he held himself back. "Have a seat," instead, he responded in a leveled voice.

Zedkiel's eyes darted from the splinters of the broken chair to the slashed-out bed. Hesitantly, he took a spot on the edge of the mattress. "There's a chance we're fighting a bigger enemy than we previously assumed. This has never been a war between mortals and vampires." Zedkiel's hesitant confession was met by a prolonged silence.

Zephyr had seen that coming. The message from the neowerevampire was enough to clue him in, but he refused to register defeat against his real opponent. "A bigger enemy? Do you mean to say Lucifer Morningstar is on the move?"

Zedkiel didn't need to answer that question. "From all the accounts I've received, yes."

"What are you implying?" Zephyr's eyes drifted towards Uriel, who somberly nodded to confirm Zedkiel's claims. "Are you saying I've been a fool? Are you suggesting I've played right into my brother's hands?" At every question, his voice raised a few octaves.

"Father, I can't engage in that dialogue," Zedkiel said sternly, bracing himself for the consequences. "I just wanted to let you in on everything I've been hearing, and my sources are reliable, so take it as you will."

Surprisingly, Zephyr took it at face value. "I see. So, how far along is he?"

Uriel glanced nervously in Zedkiel's direction as he delivered the information without any lies or deception. "Many governments across the world have agreed to collaborate with only one man. They've agreed to inject their armies with the serum, and they're patrolling borders, so we have to get out of here as soon as possible."

"That's been our plan all along. What else?" Zephyr asked.

"This man keeps his business extremely private, so there's no way of tracking him down or catching him by surprise. Arthur Morgan's project was funded by the same person. All these patterns are too uncanny to be an outcome of mere coincidence," Zedkiel continued.

"It seems like Lucifer has always been ten steps ahead of us, but all is not lost. We're heading to Antarctica, and we must operate in secrecy. The two of you will not contact anyone from the outside if you wish to continue this journey with me." Zedkiel heaved a sigh of relief at the unexpectedly sensible words. Finally, the King of Darkness had pulled himself together.

"Of course," Zedkiel agreed readily.

However, Uriel missed a beat before responding. "Sure."

Although Zedkiel was met with a far better response than he had anticipated, he still held his breath. "There's another thing, Father."

Zephyr felt like his patience was being tested. There was something in Zedkiel's voice that alarmed him more than anything he had learned so far. "What is it, child?"

"Lucifer Morningstar isn't alone. Alvira has betrayed us," the prince responded in a grave voice.

At that moment, Zephyr vowed he wouldn't rest until he broke her neck. He vowed to give his trusted warrior the most torturous death imaginable. However, his brief response was void of any emotion. "I see."

Chapter 15
The Hunt for the Original Vampire

The cruise creaked and groaned as it plowed through the dark, stormy seas of the Drake Passage. Waves crashed against the hull, sending sprays of water flying over the deck. The passengers stumbled with the constant rocking and rolling of the ship, yet the vampire remained rooted in his spot. Zephyr lowered his hood as he felt the stare of a few crew members boring into his back. The gesture filled him with a sense of shame. There was nothing more mortifying than concealing his identity from a bunch of mortals, but the risks, otherwise, were far greater.

The pureblood vampires had already lost more than half of their population in their journey to South America. All hope was lost for them, and fleeing was the only option left. At every station, they were joined by the children of the night. Vampires from all across the universe desperately sought out their father for protection in vain. The rising tension was so thick Zephyr could only look out for himself. Watching his army slaughtered wounded him just the same. The confidentiality of their destination could not be compromised; their survival depended on it.

"Father, come inside. You're raising suspicion," Zedkiel warned his father, joining him on the deck. Besides vampires, no one on the ship could stand steady against the turbulent tides. His unmoving position was a dead giveaway of his identity.

"Leave me be," Zephyr growled in response.

The King of the Darkness had spent the past few days in hiding; however, Zephyr couldn't help but feel a sense of liberation after boarding the ship. At their previous destinations, there was no one Zephyr could bring himself to trust. His frantic paranoia was bordering on insanity. At every corner, a turno-cloak neo was hiding in the shadows, biding their time. At every opportunity, a vampire was stabbed in the back. No one could be trusted, not even the fellow vampires, for even they had joined forces with Lucifer. However, the ship crew had earned the vampire's trust by offering them security when everyone had betrayed him – even his most trusted allies.

"It's not safe. We can't trust these people." Zedkiel tried to reason with his father. Zephyr's goals were beyond his understanding. The King of Darkness always had a hint of pride, but he had never let it overpower his senses. Lucifer's return had changed all of that.

"How do you plan on getting to the destination?" Zephyr ignored the prince and came up with a question of his own.

"That's another matter altogether. We must not make our intentions known by anyone," Zedkiel reminded. His patience was running thin. Uriel didn't bother with the King of Darkness anymore.

"Just keep your eyes peeled, child. There's nothing that can stop us now. We've come a long way, but home is not far. Lucifer can search all over the world, but he won't be able to find us here." Throwing caution to the wind, Zephyr went on to explain.

Before Zedkiel could lose his patience, he was mercifully joined by Uriel. Although her voice was steady, her face was etched with lines of worry. "I don't trust them at all. Honestly, I'm feeling a little on edge," she confessed with a hint of shame in her voice. The emotions were foreign to the empress.

"I agree with you. Something just doesn't feel right." Zedkiel replied, glancing in the direction of the broad-shouldered man, who kept glancing in their direction. Fernando had helped the vampires escape the ambush in Argentina. However, he seemed a little too interested in their plans.

"Enough with this nonsense! I've known these men nearly since the beginning of my time on earth. Have some pride, the two of you! How can you stand by my side, uttering such cowardly words?" Finally, Zephyr decided to assume his role as the leader. "If they turn over, they'll be slaughtered before the word goes out. We're not cornered by Lucifer's army anymore."

Zedkiel considered his father's words. They rang true since the army couldn't possibly reach them on the ship. "So, what's the plan? Where are we going to stay, and for how long?"

Uriel nervously glanced in Fernando's direction. The vampires' heightened sense of hearing kept them from having any sense of privacy. Zephyr considered it necessary to let his children in on the outcome. After all, the compromise was huge.

"We're not going to stay. We'll be entering a long slumber – that is, if you wish to join me, of course," Zephyr spoke in a low voice.

"What?" Uriel and Zedkiel shared a perplexed glance.

"We're going to go dormant and hide in the depths of the ocean for as long as necessary," Zephr elaborated.

"How is that possible?" Zedkiel looked dumbfounded.

"Child, for us, everything is impossible. We just need more time." Zephyr smiled to himself, at peace with his decision.

Uriel couldn't believe her ears. For eons, they had followed Zephyr blindly only to discover how helpless they were. They had always been fighting for a lost cause. "So, that's our solution." She couldn't help but laugh bitterly.

"We're just going to run, hide, and wait for Lucifer to kill us in our sleep? That's a very effective plan."

"How are we to know about his whereabouts in our dormant state? How are we to know about his next move?" Zedkiel tried to reason with his father. Running to the ends of the world for survival was one thing, and purposefully leaving yourself vulnerable when a predator was on the move was another. "Are you still blind to his influence, father? Lucifer has always been ten steps ahead of us! Have you considered he might already know our next move?" Zedkiel's voice raised a few octaves with every word.

Zephyr's eyes flashed with unbridled rage. "Know your place! I've lived far longer than the two of you. I wouldn't let a setback hinder me from my goal. Do you think you know better than me?"

"Know better than you? Certainly not, but we assess and understand the circumstances better than you, for sure." Uriel regretted the words as they fell out of her mouth. For a moment, Zephyr stared at her with an impassive face. Before she could release her breath, she was pushed against the deck of the ship. She struggled to twist out of his grip as Zephyr's hands tightened around her neck.

"Forgive...me," she managed to utter the words, but the King of Darkness refused to release her. From the corner of her eye, she could see Fernando observing them. The captain of the ship stared at Zephyr wearily, but no one came to her rescue. Her eyes widened as she observed Fernando passing a folded piece of paper to one of the crew members. *Something's wrong,* she thought to herself as her eyes watered.

"Father, let her go," Zedkiel cried out exasperatedly. He was tired of Zephyr's sick tactics.

As Zephyr slowly released Uriel from his grip, he spoke the words in a leveled voice, "Lucifer might know our next move, but there's a high probability he doesn't. No vampire has been able to figure out this survival strategy. I've never revealed it. If I've trusted you with it, it means you're either going to join me or die at my hands. I can't afford the word going out."

Uriel and Zedkiel shared a horrified look. Once again, their father had left them with no choice, but they couldn't possibly go up against the first vampire to walk the earth. "You're saying we need to shut our mouths and do as we're told. It's too late to turn back now. Right?"

"Now, we're on the same page." Zephyr's face twisted into a malicious smile.

"I know, you don't see it right now, but I know better, child. I know the laws of the universe," Zephyr paused before saying the next words, "And I know my brother. He would never hunt me down if I'm not putting up a fight. He wouldn't accept a victory if I'd accepted my defeat because it wouldn't humiliate me. We can only take a chance and hope for the best."

Although Uriel and Zedkiel nodded, Zephyr's words reassured his children only temporarily. It's not like they had any other choice. Uriel's distrust reached new heights every time she found the crew members interacting. She couldn't help it. Their means of interaction were highly suspicious. Whenever she found Fernando staring in their direction, she found herself on edge. However, every time she pointed it out to Zedkiel, the prince just shrugged hopelessly.

It wasn't before long her suspicions came true. A feeling of dread crept over her as a ship moved closer. "It's rather strange, isn't it?" she remarked in a weary voice, her eyes fixed on the approaching vessel a few miles away.

Zedkiel sighed heavily, accepting the inevitable. "I know. No one in their sane mind would travel to the desolate world we're headed, especially not in this weather."

The crew scurried with a mix of excitement and anticipation. Zedkiel could smell the adrenaline in the air. In response, his eyes reddened as he revealed his fangs, ready to spill blood. Although Zephyr had lost his vision and sanity, he was not to be messed with. If push came to shove, the Prince of Darkness was ready to lay down his life for him.

"They betrayed us. We're under attack," Zephyr stated the obvious, but he refused to swallow his pride.

"Yes, you think?" Zephyr responded with a hint of annoyance.

As the distance between the ships diminished, the tense silence was shattered. With agility and precision, nearly seven men scaled the rigging, swinging from ropes like acrobats. Their eyes gleamed with a combination of wild madness and greed. Uriel and Zedkiel stood back-to-back as they watched the men leaping from their ship.

Within moments, the ship became a battleground. The ancient vessel creaked under the weight of the impending battle. The vampires stood in the middle of the deck, their eyes burning with fury. Surprisingly, a ferocious hunger replaced Uriel's state of apprehension as she eyed her prey. Perhaps, Zephyr had been right all along. After all, they were the superior predators, and they thrived on hunting. The three vampires stood poised with their predatory hunger reflected in their eyes. Although the ship's confines gave them little room for retreat, they embraced the challenge.

Zephyr snarled at the crew of the ship as the enemies inched closer. The three vampires were circled by seven neos and two pureblood vampires, Fernando and his lover, Daniella. "Fernando, you'll regret this," the King of the night spoke in a low, threatening voice.

Fernando only responded with a feral snarl. The neos looked ready to pounce, fangs bared, and muscles tensed. Although they were a formidable force with their bestial nature, the vampires stood their ground.

As the skirmish commenced, the vampires moved like shadows, their movements fluid, agile, and calculated. Despite their outnumbered disadvantage, the vampires relied on their centuries-old cunning. A mere serum could never make up for the neos' lack of experience.

As a middle-aged heavy woman pounced on Zedkiel, he ducked out of the way. His face twisted into a sneer as he whispered into her ear, "Behind you."

Before the woman could react, his fangs sank into her flesh. Her piercing screams echoed through the chilly night as the vampires' venomous blood coursed through her veins. Zedkiel was attacked by another beast before he could compose himself. His self-satisfied smirk turned into a sneer as a neo clawed at his chest.

However, Uriel was just as quick to react. She straddled the neowerewolf to the weathered deck, tearing a lump out of his arms with her teeth. Her eyes glittered with sadistic bliss at his agonizing screams. Within moments, she was on to her next prey as her claws tore through the flesh, slashing and biting with lethal intent.

Despite the vampires' overpowering strength, the neos were not easily subdued. They couldn't catch a break for even a second, but the challenge only fueled their ferocity. The ship reverberated with a thunderous clash as the opposing forces collided. The scent of blood mingled with the salty sea hung in the air.

As the moon reached its zenith, the battlefield was strewn with broken bodies and spilled blood. With every fallen neo, the vampires grew more emboldened. If these wimpy brutes were sent by Lucifer, then he had clearly underestimated the King of Darkness. Perhaps, the fallen angel was only testing their strength. Whatever the cause, the battle had only rejuvenated the vampires' spirits. Zedkiel and Uriel made an exceptional team, and Zephyr didn't require anyone's assistance. The two stood victorious with their hunger sated, reveling in their victory.

"Fernando, your men have been slaughtered by just the three of us. I warned you," Zephyr growled in a low voice. His eyes burned with the fire of vengeance. As he slowly inched towards the traitor, a shiver went down Fernando's spine. The younger vampire had been a pirate, plundering and spoiling the riches for centuries, but he stood no chance against the King of Darkness.

"I'll join your side! Spare me," Fernando tried to plead with the hungry monster. His spineless response was only received with contempt and ridicule by the vampire. Zephyr's pale skin glowed under the fractured moonlight.

His regal form, his lethal aura, and his calculated moves were a reflection of his power. The king had risen in the darkness, and Zedkiel and Uriel could only feel shameful for doubting him in the first place.

"You should've known better, Fernando," Zephyr responded, smiling maliciously as the traitor's screams pierced through the dark night.

***

The moon hung low in the inky sky, casting an eerie glow upon the desolate street of Kamagasaki. The air was heavy with an unsettling silence, punctured only by the occasional gust of wind. For the surviving vampires, the slum had become their only refuge. Rows of decaying buildings lined the filthy street, and one such abandoned building was habited by the vampires, Shadow, Star, and Dorothy. Eight months ago, the trio was hunted out of their dojo and driven to one of the most poverty-stricken areas of Japan.

Dorothy had given up her attempts at maintaining the three-story building. Its once vibrant red paint had faded to a weary gray. The stairs were battered, revealing the grainy texture of weathered timber underneath. Weeds sprouted from the cracks in the pavement. The stench of dampness and rot hung in the air, tormenting the vampires due to their heightened senses.

"Any word from him yet?" Shadow tapped his sharpened nails restlessly over the armrest. As he sat poised on a chair, no one could suspect the gloominess of his circumstances. Months had passed, but he continued waiting patiently for a message from their leader.

"No, nothing. You better give up, Shadow. We're on our own, I'm telling you." Dorothy failed to hide the frustration in her voice. Their refuge in this shithole was supposed to be temporary. At least, that's what Shadow had initially planned. However, every time Dorothy brought up the subject of relocation, Shadow turned her down flatly.

"Lord Zephyr will reach out to us. Don't lose hope," Shadow answered with a blinding conviction.

Dorothy sighed heavily. It was the same argument all over again, and she was sick of going in circles. "Honestly, I don't see a flicker of hope in this darkness. We can't hide in here forever." Her voice rose a few octaves as she tried to reason with Shadow.

Shadow's eyes flashed with anger as he sprang to his feet. "Look, he has had only one purpose from the start to time – to seek vengeance. Do you seriously think he's going to give up now? Believe me, he's just biding his time. He's going to need us to win this war, and sooner or later, he's going to reach out."

"If he wanted to communicate with us, he could reach us out anywhere in the world. I still don't see why we're holed up here," Dorothy argued.

"Because this place is inconspicuous, and we're safe here. It may have escaped your notice, but we haven't been able to stay put anywhere for more than a month. We'll be hunted down the moment we step out of here. Do you understand?" Shadow spat angrily, his voice was laced with bitterness.

Giving up, Dorothy raised her hands in the air. "Fine, believe whatever you want, but I'm leaving. You're delusional if you think we still stand a chance." Although Dorothy said the words, she showed no signs of leaving. Instead, she tried another tack. "Just look at her! She's going to die!"

Dorothy pointed in Star Reaper's direction, who was huddled in a corner of the room. Her face was gaunt and pale – paler than usual. Her gown was reduced to tatters, barely shielding her from her harsh surroundings. Although her eyes glowed with an insatiable hunger, she showed no other sign of life. Save for her occasional fits, she couldn't bring herself to move. She went rabid at the slightest smell of blood, devouring her prey without a shred of conscience.

Shadow's eyes softened as he regarded his sister, but he continued to speak ruthlessly. "Come on, Dorothy. Do you hear yourself? We're pureblood vampires! She's not just going to die on us." Shadow laughed nervously, trying to convince himself, but his words sounded hollow to his own ears.

Dorothy's eyes hardened as she realized she couldn't reason with the older vampire. "You're right. She'll just go insane out of starvation. Not the same thing, of course – just slightly worse," she spoke through clenched teeth. "I can't believe you're the same man I once admired."

Shadow lowered his gaze, his voice tinged with resignation. "You're right, Dorothy. I won't let us starve to death in this wretched place. I can't allow her to wither away in obscurity," he nodded in Star's direction, "I know we need to venture out, but they're everywhere. They roam the streets disguised as ordinary men. They'll hunt us down without mercy."

As Shadow continued speaking, he realized he was confined in this desolate place by the grip of fear. Dorothy's eyes welled with tears at the display of vulnerability. When the mighty vampire accepted his vulnerability, Dorothy acknowledged the imminent danger lurking in the dark. She gently reached for his hand, trying to offer some comfort. "We'll find a way, Shadow. We'll regain our strength. I know how terrifying this is, but we have to get out of here. We'll navigate this treacherous path with caution, and we'll survive."

As Shadow nodded slowly, the brief moment of intimacy was shattered by the sound of distant howls. Dorothy froze in her spot, trying to compose herself, but a single thought consumed her mind. *They can't be here. How can this be?* A chill went down Shadow's spine as he detected a foul scent – the scent of neowerewolves.

Shadow sprang into action before Dorothy could react. With one arm, he lifted his incapacitated sister while reaching for his katana with the other hand. "We have to get out of here, Dorothy. Let's go!" His voice was laced with urgency as the younger warrior tried to gather her senses.

Before they could make their escape, the sound of shattering windows punctured the silence. The two vampires exchanged a desperate glance. Dorothy remained rooted at the head of the stairs, but Shadow retraced his steps. In the abandoned room, he struggled to find a spot to hide his sister from the approaching harm. Star whimpered as he gently lowered her. Although a desk concealed her from sight, Shadow knew his efforts were in vain. Quite possibly, the neos had already detected her scent.

As he turned his head, his eyes widened with fear. Emerging from the shadows were three neos, accompanied by the scientist, Arthur Morgan. However, Dorothy was nowhere in sight. "Well, well, well... If it isn't the bloodsuckers who raided my lab. Am I mistaken?" Morgan's face broke into a twisted smile as Shadow's eyes searched for an escape. "Not so quick, my friend. I hope we can have a little chat. Do you know how devastated I was when you destroyed my serum? Well, it doesn't matter now. I came up with a better formula. What do you think, friend?"

"Do you want my honest opinion?" Shadow tried to keep his composure. "You could've done a little better. They smell awfully bad."

Shadow's retort was met by ridiculing laughter. The scientist turned his head in the neos' direction, his eyes burning with admiration. The largest neo, the alpha of the pack, stepped forward, his voice dripping with malice. "One, two," he nodded in Star's direction, "Where's the third one?"

His tall and burly appearance exuded raw power, and his eyes flickered with primal hunger. His thick, tousled hair framed a rugged face. As for his companions, they shared a similar aura of animalistic strength. Their bodies were lean but well-defined with sinewy muscles. Their dark eyes also bore a wildness that pierced through their façade of humanity. Their shoulder-length brown hair was disheveled and unkempt. Shadow could smell a trace of blood in their hair. He could tell without a doubt another vampire had only recently fallen prey to their untamed nature.

"I'd like to know that as well," Shadow uttered every word tentatively, trying to stall his enemies. "She was just here a moment -"

Shadow's response was cut short as he spotted a flash from the corner of his eye. The neos noticed it just a little too late. Sensing an opportunity, Dorothy materialized behind one of the neos. Distracted by the vampire before him, the neo failed to detect her looming presence behind him. With a swift and precise strike, Dorothy brought the blade down in a fluid motion. Before any of the neos could react, a severed head was rolling on the ground. Blood spurted from the neck, showering the surroundings in a crimson mist.

Chaos ensued as Shadow assumed his fighting stance. With a burst of speed, the other werewolf lunged at Dorothy while the alpha charged in Shadow's direction. He danced around the werewolf, his katana striking with lethal precision. As he parried the blows with deftness, he continued to draw blood with each strike. However, the alpha remained calm – almost impassive and calculated. Whether Shadow managed to strike or failed, his adversary continued to frustrate him. The alpha remained unaffected.

Dorothy swiftly dodged the attack, her movements agile and graceful. The sound of metal clashing against claws echoed through the decaying walls. She evaded clawed swipes, retaliating with swift slashes. Her katana gleamed in the dim moonlight, piercing through the window. "Oh, look at you. All bark and no bite," she jeered at her opponent, her courage fueled by the rush of the combat. "I thought wolves were supposed to be fierce."

The neo accepted the challenge with grace. "You know, I can smell your fear emanating from you. Right, Deathdealer?" He lunged at her, snarling and baring his teeth. Dorothy managed to roll out of his way in time; however, before she could get to her feet, the neo's claws slashed her arm. She felt severe pain, along with a burning sensation. *What's happening?* As the claws made contact with her arm, she felt her mobility becoming restricted.

"Can't move! Shadow, there's something," she called out feebly. In a single moment of vulnerability, the neo managed to land a fatal blow. Its razor-sharp claws pierced through her heart. As Dorothy stumbled, the neo's fangs pierced into her throat.

A split second of shock registered on Shadow's face. However, before he could rush to her side, his attention was stolen by his opponent. Frozen in a moment of disbelief, Dorothy tried to cling on to life.

"Dorothy! No, no," Shadow called out desperately as her body crumpled to the floor. The weight of its loss echoed through the dark room.

A whirlwind of fury and despair engulfed Shadow. He felt a crushing sense of hopelessness as a singular thought consumed his mind, *I'm alone. I'm all alone.* From the corner of his eye, he watched as the other neo dragged Star across the floor. "Stay away from her! No!" His throat was raw from screaming, but his desperate cries fell on deaf ears. "Leave her alone!"

Shadow cried out in agony as the neo's fangs sank into Star's exposed throat. His sister's life force waned before his eyes. Once, a fierce warrior embraced death in silence.

"Where's your attention? I'm your opponent." Shadow felt nothing as the alpha's fangs sank into his arm. Silent tears ran down his face as his eyes gleamed with the fire of vengeance.

Consumed by rage and grief, Shadow unleashed his rage upon the alpha. He pounced with supernatural speed, his blade slashing through fur and flesh. Surprisingly, the blows seemed to have no effect on him.

"Do you understand what you're up against?" the alpha lifted Shadow with a tuft of his hair. "I'll give you credit for trying, but your efforts are futile."

As Shadow lost the mobility in his arm, his katana slipped from his grip. From the corner of his eye, he could see the look of satisfaction on Morgan's face. With the remaining strength in his body, he tried to hold on to his consciousness. As the life drained from his body, he felt the alpha's fangs pierce his throat, sealing his fate. The neos' victorious howls echoed through the dark night.

With every passing day, Alvira dreaded the inevitable. Every moment, her mind was plagued by a combination of fear and despair. Most days, she spent isolated in Lucifer's tower, waiting for the moment that would seal her fate. Despite the fear, Alvira didn't once regret joining Lucifer's side. Perhaps, her unwavering loyalty to her new leader also had to do with Lucifer's clutches on her heart and mind. However, Alvira had seen many a times what became of those who lost their utility to Lucifer – they were cruelly discarded by him.

Alvira paced her room, trying to recall the details. Although Lucifer hadn't threatened her, the warning hung heavy in the air. No words needed to be said. She could feel Lucifer's sense of restlessness and rage directed at her. After all, their contract was built on the information she had on her former master. She knew she only had a few hours to locate the King of Night.

Did Zephyr ever reveal his hideout in passing? No, not really. Alvira couldn't even imagine him running off when challenged by Lucifer. No matter how hard she tried, she couldn't come up with an answer. She had already named every possible place where Lord Zephr had allies, and Lucifer had sent his warriors only to be met with disappointment. It was like the King of Darkness had disappeared into thin air.

Alvira knew she was only a prisoner, caged behind these walls. This beautiful room had once held her in awe. Tall, arched wind draped with velvet curtains allowed her the view of the desolate world beyond. A collection of plush armchairs and a grand Chesterfield sofa were arranged around a black coffee table. The upholstery, in deep shades of ruby and emerald, added a luxurious touch to the room. The sophisticated interior had now become a painful reminder of her mistake. She could only feel nothing but suffocation in fear of what lay ahead.

Alvira's hopeless musings were interrupted by the butler. "You have been summoned by Lord Lucifer immediately." Once again, he didn't bother to knock. "Meet him in his study."

"Would it kill you to knock?" Alvira glared at the butler, subjecting him to her pent-up frustration.

"Why bother? You realize you're being monitored all the time, don't you?" His remark only aggravated the princess even more. A chill went down her spine as she felt a tug towards her master. Alvira decided to ignore the butler lest she suffer Lucifer's wrath.

Alvira's breath was caught in her throat as she stepped into the study. Lucifer sat back in his armchair, poised and elegant. His dark eyes burned with unbridled rage. However, the malicious smile playing on his lips contrasted with his emotions. His hands were resting on the armrest. He impatiently tapped his fingers as Alvira eyed him warily.

"Don't keep me waiting. Take a seat, Alvira," Lucifer instructed in a low but crisp voice. Terrified, Alvira hesitantly pulled up a chair in front of him.

"I presume you understand why you're here." There was a hint of threat in his voice. "I've been patient with you."

Alvira knew she served no purpose anymore, yet she held on to a glimmer of hope. "My lord, I understand you're not pleased with me, but I'm trying. There's a chance Zephyr already knows about my motives. Otherwise, he would've reached out to me. I've been investigating his whereabouts to no avail."

"Excuses!" Lucifer spat angrily. Alvira could barely keep her composure. Her nervousness grew, held under Lucifer's piercing gaze. "You're wasting my time and resources. Is it possible your allegiance has shifted? Are you protecting him?"

Alvira's eyes widened at Lucifer's words. He couldn't possibly mean those words when he had consumed her mind, and invaded her thoughts. "Pardon me, my Lord, but I wouldn't switch sides. You know that," she paused for a moment before speaking the next words, "There's a society of surviving vampires in Kamagasaki. Perhaps, there's a chance, Zephyr is hiding there, trying to unite the pureblood vampires once again. It's rather uncharacteristic of him to run and hide."

Alvira's words had the opposite effect as what she had hoped. Her narrowed his eyes as he responded, "Not when he's up against me, it isn't. About Kamasaki, I've already taken care of it. However, there was no sign of Zephyr in the area."

"I see," Alvira's desperation grew with every failure. Their contract was based on her prior close relationship with the King of Darkness. Without the information, she was nothing but a waste of space. Lucifer made sure she was aware of the fact. "Give me a few days. I'll locate them," she promised resolutely.

"A week."

As Alvira met Lucifer's gaze, she knew she wouldn't be getting any more passes. Her life was on the line.

Four days later, Alvira was still searching for the first vampire in vain. Driven by her desperation, Alvira pulled out all the stops. Her mind was still connected with Lucifer's, so he could track her every move. There was no way to escape his clutches. Throughout her journey, he followed her like a shadow. Initially, she had felt blessed for the connection. The enmeshment gave her remarkable power. However, now his invasion into her mind only drove her insane.

Apparently, the vampire had been staying at shabby bars and inns – something she never expected from Zephyr, given his pride and exquisite taste. Following his trail, Alvira was eventually led to Ushuaia with only a few hours to spare. She scanned the bustling Usuaia Dock in search of answers. As her gaze landed on a man eyeing her, she approached him hesitantly. There was something distinctive about him. A predator never failed to detect another beast's presence.

The man stood there, leaning against a weathered wooden post. His rugged appearance seemed to reflect a life at sea. With piercing eyes, Alvira observed the sailor, measuring his intentions. A slight smile played at the corner of his lips, betraying the secrets he held. She could tell he somehow recognized her and her motives.

"Princess, I know why you're here," the sailor said before Alvira could open her mouth.

Alvira did a double take at his words. She studied him with a hint of curiosity. As he grinned at her, Alvira's sharp eyes caught the sight of his pointy fangs. *A neo, as expected.* Despite the lurking threat, she felt confident in her abilities. She could take him out within seconds, but the neo's newfound abilities made him rather smug. This wasn't the first time a neo had foolishly underestimated her capabilities.

"Then, you should know better than to fight me. Don't resist me if you know what's good for you. You better give me the answers I seek."

Alvira's threats were met by mocking laughter. "I've seen a fair share of travelers come and go through these parts. What's in it for me?" The sailor tried to play smart.

"Let me think," Alvira returned his sly smile with a grin, "I'll spare your life."

Once again, the sailor burst into a fit of laughter. "Princess, don't pretend otherwise. You know, I can smell fear on you."

At the provocation, the vampire's demeanor changed, revealing her predatory nature. Of course, the source of her fear was another – an unmatched mightier being. Before the sailor could react, Alvira moved with lightning speed. She moved behind the sailor, catching him off guard. With a grip of iron, Alvira clasped her hands around his neck. Tightening her grip, she threatened to snap his neck.

The sailor's eyes widened in shock and fear, realizing the dire situation he was in. Any attempts to resist or escape proved to be futile against Alvira's superior strength. The sailor croaked as he realized he was at Alvira's mercy. Her face, once seemingly calm, now carried a sinister gleam.

"I'm running late. You better start talking, sailor."

***

When Caius set about investigating a society of vampires in Kamasagaki, he didn't expect to come upon a dead one – well, a nearly dead one. Although Dorothy and

Star Reaper had perished, Shadow Reaper still showed some signs of life.

Caius found the wounded vampire sprawled on the ground in an abandoned building. Shadow's once regal appearance was now marred by his weakened state. His pale skin, which once exuded an ethereal glow, now seemed ashen and sickly. The wounds inflicted by the neos were still raw and bleeding. Deep claw marks crisscrossed his chest. For some reason, unbeknownst to Caius, the vampire's wounds refused to heal.

A few feet away, he found Star Reaper's decapacitated bodies. The other corpse, Caius recognized as Dorothy's. With a swift motion, Caius moved the corpses, before attempting to awaken the survivor.

"What misfortune has befallen you, Shadow Reaper?" Caius inquired the barely-alive vampire. His voice was tinged with concern and sadness.

The weakened vampire managed to muster a feeble response, "Dor-othy?" Shadow's voice was barely audible. Although he tried to adjust his vision, he could barely make out the vampire leaning above him.

"She's dead. So is your sister," the vampire answered in a coarse voice without sparing Shadow's feelings. Although Shadow didn't expect otherwise, he felt an intense pang in his chest. It was worse than any neo bite. If he had any tears left to shed, Shadow would have cried out in pain.

As Shadow tried to focus his vision, he noticed emerald-green eyes staring down at him. He struggled to piece together his memories. The last thing he remembered was the neos slaughtering Dorothy and his sister. He recalled fighting the alpha, and... the vision of a winged silhouette against the moon as he drew his last breath. “Caius? Did you save my life?”

“Yes. And never mind the pleasantries,” the vampire answered, urgently nudging the pale vampire. “Get up, Shadow. We must leave before they return.”

“I appreciate it, but Star-”

Caius cut him off impatiently. “You can’t do anything for them anymore, and it’s better if you didn’t see them. Make haste.”

As Shadow tried to stand, his limbs trembled, unable to support his own weight. His state was beyond humiliating. The elegant vampire had never felt so weak in his lifetime.

“How did you find me?” Shadow asked as Caius supported him.

“Word gets around. Don’t you think you overstayed your welcome?” Caius asked the weakened vampire mockingly. Shadow couldn't help but wince at the jab. Had he listened to Dorothy earlier, she wouldn't be dead.

"I should've listened to Dorothy," he said in a feeble voice. It took everything in him to drag himself. Half of his body was paralyzed from the strange effects of the serum, while the other half was brutally wounded.

"No point lamenting."

For a moment, Shadow stayed silent before another pressing question crossed his mind. "Have you managed to locate Lord Zephyr?"

"No one knows where he has disappeared. Some say that he's dead, while others claim that Lucifer has taken him captive. It's highly unlikely," Caius explained. Although they had always done Zephyr's bidding together, the two vampires had never been close. However, Caius found it sickening to see his own kin in such a pitiable state.

"Where are we going, anyway?" Shadow asked, descending the stairs of his desolate home. A part of him wanted to stay within the darkness – with his dead kin. His undead heart bled for the loss, but he had no time to grieve.

Finally, Caius turned to face him. "You'll see."

***

The secret society of vampires existed as a clandestine enclave tucked away in the depths of an isolated land. The remaining vampires found their refuge in a fortress built on the crater of a dormant volcanic island. Although the bright and warm weather was quite unsuitable for the vampires' habitation, they remained safe from the prying eyes of the mortals and the neos. No one expected to find the vampires on the island. Most of them spent their days deep within their caves or in the fortress and only went out to hunt at night.

The remaining community was known only to those initiated into its ranks. Its very existence was shrouded in mystery and secrecy. Access to the society was granted through a highly-guarded entrance to the island. Once inside, a labyrinth of underground tunnels and passageways led to the fortress.

The majestic fortress was constructed with a fusion of ancient architecture and supernatural craftsmanship. Its massive walls were fortified with dark stones. The entrance to the fortress was guarded by a pair of ornate iron gates.

As Shadow was led inside, he observed warily as starving vampires snarled at him, but Caius paid them no heed. Some were in a deranged state of mind – a state of insanity Star had descended to before her demise. Within the fortress, each chamber housed three to four vampires at a time. Several cages were built within the chamber to contain them. Shadow couldn't help but wonder why they hadn't been put to rest.

"How long have you been here?" Shadow asked the other vampire, impressed. Nestled within the walls of the ancient fortress, the society was an impenetrable bastion against the outside world.

"It nearly took us a decade. Well, it was initially Cain's evil ploy against Zephyr," Caius explained, "However, when the vampire kind was on the brink of extinction, I built this society with him. This fortress has now become a safe haven for our kind."

All of a sudden, Shadow halted in his steps. "How do you know we can trust him?" he asked warily.

"We can't," Caius answered, shrugging nonchalantly. With a start, Shadow realized he was a stranger in this world.

Shadow was led to an expansive chamber at the heart of the stronghold. The grand assembly hall, with its vaulted ceilings and majestic pillars, acted as the central gathering place. As he entered, his eyes fell upon the figure seated upon a grand throne. It was Cain's dream all along!

As Shadow stepped into the majestic throne room, he was, at once, struck by how healthy Cain looked. His porcelain white skin was a stark contrast to his dark hair. He exuded an aura of power and elegance. He donned a tailored shirt of linen in a deep shade of burgundy. The shirt had a high collar; however, its sleeves were short.

Although he occupied the throne, he looked unlike any ruler Shadow had ever seen – a modern-day monarch with a touch of antiquity.

Caius hung back as the vampire greeted Shadow with a nod, weighing his worthiness and resolve. Cain had taken a commanding stance. As he spoke, his voice had a hint of caution mingled with authority. "Welcome, Shadow. Welcome to our humble society."

"Cain," Shadow nodded in response with reverence; however, he refused to bow down before him – not without understanding his motives. With a wary gaze, Shadow eyed his surroundings. Built upon ancient ruins, the hall was a blend of sturdy stone walls - vines of ivy and creeping moss adorned the walls. The hall was illuminated by tall, narrow, painted glass windows, allowing streams of colorful light to filter in.

Shadow could clearly observe the power hierarchy within this little kingdom. He could tell it was determined by age, lineage, wealth, and, most of all, prowess.

A long, grandiose table stretched the length of the hall, where a group of vampires were huddled together. They were engaged in an intense conversation, indifferent to Shadow's unexpected appearance. These vampires were part of the elder council, comprising the oldest and most powerful vampires. Shadow's savior, Caius, also belonged to this group.

Some vampires sat on the grimy floor, slumped against the wall. Occupying the lowest rung, they were responsible for the menial tasks. Unlike the vampires seated at the table, these vampires were in a far more impoverished state. Their parched lips and hollow eyes were a reflection of the meager rations of blood and the tyranny of Cain's rule.

Shadow's gaze was drawn back to the throne at the far end of the hall. It was crafted from dark, polished wood, intricately carved with ornate motifs.

"I see, you take after your father," Cain remarked with a low chuckle. "However, if we want to survive, we must set aside our differences. Our community grows at a slow pace, but it matters not. We grow in number and strength every day. Our resources are limited, but we work as a single unit."

Cain's words were met by surprise. An offer of the treaty was far from what Shadow expected from the vengeful vampire. "I'm not seeking any confrontation either," Shadow responded carefully.

Cain continued, his words measured and careful. Although he had done this more times than he could remember, every reception seemed like a test. "Before you can fully embrace our society, there are certain protocols that must be observed. These protocols serve to protect our collective well-being and ensure our survival."

He continued, his voice echoing through the hall, "You must swear a binding oath, a contract that solidifies your commitment to our society."

At Cain's words, Shadow was given a contract with the rules of the society listed in the order of their significance. From secrecy, loyalty, and respect for authority to sanctuary protection and feeding etiquettes, there was nothing Shadow didn't already expect. However, there were specific rules for the preservation of the bloodline. Interference or endangerment of the bloodline was strictly forbidden. It was necessary to pass down powers, train newcomers, and turn humans into vampires with their informed consent.

"How are we supposed to transform humans into vampires while ensuring our secrecy?" Shadow asked, already knowing the answer.

"The act of revelation and turning requires careful consideration and approval by the council. Intruders or any threat to our sanctuary will be swiftly dealt with," Cain answered simply.

"Should a human refuse to turn, they must be killed," Shadow asked for confirmation.

Cain's face twisted into a malicious smile. "Precisely." He marveled at the power of desperation. Using fear as his instrument, he could get anyone to do his bidding. His eyes narrowed, his gaze unyielding as he continued, "While we're on the topic, I must warn you; if you refuse to seal the contract at once, you will also be deemed a threat to our existence, and your fate will be sealed. You'll be beheaded on the spot. Should you breach the contract, you'll meet the same fate."

Shadow glared at Caius, enraged at the vampire for withholding the truth from him. However, Caius refused to meet his gaze. With an impassive face, he stared ahead at the authoritarian.

"If I sign the contract, what benefits do I get?" Shadow asked, weighing his only option against imminent death.

"Well, you'll get to live, first and foremost. What else do you want?" Cain let out a provoking laughter at Shadow's stern expression. When Shadow refused to react any further, Cain went on, "Your wounds will be treated here. These bites of these beasts are venomous, but you already know that, don't you? You can already feel its effect on your body."

With each passing minute, Shadow could feel the poison sapping the life out of him. A sense of dizziness intermittently came over him, and he struggled to remain on his feet, but he gave away no signs of weakness. He knew his efforts were in vain, but his pride sustained him.

Shadow considered death a better alternative to a life of slavery. "You do understand you need us just as much as we need refuge in your little kingdom?" he said, refusing to give in.

"That's true," Cain could see right through Shadow's weaknesses, "but we need to stick together. Shadow, you know Lord Zephyr lives on, ever-present in the shadows. You also realize your beloved father's loyalty knows no bounds. Though they might dwell in a realm beyond our reach today, the day will come when they will make their return; perhaps, centuries might come to pass, but they'll return. Shadow, do you want to be a witness to their triumphant homecoming?"

"Yes." As Shadow uttered the word, he knew he was trading his freedom in favor of his unwavering loyalty.

***

Zephyr's thoughts were plagued by his children's cries from all over the world. Every day, horrifying images of their merciless slaughter flashed before his eyes. Although he had severed his connection with them, their pleas still reached him, and it took everything in him to cling to his sanity.

As he neared his destination, the visions grew more frequent. More often than not, he woke up snarling and fuming with rage. His episodic outbursts had ceased to worry Zedkiel and Uriel. The duo had long gotten accustomed to their father's ailments.

"LEAVE HER BE!" Zephyr's furious voice echoed through the silent white land. "NO! GET AWAY!"

Zedkiel and Uriel exchanged a worried glance. "He must be having one of his nightmares again," Zedkiel spoke, warily observing his father.

Uriel's brow furrowed at Zedkiel's offhanded remark. "You know, they're not mere nightmares. Don't you?" Her honeyed voice turned softer as she continued, "They need him. They're trying to reach out."

The bond between vampire kind ran deeper than blood. Although many often strayed away from the King of Darkness, they primarily existed for his servitude. Without their lord, they had lost their purpose for living. Their immortality was in vain. Zephyr's heart ached for the loss. The cursed vampire couldn't help but feel the weight of responsibility.

For a moment, Zedkiel was surprised by the cold empress' display of vulnerability. "I'm aware, but it all seems like a dream now." His red eyes pensively stared off into a distance, fixed on the vast expanse of glistening white. Zedkiel chuckled in a low voice before continuing, "It's beyond my capability. Moreover, we're so far removed from the rest of the world. Everything seems so surreal – the war, the outcome, and this foreign eerie land."

Uriel sighed heavily, joining the prince on the icy ground. Zedkiel sat cross-legged at the entrance of the jagged glacier cave. There was a strange sense of serenity about him that Uriel had never seen before. "It's only natural. However, it doesn't mean I'm not pained by the loss. I care."

Zedkiel's eyes flashed with surprise at the unexpected words. The guarded empress had never before expressed herself so. There wasn't much he could say to comfort her, so he chose to assume silence. Only the whisper of a chilling breeze punctured the silence. The air was frigid and crisp with a faint aroma of distant saltwater.

"I have to admit, I never expected *you* to survive. From the start, my bets were on your sister," Uriel confessed good-naturedly. The uptight prince had been her least favorite from the council. However, after their shared journey, she had developed a sort of reverence, and even affection, for Zedkiel.

"Of course. Ariel was," Zedkiel paused, trying to come up with a word which wouldn't dishonor the late princess, "calculating. Well, I, on the other hand - I wear my heart on my sleeves." His voice was laced with bitterness.

"Well, turns out, unwavering loyalty was just what we needed for survival. Perhaps, it's not such a bad attribute." Uriel offered him an awkward smile. "It's about time. We should wake Father up."

"There will be no need for that."

The pair was startled as Zephyr appeared from the depths of the cave. Their senses failed to detect the silent figure; however, Zedkiel could detect a sympathetic look on his face. Zephyr's hollow eyes were cast down as if in a solemn prayer.

"Father, what's wrong?" he asked in a low voice.

"Son, your children – the Reapers and the Deathdealer…" Zephyr trailed off. His voice carried the weight of sorrow. "We will avenge them. Centuries might pass, but this atrocity against our kin will not go unpunished. Their death will not go in vain."

Zedkiel was speechless, but he nodded understandably. He turned away as his eyes welled up with tears. His body shuddered with unbridled rage as he tried to come to terms with the truth. His children were brutally hunted down just like the rest. Although he wanted to tear about the killers limb from limb, he could do nothing but weep silently.

"Father, time is of the essence. Before the crack of dawn, we need to perform the ritual," Uriel reminded the King of Darkness in a somber voice.

Nodding, Zephyr took his mournful son's hand. The icy tunnels led the vampires to a hidden chamber deep beneath the frozen expanse of land. The chamber was adorned with ancient symbols etched into the ice walls, casting an eerie glow in the dimly lit space. In the center, rows of intricately designed caskets lay open, waiting to receive their occupants.

The vampires, their eyes gleaming with a mix of anticipation and trepidation, stood in a triangle formation, facing one another. A subtle smile graced Lord Zephyr's lips. Despite the odds, he couldn't help but feel proud of his children. "You stood by my side through the rough storms. I never imagined it possible, things would come to this."

"Father, we didn't stay because we're bound by some oath," Zedkiel spoke honestly, eager to express his genuine devotion to his father after having lost his own children.

"Neither did we stay because we feared for our lives," Uriel added.

As Zephyr peered at his children, he could almost feel emotions welling up in his chest. The apprehension of their inevitable fate hung heavy in the air. "Your faithfulness is commendable. However, you must know; there's a possibility this slumber might be eternal. Should we remain undiscovered for the rest of eternity, the spell of our dormancy will remain intact."

Uriel and Zedkiel exchanged a resigned gaze before nodding solemnly. The vampires knew that their commitment and the power of their shared blood would be enough to bind them to their fate.

The vampires chanted in a low, commanding voice. “We gather here tonight, bound by our immortality. We pledge our lives and our essence to the deep embrace of the ocean's depths.”

With a flick of his wrist, Zephyr drew a small ceremonial dagger and sliced open his palm. Crimson blood welled up, dripping onto the pristine ice beneath their feet. The two other vampires followed suit, cutting their palms in turn and allowing their own blood to mingle with their father’s.

As the drops of blood fused together, a radiant light enveloped the chamber. A surge of energy coursed through their veins, binding their fates inextricably together. Once again, the children felt the depths of their father’s sufferings. They felt the agony of his curse. The slaughter of every child of the night flashed before their eyes. The pain was crushing, but none of the vampires broke away.

The air grew heavy as their combined energy filled the space. The ground trembled beneath their feet as the ritual reached its crescendo. The ancient symbols etched into the ice walls flickered and glowed. Cracks snaked their way across the icy surface, splitting it apart. Chunks of ice tumbled from the ceiling, crashing to the ground with thunderous roars. The rumbling intensified, causing deep crevices to form in the chamber floor. Crystalline stalactites shattered, shattering the eerie silence with a cacophony of splintering ice.

The vampires' grip on each other tightened as silent tears streamed down their faces. They could feel their muscles freezing, blending with ice. As they lay in the caskets, they could feel their senses fading. They sank deeper into slumber.

As the caskets closed, a final echo resonated through the chamber. "I await the day when our dark spirits would rise once more."

Chapter 16
Vampire God

Shadow couldn't bring himself to bow down to Cain's will. Although he was bound to him by a blood oath, he felt no sense of devotion towards him. It was still difficult to come to terms with reality. In the span of a few years, he had lost his home, his family, and his purpose for existence. For eons, he built his strength to serve Lord Zephyr's goals, but it all came to nothing. What little link he had with the king of darkness had disintegrated into nothingness. Everything Shadow held dear had crumbled before his eyes. Now, under Cain's reign, he lived for only hope of his former master's return. The world outside the sanctuary had turned into hell. The memories still continued to haunt him day and night, and he could acquire no peace. As he lay brooding in his chamber, he contemplated the purpose of his existence yet again.

"Survival," Devon responded to his unspoken uncertainties. "That's what keeps us going. That's what it has always been about."

Shadow eyed him warily. After having lost his family, he had begun to distrust friends and foes alike. "Has it?"

Looking back, he could recall feeling tempted by supernatural abilities. However, he walked the path of darkness for survival. It's true that Zephyr's thirst for vengeance motivated him. "Something else tied us together. Although there was strife amongst us, we didn't spend our old days watching our backs."

"Yeah. No one can be trusted anymore. It can't be helped, so quit brooding. Come," Devon insisted. The two vampires shared a chamber in the fortress. Although Shadow didn't reciprocate the sentiments, Devon had grown fond of the vampire. In fact, he tended to Shadow's wounds when he first arrived. "The council meeting is about to begin."

Devon never rebelled against Zephyr, but he could never completely align with his motivations, either. Despite his hesitations, he remained loyal to Ariel. Her unexpected death only fueled his faithfulness toward her.

"I'll be there in a minute," Shadow answered grudgingly.

The gloominess in his chamber reminded him of that dark derelict building. It was enveloped in perpetual darkness, save for a single stained glass window that filtered feeble rays of moonlight, casting a mosaic of ethereal colors upon the decaying tapestries that adorned the walls. A grand four-poster bed, draped in faded velvet curtains, stood against one side, its intricately carved wooden frame showing signs of age. A worn armchair rested near the window, its once opulent upholstery now tattered and threadbare. Cobwebs clung to the corners of the chamber, weaving a macabre tapestry of neglect.

The silence was broken only by the distant echoes of dripping water. Once again, his thoughts led him back to the moment he lost his family. Had he been stronger, he could've saved Star and Dorothy. His own limitations had become a bane of his existence. He yearned to go out into the night – to hunt down those monsters, but his wounds hadn't completely healed yet.

Sighing heavily, Shadow got off the bed. Although he hadn't recovered his strength, his presence was required at the council meeting. The meetings were held in the grand hall and were led by Cain, of course. Devon, Caius, and two other vampires, Elizabeth and Samantha, also attended the meetings. Once, Elizabeth was a trained assassin. How Cain managed to find her remained a mystery, just like Samantha's origins.

As Shadow winded down the stairs, he could hear the agonizing screams from the dungeons. Just like Star, many vampires had lost their sanity due to starvation. However, for some reason known only to him, Cain refused to put them to mercy.

"Welcome, my trusted companions," he greeted the vampires in an uncharacteristically cheerful voice. For a few days, he had been in quite an unpleasant mood due to low rations of blood.

The rest of the vampires silently took their seats. None wished to attend the meeting, save for Elizabeth, who served as his advisor. "You look pleased," she mentioned the obvious.

"Indeed, I am pleased! As it turns out, a herb has been found in Zimbabwe which counters the venom found in neo's bite. In fact, a small dose of the plant is lethal to them."

Shadow's ears perked up at the news. It was, indeed, worth celebrating. Caius face split into a smile as he suggested, "If that's so, we should start taking them out."

Elizabeth, however, disagreed, "No. I think not. Humans are quick to adapt to such circumstances. If we don't take action on a large scale, they'll just come up with an antidote. We need to find a strategy that will ensure mass slaughter."

Although Cain trusted Elizabeth with his life, Shadow could detect something awry about her. However, he couldn't quite put his finger on his suspicions. Elizabeth emanated an aura of mystery and danger. Her smooth ebony skin accentuated an otherworldly aura. Her deep eyes remained impassive like hollow pits. Sharp, angular features framed her face. Silken locks of raven-black hair cascaded down to her narrow shoulders. A form-fitting jet-black attire clung to her lithe, sinewy form.

Although Shadow could barely stand the pompous vampire, he couldn't help but agree with her. "I stand with Elizabeth. Our enemies have always been sly. We have to assume similar tactics. We have to let them think they have annihilated us while we build our strength in shadows."

His words were met by a self-satisfied smile from Elizabeth's end; meanwhile, Devon and Cain fell into a contemplative silence.

"How do we build our strength?" Cain asked.

Caius looked at the ruler indignantly. "What do you mean by that? Just like we always have! That is if you bend your senseless rules a little."

Although Caius did Cain's bidding, he didn't agree with his ways. The clandestine society served as a sanctuary for the vampires, but Cain's pride hindered their growth.

"The rules are in place to ensure the discretion of our society. I'm sure you understand -"

Cain's words were cut off mid-sentence as Shadow slammed his fist on the table. "Don't you play us for fools! These rules you impose upon us are senseless and serve no purpose other than to maintain your grip on power. You silence dissent and force us into submission, ensuring your reign goes unquestioned. How long do you think you can keep up this charade?"

From the moment Shadow passed through the walls of this fortress, he had felt enslaved. Shadow was almost trembling with rage as he voiced out all his suppressed thoughts. It was beyond his belief how someone could be so drunk on power. Cain refused to see the consequences of his actions.

At Shadow's outburst, Cain couldn't help but smirk. "Ah, so you have found the courage to challenge me, have you? Pray tell, what gives you the audacity to question my rule?"

Before Shadow could retort, Devon mustered the courage to voice his opinions. "He's right. Don't you see? Our community is weak! They're remaining vigilant. What will happen if we get discovered? You need to build an army. Just because you're afraid someone might overthrow your ridiculous monarch does not mean you're safe."

Blood rushed into Cain's face. His eyes darted from one vampire to another; however, he found no support. Finally, Samantha spoke up in a rather timid voice, "Cain, it's best we start training. We should be able to defend ourselves."

Shadow eyed the mysterious vampire with intrigue. She was so coy she barely looked like a vampire. However, Cain's eyes softened at his words. Gingerly holding her hand, he nodded slowly. "I believe we're stronger together than we're apart. However, we must do what's necessary for our survival. So, what do you propose?"

"Moon Village," Caius answered at once, his emerald eyes sparkling. If the whispers were true, there already was a small discrete community of vampires in the region. "I'll build my empire in the north."

"I'll head to the east," Shadow proclaimed. Everyone was caught off-guard at the declaration, but Caius had a knowing look in his eyes. Shadow had always reigned in the south alongside his father, so the revelation was surprising, after all. After a pause, Shadow explained, "There's a small community of vampires in the east. They have no sense of direction."

"Then, I should take the South," Elizabeth exclaimed in a bubbly voice, flashing Shadow a grin.

"Fine by me," he answered in a cold voice.

"I'll overlook the West alongside Samantha." Cain offered the woman a warm smile. "How does that work for you, my queen?"

Samantha flushed at the term of endearment. "I'm pleased with your decision," she answered in a hushed voice.

The rest of the vampires were greatly intrigued by their relationship, but no one remarked upon it. There was nothing remarkable about Samantha to capture the brute vampire's attention. Her eyes were a muddy shade of brown, tinged with red. Her pallor looked almost sickly, and her flaxen hair had a rough appearance of a haystack. She had no remarkable fighting talents known to the vampires, yet Cain was completely enthralled by her.

Cain's grin widened at her response. "I'm glad," he answered with a hint of relief in his voice.

No universal purpose connected the race of vampires any longer. No pact was sealed between the council members. Every creature of the night lived for survival, yet their own selfish motivations bound them to his will.

***

Shadow possessed an unquenchable thirst for vengeance that surpassed his need for blood. His impatience grew with each healed wound. He could barely wait to fly out of his nest – to exit the clandestine society with senseless rules. Although he had successfully managed to convince Cain to bend them, he knew the older vampire would continue surveying him. No matter how far he went, he'd never be able to escape the clutches of his. However, the flames of vengeance burned brighter. After all these centuries, he could finally understand his lord's motivations – his rage at the unjust circumstances.

He began his journey by traversing treacherous landscapes, traversing vast deserts, and scaling formidable mountain ranges. He used his supernatural abilities to blend seamlessly into the human world, disguising himself as a weary traveler seeking shelter and companionship. His knowledge of ancient cultures and languages aided him in adapting to the customs and traditions of the lands he passed through.

Whispers carried on the wind, hinting at the existence of a small community of vampires nestled within the borders of China. Shadow, driven by a need for camaraderie, sought out the elusive group. After years of discreet investigations, he finally discovered their secluded haven.

Deep in the heart of rural China, nestled amidst rolling hills and rice fields, lay the sacred haven of Xiangyuan Valley. This valley, hidden away from prying eyes, boasted an ethereal beauty. Lush, emerald-green forests blanketed the landscape, while a crystal-clear river meanders through the valley. The refuge remained secure due to its remote location and rugged terrain. Tucked away in the depths of the countryside, its treacherous paths, dense forests, and rocky cliffs made it inaccessible to humans and neos, alike. Once Shadow regained his wings, the valley became the perfect setting to establish his dynasty.

After much investigation, Shadow finally decided to approach the grand mansion nestled within the mist-shrouded valley. The moon's pale light illuminated the ancient stones, casting an eerie glow upon his path.

As he neared the entrance, the doors creaked open, revealing a young lanky boy. Shadow recognized him as the messenger he had met earlier at a ship harbor. The boy had his transformation when he was only fourteen, and the signs of his youth remained in his eager, opal eyes.

The weight of anticipation hung in the air as the lone messenger greeted him cautiously, "Welcome, Lord Shadow."

"Marcus, you can call me Shadow," he corrected the boy as Marcus helped him out of his traveling cloak.

Marcus' eyes glinted with recognition as he acknowledged the formidable power emanating from the newcomer. "We have awaited your arrival. Our kind is in need of a leader, one who possesses the strength and wisdom to guide us through these perilous times." His voice was laced with a mix of curiosity and reverence.

Shadow couldn't help but observe the dimly lit hallways and the deadly silence. "Where are the rest?" he inquired, perplexed.

"They fear what you may bring."

Shadow remained silent, his gaze fixed upon the messenger, regarding him with a measured gaze. He understood their apprehension, for trust was a fragile currency among their kind, earned through time and proven intentions.

"The responsibility of leadership rests not in lofty promises, but in actions that speak of the purpose. In Lord Zephyr's name, my sole purpose is survival. I believe, our common resolve unites us. I shall demonstrate my worth and earn the trust of your hidden brethren."

Marcus' face gave away his curiosity. He motioned for the leader to follow, leading him through the mansion's labyrinthine corridors, their footsteps the only sound in the haunting stillness.

As they traversed the dark halls, Shadow's senses were heightened, his eyes scanning the surroundings for any hidden observers. The mansion seemed to hold its breath as if anticipating the revelation of their enigmatic visitor.

Finally, they reached a hidden chamber, the door revealing a sliver of light amidst the darkness. The messenger pushed it open, revealing a gathering of vampires concealed within. Their appearance reflected their somber circumstances. Clad in once-fine silk garments, now tattered, their attire reflected their former grandeur. Symbols of their Chinese heritage – an embroidery of lotus flowers – adorned their garment. Emaciated and disheveled, their gaunt faces bore traces of exhaustion. Yet, amid their downtrodden state, an air of muted power emanated from a few individuals. Their eyes glittered with similar defiance, reflected in Shadow's eyes.

The room was cloaked in an air of cautious watchfulness. Shadow stepped forward, his presence commanding yet serene, and spoke in a voice that resonated with quiet authority, "I come not as an invader, but as a protector," he began, his words echoing through the chamber. "I understand your apprehension, your instinct to remain hidden. It is a sentiment born of centuries of survival. But now, I offer you something more—a chance to thrive, to reclaim our rightful place in this world."

The vampires watched him intently, their gazes shifting between skepticism and flickers of hope. They had heard whispers of Shadow's arrival, tales of his unparalleled martial prowess, and his ability to survive undetected for centuries. Now, faced with his enigmatic presence, they sensed the promise of strength and salvation.

Shadow continued, his words carefully chosen to inspire trust, "I have traveled far, enduring trials and tribulations to arrive at this moment," he declared, his voice unwavering. "I seek not dominion over you, but unity—a covert dynasty that safeguards our existence and preserves our ancient legacy."

A murmur of intrigue rippled through the chamber, mingling with a newfound sense of curiosity. Although uncertainty was etched upon their faces, Shadow sensed their desperation.

"Let us stand together, hidden yet powerful," he concluded, his tone imbued with quiet conviction. "For within the depths of secrecy lies our strength. Trust me, and together, we shall forge a path to protect our kind and ensure our survival in this ever-changing world."

One vampire stepped forward. He was a sturdy man in his late thirties. *A warrior,* Shadow thought as he observed the scar marring his face. His sleek black hair was tied up in a ponytail, and he donned a cheongsam blouse. Introducing himself as Xiang Li, he continued, "Tell us, Shadow, what will be our role in this new dynasty? How can we aid you in preserving our existence?" His voice was mingled with authority and distrust in equal measures.

Shadow responded, each word measured, "Our roles shall be many, but our foremost duty is secrecy. We must remain hidden from the prying eyes of mortals, for they would seek to eradicate our kind. Each of you has unique talents and skills to contribute. Some shall be protectors, safeguarding our hidden enclaves, while others shall gather intelligence and ensure our anonymity within the mortal world. Some would be assigned to procure bloodstock.

A sense of purpose began to settle among the vampires, their doubts slowly dissipating. They recognized in Shadow a leader who could inspire and guide them in this clandestine existence.

"United, we shall prevail," Shadow declared, his voice resonating with a quiet strength. "Our dynasty shall remain concealed from those who hunt us. We shall blend among the shadows, adapting and evolving, while holding steadfast to the ancient traditions that bind us."

With those words, the small community of vampires bowed their heads in acceptance and reverence. Their destinies intertwined with that of Shadow, they pledged their loyalty and unwavering commitment to the dynasty that was yet to be unveiled to the world.

Under the rule of Shadow, the vampire dynasty in China began to flourish, and he proved himself a wise and just leader. His drive was fueled by inextinguishable flames of vengeance. It was remarkable how he built a dynasty greater than his father's under such perilous circumstances. Unlike Cain, the secrecy and strength of his reign was rooted in trust, integrity, and discipline. Once he replenished the blood supply and brought order, he learned about the secretive talents and martial prowess of the Chinese community and utilized this talent for the development of vampire society.

As the dynasty prospered, Shadow sought to establish a council within the community that would oversee their secretive operations and maintain harmony among the various vampire clans. The council comprised representatives from both the clans, Feng Yang and Rishi Ren. The meetings were held every month. Initially,

Shadow focused on three crucial aspects of the community – blood supply, espionage, and secrecy.

As the council sessions continued, each clan brought their unique abilities to the table, and the vampire dynasty's strength grew exponentially. Shadow marveled at the exceptional talents hidden within his community. With each clan specializing in secrecy, council, blood supply, and warriors, they formed a cohesive and formidable force.

The clan, known as Rishi Ren, was assigned the responsibility of replenishment of blood supply. Comprised of veiled dancers, the members of these clans performed intricate dances in the darkness, mesmerizing their victims and drawing blood without leaving a trace. Moreover, they could infiltrate the human world unnoticed and extract vital information. Shadow's appreciation for their skill in secrecy and sustenance earned the clan a significant role in safeguarding the vampire community.

Li Wei, an influential woman of timeless beauty, was the leader of the Rishi Ren clan. She was a character of mysterious allure and quiet dignity. A master of deception and stealth, Li Wei's movements were as graceful as a moonlit dance, and her silvery laughter echoed through the shadows, leaving her enemies captivated and ensnared in her web of mystery. Beneath her serene exterior, she concealed a shrewd mind, always strategizing to protect her clan and ensure the survival of the vampire dynasty.

The other clan, Feng Yang, was a tribe of warriors and assassins. Their martial prowess made them the frontline protectors of the vampire community. Xiang Li was the leader of this clan, and Shadow trained and appointed him as the guardian of the secret community, entrusting him with the responsibility of keeping the dynasty safe. Moreover, the skilled Sifu not only trained his subordinates but also helped Shadow advance his martial prowess.

The vampires of the Feng Yang clan trained in the tranquil training grounds. The council had decided to train secret assassins to hunt down the neos in an efficient manner.

Although Shadow was considered among the most deadly vampires alive, his defeat against the neo, his failure to protect his family, had sparked a fire within him. He was driven to become stronger – so strong that no neo could stand a chance against him. As a leader, he wanted to become an inspiration for the clan, and without fail, he had managed to do so. Everyone in his small dynasty looked up to him. Despite his exceptional strength, he strived to become stronger, encouraging the rest to follow.

Shadow stood poised, facing Xiang Li, the revered leader of the clan. The air crackled with anticipation as the two masters prepared to engage in a spirited bout of Chinese martial arts.

"Focus your mind, Shadow," Xiang Li advised in a low voice. "Let the energy flow through you, harmonize with the movements."

With the grace of a predator, Xiang Li struck, his strikes swift and precise. Shadow deftly parried each blow, his movements becoming more fluid and assured. Their clash echoed through the courtyard, drawing the admiration of other vampires who were practicing their own forms nearby.

As Shadow missed a strike, Xiang Li continued to impart invaluable wisdom. "In stillness, find strength. In movement, find purpose. Your rage and shame distracts you. You must let go of the past, Shadow."

"Never," Shadow's eyes burned crimson as he let his fury take over his senses. For a moment, the vision of Star's beheaded form flashed before his eyes. Gritting his teeth, he swung his katana once more. However, Xiang Li blocked the attack with a swift *Peng*—a powerful palm strike aimed at Shadow's chest. Reacting swiftly, Shadow countered with a *Beng*—blocking the attack and diverting the force to the side.

"Good, Shadow," Xiang Li commended, his voice calm yet encouraging. There was a hint of amusement in his voice. He had never before seen a warrior, who channeled his emotions to establish acute focus. "Now, let us see your *Peng Jin* in action." Other vampires watched them in awe, trying to mimic the deadly dance to the best of their abilities.

Shadow's focus intensified, channeling his inner strength into his next move. With a burst of energy, he unleashed his own *Peng Jin*, sending a wave of power rippling through his arm and meeting Xiang Li's force head-on.

The exchange continued, the two martial artists engaging in a mesmerizing dance of strikes and counterstrikes. Xiang Li's footwork was swift and precise, evading Shadow's advances with almost preternatural grace. He moved like a phantom, making himself a challenging target.

"Remember, Shadow, every technique has a purpose. You can't get stuck up in your memories – in your old ways," Xiang Li reminded, his voice carrying the weight of years of experience. "We're not beasts, who fight without technique."

"I mean no disrespect, but your bickering is the biggest distraction." Shadow spat blood as Xiang Li's katana made contact with his jaw. "Of course, I'm nothing like those savages."

Xiang Li continued striking his mentee relentlessly. Narrowing his eyes, he continued, "Precisely! Which is why you must not let your primal urges rule over your senses. Your energy must flow seamlessly, like water through a river. There's so much hatred in your eyes; it clouds your vision."

"It fuels my strength!" Shadow exclaimed, adjusting his approach, combining fluid footwork with precise strikes. His movements became more fluid, the grace of his form now blending harmoniously with his techniques.

In a daring move, Xiang Li executed a series of *Fa Jing* strikes—a quick and explosive release of power. Shadow, undaunted, met each strike with deft blocks and counterattacks. Their strikes resonated through the courtyard, punctuating the night with a symphony of martial prowess.

"Excellent, Shadow!" Xiang Li praised, a hint of satisfaction in his eyes. "Your understanding of *Fa Jing* is growing."

Shadow couldn't help but smirk as Xiang Li ate his words. As the intensity of the duel reached its zenith, a sudden shift occurred. Shadow launched a series of *Chin Na* joint locks, seeking to immobilize his Sifu. With swift precision, he targeted Xiang Li's wrist, seeking to control his movements.

However, the master's reflexes were nothing short of extraordinary. In a breathtaking display, Xiang Li countered Shadow's *Chin Na* with a fluid *Hua Jin* redirection, deftly breaking free from the lock and seamlessly transitioning into a counterstrike.

Their movements became a blur of speed and precision, each martial artist pushing the other to the limits of their skill. The duel continued, reflecting the rage they harbored for the loss of their fellow kinsmen.

***

The laws of their little kingdom kept Shadow chained. Every day, he was struck by a state of restlessness. Although the rest of the vampires had made peace with their clandestine existence, Shadow couldn't come to terms with it. The pacifism of his fellow kins infuriated him to no ends. The vampires had significantly grown in numbers and power, but they were still unwilling to strike back – to retaliate or seek vengeance for the comrades they had lost. Although Shadow had built a family and an army at Xiangyuan Valley, they remained unaware about Shadow's true purpose. He lived by one single principle – vengeance. *Every vampire on Earth be damned if I don't get my retribution.* However, Xiang Li often witnessed glimpses of his true darkness.

Decades had gone by, yet Dorothy's hopeful words still rang in his head. Star's helpless form as her head was severed from her body was still fresh in his mind. Time and again, he had raised the matter before Cain to no avail. However, he tried his luck once again.

"They'll keep growing in number. Should we get discovered and a war unfolds, do you plan to run away with your tail between your legs?"

"You'll watch your mouth if you know what's good for you," Cain tried to intimidate him into silence, but Shadow didn't give in.

Coming from Cain, the warning was amusing, but he chose to keep a straight face. The older vampire was comfortably seated on a dragon chair with Samantha on his left, and Caius on his right, meanwhile, Elizabeth and Xiang Li sat on Shadow's either side. The vampires were gathered in the inner hall of Shadow's grand mansion, and Cain was surrounded by the emperor's trained assassins, yet he had the nerve to make empty threats.

"Right. You'll isolate yourself at an island, and stay hidden until the war dies down. Later, you might build a pathetic empire, and revel in its glory just for compensation," Shadow snapped. His eyes glowed red from suppressed rage, and Xiang Li placed a gentle hand on his shoulder to calm him down. Although he generally remained calm, Cain always somehow managed to aggravate Shadow.

Cain couldn't believe his ears. He could sense a rebellion from Shadow, and he only knew a single effective way to rule effectively. "I'll have your tongue if you continue spouting this nonsense."

"No, you won't. Look at the size of my army." Shadow knew he could easily overpower his pitiful leader, but he didn't want any more vampire blood spilled. Why Cain chose to make appearance at council meetings when he only wished to dictate, Shadow could only guess.

Composing himself, Cain tried to reason with the blood-thirsty vampire, "Look, Shadow, we can't make any ripples. We can't stir the beast."

"It's too risky, pal. Try to understand the consequences," Caius agreed, blindly following the ruler. It was beyond Shadow's understanding how Cain had managed to get into Caius head when the younger vampire had been loyal only to Princess Ariel. Falling prey to his fear and desperation, he had turned into Cain's lap dog. It was beyond disappointing and shameful. Samantha obviously always stood by Cain's side. However, Elizabeth had rather divided loyalties.

Throughout the debate, Elizabeth remained silent. Feigning disinterest, she painted her nails in a shade of burgundy. Finally, she cleared her throat, and spoke deliberately, "Cain's right. We can't just make a declaration of war."

Somehow, her nonchalant attitude irritated everyone but Shadow. "Oh? He's right?" he asked with a hint of skepticism and warning in his voice.

"Of course. You're hot-headed and impulsive. Had it not been for Cain, your blind loyalty to the dead would have gotten you killed. Oh, it nearly did," she spoke languidly, flashing him a grin.

"There's a fine boundary between courage and stupidity, and I assure you, I don't mean to cross it," Shadow responded calmly. He returned her provocation with a smirk. "So, you agree with Cain's methods of ruling."

"Correct," she replied in a clipped voice.

"Are you implying, you wish to remain helpless? You don't wish to have your army trained by my men?" His words were lost on the other attendees of the meeting. However, Elizabeth's eyes widened in response.

Laughing sheepishly, she said, "No, Shadow, I'm not implying anything. I'm just saying, you could practice a little bit of diplomacy."

"And I say, you could do a little less without it."

In secrecy, Elizabeth ployed with Shadow, but she was as cunning as they come. The young warrior employed clever strategies to strengthen her empire. She allied with Caius to acquire rations of blood for Moon Village had an exceptionally good supply. Due to his association with the late formidable princess, even the neos never dared to pillage the village. Meanwhile, Elizabeth sent her juvenile vampires to train with Shadow. The Chinese' martial prowess was talked about all over the world. Over time, Shadow had managed to built a large army of trained assassins. His' was the only kingdom which made any attempts to avenge the fallen vampires.

The Chinese assassins skillfully targeted the neos without alerting humans or Lucifer's forces. They used a rare breed of a poisonous plant, *Lunarbane* to secretively poison neos. Somehow, the plant's traces were flushed out of the system before the death of the victim. More importantly, there was no way humans could trace back the poison to vampires. They couldn't even begin to figure out the cause of unexpected deaths. Consequently, they found faults in the serum, giving rise to fear, doubts, and uncertainty. Year by year, more and more people turned away from the serum, growing distrustful of the scientific community.

Such secret operations brought a sense of satisfaction to Shadow. Unlike Cain, he wasn't a sheep, waiting to get devoured by wolves. Not for a moment, did he forget his own predatory nature. Although the retaliation gave him a sense of purpose, the idea of the assassination had been Elizabeth's. The warrior of the South impressed, infuriated, and intrigued him in equal measures, but heaven forbid he ever expressed that.

The heated argument between Shadow and Elizabeth was interrupted by Caius. "Look, Morgan monopolized the supply of his serum. I'll give credit to the man for his genius. He even managed to prolong men's lifespan, but he's just a crippled old man now."

"For now, yes," Shadow continued arguing, "Just as long as our existence remains a secret. Don't forget the scientific community doesn't work alone. Lucifer Morningstar continues to support them from the shadows."

"It's true, they bested Lord Zephyr," Elizabeth finally put in a word in Shadow's favor. "Do you seriously think you stand a chance? There's no way Morgan would take the formula of the serum to his grave. The invention is his bloody legacy. A single sighting of a vampire would lead to our hunt inevitably."

"Thank you!" Shadow exclaimed, and Elizabeth genuinely smiled in response. Turning to face Cain, he continued exasperatedly, "Quite honestly, I can't even begin to understand the root of your hesitation. I mean, if we use Lunarbane to poison them, the neos won't be none the wiser. From the start of time, they've attributed plagues to any calamity that has befallen them."

No one could disagree with Shadow's argument, yet an inexplicable fear gripped their hearts. After all the struggles and sufferings, their survival could be considered nothing less than a miracle, and Cain refused to meet the same tragic end as his master.

"We must wait a few –"

"Osmund still walks amongst us!" Shadow spoke through clenched teeth. His eyes flashed crimson at the mention of his family's murderer.

"Shadow," Cain began softly, trying to reason with the infuriated man, "Vengeance became Lord Zephyr's downfall."

"It was his strength." Shadow let out a low chuckle. "His misplaced trust, unchecked pride, and reckless decisions became his downfall."

There was a look of concern on Elizabeth's face. Although she deeply cared for Shadow, she hid it behind her cutting words and sarcastic remarks. "Cain, the strength of one solitary assassin sufficed to eradicate an entire population of werewolves in the east," she recounted. "A masterstroke executed without a hint of suspicion; the world believed a plague had claimed them. This triumph shall fortify our cause."

Her tone turned somber as she continued, "It is high time that we reclaim our power and fight back against those who threaten us. Let it not be forgotten that vampire blood has been spilled all too frequently. The time has come to mend our fractured unity and rise once again."

Vampires didn't age, but Cain felt wearied by his years. Sighing heavily, he gave in to the younger vampire's demands. "Fine. We'll fight back."

"What?" Shadow shared an astonished glance with Elizabeth, who had a look of victory plastered across her face. Convincing the leader turned out to be easier than they had expected. Shadow had dreaded three to four futile council meetings. If push came to shove, he had been willing to go as far as threatening Cain. Fortunately, it didn't come to that.

"You heard me," Cain rolled his eyes, "Look, you might think you know better than me, but in the midst of the hunt, I managed to survive. Don't forget that I gave you shelter."

Shadow heaved a weary sigh. "Here we go again."

"We're going to have rules in place to ensure the secrecy of our existence."

"Well, of course."

Before they could start bickering again, Elizabeth interrupted their conversation, "So, what's our plan?"

Cain turned towards her with a knowing look. "Well, shouldn't you propose something? Aren't you the clever one?" Shadow couldn't help but snort as Cain's remark was met by an indignant look from Elizabeth. "Don't look so surprised. Did you seriously think you would start an assassination training right under my nose and I wouldn't find out?"

Elizabeth quickly composed herself and spoke in a dignified voice, "Well, you have to admit, it's a pretty good plan."

"So it is. What do you say, Samantha? Should we continue this operation?" Cain turned to his wife, whose attention was preoccupied with a raven at the window.

Her eyes lit up at the unexpected attention as she responded in a honeyed voice, "Definitely! I want to see neo blood spilled."

"There shall be no spilling of blood," Cain said, turning to face Shadow with a hint of warning in his voice. "Our approach to the termination of the neos shall be characterized by the utmost precision and organization. We aim for a resolution devoid of unnecessary violence. To achieve this end, we'll employ only trained assassins. Poison will be our only weapon in this fight."

"I understand the conditions very well," Shadow responded, his brows furrowing out of irritation. Xiang Li watched the exchange in silence, seeing right through Shadow's façade of composure.

"I don't wish to get involved in this operation," Caius stood up abruptly with a resolute look on his face. "Moon Village already has a reputation. They'll suspect us before anyone else."

Shadow nodded understandingly. Moreover, Caius already had the responsibility of the collection of blood supplies. "Fine by me."

As the room gradually emptied, only Elizabeth and Shadow remained. The air seemed to thicken with an unspoken tension, a palpable connection that went beyond mere words.

A subtle smile played at the corner of Elizabeth's lips, her gaze locked onto Shadow's. She traced the rim of her wine glass with a delicate finger, her movements deliberate. Without a word, she offered him a silent toast, her eyes inviting him to partake in the private victory they seemed to share.

Shadow met her gaze, his demeanor poised. "Thank you," he repeated in a hushed voice. No words were enough to demonstrate the gratitude he felt toward her. "You don't plan on sticking with *his* conditions, do you?"

Elizabeth let out a throaty laugh. "Hell, no."

"Good," Shadow's crimson eyes darkened as he moved closer to Elizabeth. "Then, I'll bring you a trophy of

Osmund's head. What's one less neo in the grand scheme of their imminent doom? I shall have my vengeance!"

And thus, the cycle of retribution continued, an unbroken legacy passed down from one beast to another. In the dark veil of the night, the sins of the past continued echoing into eternity.

Epilogue

In the heart of the icy expanse, the frigid wind whispered the land's long-forgotten secrets. Despite the hushed conversation, an otherworldly stillness reigned. The breeze itself seemed to crystallize, and icebergs loomed ominously in the distance. The pale sun hung threateningly low on the horizon, foreshadowing the imminent arrival of darkness.

"Come on, Lawrence! We should really think about our safety first," Evelyn, a renowned marine archeologist urged, her voice laced with concern. "It might be wiser to seek shelter and wait until tomorrow when the sun is brighter before we continue our exploration."

A shiver went down Evelyn's spine as her gut instincts warned her against impending doom, but her colleague, Lawrence, remained adamant about sealing his fate. He continued directing the spotlight of his submersible to illuminate the mysterious coffins, his eyes gleaming with a mixture of exhilaration and trepidation. The harsh light reflected off the glacial walls, revealing the depths that held the secrets of time.

"Evelyn, they've been buried here for centuries!" he stated the obvious. As the feeble flashlight pierced through the darkness, illuminating the wooden boxes, Evelyn instinctively reached for the cross resting between her collarbones.

"Lawrence, I want to leave now," she spoke sternly, but her partner continued operating a complex array of controls. He navigated the submersible's robotic arms, which extended into the icy depths.

"Hey, relax! There's nothing to worry about," he tried to reassure her, chuckling slightly. "Are you seriously scared of coffins?"

As the submersible's arms reached the ocean floor, they grasped onto the massive wooden coffins resting among the submerged rocks. With a series of mechanical whirrs, the coffins were slowly brought to the surface, and the marine archeologists followed their ascent.

Evelyn stood back, staring at the mysterious boxes with a look of apprehension across her face. Although Lawrence shared her expression, he knelt by their side, tracing the surface of the largest coffin with his palm. "It's beautiful," he spoke in a hushed voice, and Evelyn couldn't help but agree with him.

"They are."

The centuries-old wood glistened with an ethereal beauty, contrasting sharply with the bleakness of the surroundings. Hesitantly, Evelyn inched closer to the coffins, and a sense of reverence washed over her. They were really a sight to behold. Despite having been buried beneath the ocean's depths for an eternity, their mahogany surfaces gleamed as if freshly polished. The wood retained a rich, deep hue, and the intricated carvings adorning each coffin were a reflection of a long-gone era.

Lawrence's hands trembled as he reached for the coffin's lid, his fingers brushing against the carved engravings. As he carefully opened the lid, the mournful creaking of its hinges pierced through the whispering winds. A gasp of awe escaped the duo at the fascinating sight. Inside the coffin lay three mummies, cocooned in pristine-white linen, unaffected by time.

"Evelyn, can you believe it? This could rewrite history!" Lawrence's eyes glinted with excitement, his breath visible in the chilled air.

A shudder went through Evelyn's body as her eyes fell upon the mummies within. She could almost feel the weight of time pressing down on her, a silent warning from the past. Somehow, she could sense the otherworldly energy – the sinister forces at play. Her voice quivered as she insisted, "Lawrence, we can't tamper with unknown forces."

Paying her no heed, Lawrence continued assessing the mummies with his gloved hand. His enthusiasm remained undaunted. "Evelyn, think of the knowledge, the discoveries -"

"Lawrence," she breathed, her voice barely more than a whisper. "Please! We need to get out of here!"

Lawrence's eyes were alight with excitement, his words tumbling out in a rush. "Evelyn, we've struck gold here! These coffins, these mummies - they're the most well-preserved specimens ever found. Can you believe? This discovery could redefine our entire careers, even the field itself! Imagine our findings displayed at a museum!"

Evelyn's expression remained cautious as she tried to reason with her partner. "Lawrence, I can't help but feel a sense of unease. We're treading in the realm of the dead here."

He chuckled lightly, dismissing her concerns. "Oh, Evelyn, you've always been one for the mysterious and the superstitious. But we're scientists. We deal in facts, not folklore."

Evelyn's gaze hardened as she met his eyes. "I understand the excitement, but these mummies have rested beneath the sea for untold years, and there's a reason they've remained undisturbed."

"Yes, and the reason happens to be the obvious. No one else ever dared to explore the mysteries of this icy land."

A feeling of dread gripped her heart, and the urgency in her voice grew. "Lawrence, we're going to return them to where we found them – to the depths of the sea."

Lawrence's enthusiasm wavered at her somber voice, his brow furrowing in disbelief. "Are you serious? You think we should just leave this incredible discovery untouched?"

Evelyn nodded, her voice firm. "Yes, Lawrence. I do."

He couldn't hide his incredulity, his tone tinged with sarcasm. "So, what, we're supposed to throw away the opportunity of a lifetime because you believe in ancient curses? Come on, Evelyn! We have a chance to make history!"

"Sometimes, history is best left undisturbed."

Their debate was abruptly shattered by the sharp flap of wings. The sound cut through the air like a chilling prelude, freezing both Lawrence and Evelyn in their tracks. Their heads snapped towards the source of the disturbance, eyes widening in disbelief.

"What was that?"

Before Evelyn could answer his question, Lawrence was engulfed by a swirling vortex of movement. The air filled with the frenzied rustle of wings that drowned out all other sounds. Bats – a dark, frenetic frenzy of them – swarmed around him, a swirling mass that seemed to materialize from the very shadows.

Evelyn's heart raced as she watched in shock, unable to do anything but watch the surreal spectacle unfolding before her. White linen fluttered like ghostly remnants in the empty coffins. Lawrence's screams pierced the stillness as the bats continued to engulf him. In the blink of an eye, he vanished, swallowed by the whirlwind of creatures that had materialized seemingly out of nowhere.

Evelyn struggled to comprehend the scene before her. And then, as swiftly as they had appeared, the bats dissipated into thin air. The frenzied flapping faded, leaving her alone amidst the chilling silence, staring at the empty coffins.

Amid the desolate expanse of the Antarctic, only one woman bore witness to the unfathomable horror that unfolded that day. Years had gone by, but the spectral sight of bats and linen disappearing into the abyss continued haunting her.

Following the incident, rumors swirled like snowflakes in a blizzard – tales of mummies with red eyes stalking the night and whispers of a curse that lingered. Skeptics dismissed the survivor's tale as a delusion, a mind fractured by fear.

Yet in the realm beyond, Lucifer Morningstar knew her truth. He felt a disturbance at the resurgence of a foe whose power matched his own. And so, the tale endured, shrouded in mystery, a haunting omen that would once again alter the course of the world.

Made in the USA
Columbia, SC
16 January 2024

1f2b15e8-f067-45ab-b289-a61eafcbcc09R02